FLASH POINT

A MASON SHARPE THRILLER

LOGAN RYLES

INKUBATOR
BOOKS

Published by Inkubator Books
www.inkubatorbooks.com

Copyright © 2023 by Logan Ryles

Logan Ryles has asserted his right to be identified as the author of this work.

ISBN (eBook): 978-1-83756-301-2
ISBN (Paperback): 978-1-83756-302-9
ISBN (Hardback): 978-1-83756-303-6

For my mother, Karen, who has inspired my creativity since childhood. I love you!

1

—————

"**G**et that joker!"

The bar fight erupted with all the suddenness and violence of a nuclear blast. Fifty sweaty bodies were packed around the stage, swigging beer and enjoying the music. I stood just left of the bass guitarist, violin pressed under my chin, my bow arcing across the strings as I launched into a twenty-second solo—the climax of Charlie Daniel's famed "The Devil Went Down to Georgia". It took me a solid month to learn it, and I was too focused on the finger work to see the barstool hurtling toward me like a Patriot missile.

The stool made impact against my right shoulder. I hit the stage in a tangle of guitar cables, the violin flying from beneath my chin. My head smacked the plywood, and stars whirled overhead. Beyond the stage, the tangle of sweaty bodies had descended into a mosh pit of flying fists and hurtling bottles. Glass broke and beer exploded across the floor. I fought to my feet, abandoning the violin as the rest of the band scrambled for cover. From across the room,

Brandon and Braydon, the bar's bulky pair of steroid-inflated twin bouncers, rushed to calm the tempest.

There was no calming it. It was one of those perfect storms—those spontaneous bar fights where all at once everybody is hitting anybody, with no rhyme or reason, no teams and no battle lines. It was too much beer, too much Florida heat, and too much testosterone. The devil had left Georgia and headed straight for Tampa.

I leapt off the stage and grabbed a muscled redneck by his right arm, pulling him off balance before he could ram a table chair into the face of a Cuban guy with blood running from his lip. The redneck reeled but failed to go down. The chair fell from his grasp and he whirled on me with a fist cocked.

I ducked the drunken blow and drove a knee into his groin. His eyes bulged and he swayed on his feet, then hit the floor like a falling oak tree—colliding with another beefy redneck on his way down.

The new guy whirled in bristled fury, face crimson red, a broken table leg brandished in one hand like a baseball bat.

"Just calm down!" I said, raising a hand. "Let's take a breath."

He wasn't taking a breath, and he wasn't calming down. Somebody rammed him from behind, and he tumbled toward me. I sidestepped the table leg but was unable to miss a flying beer bottle. It glanced across my temple, and my head spun. Then the fight enveloped me, nothing but chaos on every side.

There was no escaping it, now. I was caught in the pit amid a hurricane of flying fists and projectiles. I landed two good hits on the redneck with the table leg—enough to disable him and send the weapon crashing to the floor—but

I couldn't protect my undefended back. An elbow caught me in the ribs, and a boot struck my shin. I maintained my footing and pivoted to a new target just in time to catch a random fist to my nose. Blood sprayed across my T-shirt, and I blinked through the pain. It was the Cuban guy again—the one with the busted lip. He looked semi-apologetic as he withdrew his fist, as though I hadn't been his intended target.

I no longer cared. Pain and the fog of combat had overwhelmed any desire to reason with madness. I was ready to break bones, now. I was ready to do what I do best.

I found the table leg between my feet and flicked it into the air with the toe of my boot. The Cuban guy's bleeding face flooded with panic, and he lost himself in the crowd. I pivoted toward the first drunken fool I could find and clocked him over the head with the busted leg—hard enough to send his eyes rolling back in his head and his body toppling to the floor. The next guy caught the makeshift weapon in the gut, driving the wind out of him. Then I backhanded him across the side of his left knee. He screeched and hit the floor. I let him fall as a beer bottle raked across my shoulder blades, shattering and tearing my shirt. I pivoted with the table leg, ready to smash more bones than the human body contains.

Then the shotgun blast erupted like a thunderclap, belching fire and fury. In unison, every face in the joint spun toward the polished counter that ran the length of one wall, behind which Hank the bar owner wielded a Mossberg 500 shotgun, pointed first at the ceiling, but now dropping toward the crowd.

"Clear out!"

Nobody argued. Bottles, chairs, and table legs rained

across the floor, then everyone moved like a tidal wave for the parking lot. Through the doorless doorway, onto the gravel. Trucks and motorcycles roared to life in a cacophony loud enough to drown out any further shotgun blasts. The wounded limped and dragged busted legs. The healthy ducked their heads and feigned innocence. Brandon and Braydon brandished fists and drove the sweaty crowd like a pair of sheepdogs, landing a few revenge blows as the last of the revelers were ejected from the building.

When I turned around, even the guy I had knocked unconscious was gone. The Cuban was gone. The band was gone.

All that remained was a field of smashed furniture and broken glass...another Sunday night on the beach.

2

I spent the next hour helping to clean up the mess, sipping on free beer while I swept up shattered bottles and stacked broken tables. A collection of personal items had been left behind—purses, phones, wallets. All things that Hank happily impounded, pending settled tabs and damages repaid.

When the last of the debris was cleaned away and some order was restored, I laid my violin on the counter and went to work wiping away the smattering of blood and beer that speckled the bout and fingerboard. It was a battered instrument, several years old and the longtime victim of my transient, unstable lifestyle. Miraculously, it was undamaged. A quick wipe down with a bar rag and an adjustment of the strings brought it right back to performance standard...not that I was interested in further performance that night. A quick glance at my own reflection in the bar mirror confirmed an inflamed nose, both nostrils sealed off with wads of toilet paper to stem the blood flow.

That Cuban had a mean right hook. I didn't think my

nose was broken, but I'd be purple with bruises in the morning.

Figures.

Behind the counter, Hank stood with his head cocked, bulging arms folded, regarding the ceiling. I traced his line of sight to find a hole blown clean through the shingle roof, about the size of a grapefruit. The handiwork of the Mossberg.

"Nice shooting," I quipped. "The Corps would be proud."

He glowered at me, muttering curses under his breath. Then he walked to the cash register and counted out ten twenty-dollar bills. He folded them in half and passed them across the counter.

"What's this?" I said.

"Your share of tonight's tips."

"Two hundred bucks?"

Hank shrugged, jabbing a thumb toward the empty stage. I hadn't seen any of my bandmates since the shotgun blast.

"They split, they forfeit their share. You stayed, you get to collect."

I pushed the money back across the counter. "Count it toward next month's rent."

Hank nodded and poked the money into his pocket. I ran a hand across my lip to wipe away dried blood, casting a weary glance around the room. Despite the busted nose, battered back, and pounding headache...I couldn't resist a grin.

I'd given as good as I got. Maybe better.

"I'm clocking out, Hank. See you tomorrow."

Hank lifted a hand in dismissive farewell as I cradled the violin under one arm and headed for the open doorway. The early summer air was thick with humidity, and I slapped my first mosquito only inches outside the bar. Ruts lined the gravel parking lot, the knot of pickups, SUVs, and Harley-Davidsons from earlier that night now long lost amid the sagging hardwoods.

They would be back, I knew. Probably with heads hanging, shuffling in to settle tabs and pay for damages before they sheepishly requested more beer.

Just another Sunday night on the beach.

I sighed and turned toward the campsites, mentally fast-forwarding past any consideration of dinner and setting my course straight for bed. It might be midnight, it might be two a.m. Whatever the case, I was done for the day. My air mattress and mosquito net would serve as a welcome landing zone until sunrise.

I made it halfway to the edge of the gravel before the disturbance caught my attention. A muted female cry was joined by a gravelly male voice—a little slurred, a lot insistent. The woman snapped a curse, and the guy shouted something unintelligible.

My gaze flicked right, through the shadows, behind the trash cans loaded with beer bottles, to a shaded spot beyond the slouching cedar-sided building. There was a red Volkswagen Beetle parked on the grass there, and standing next to it two figures appeared as silhouettes outside the perimeter of a security light—both relatively small people, but still divisible by gender. A man and a woman, matching the voices. The woman stood with her back to the car, shoving the guy away. The guy stumbled, swaying on his feet and nearly toppling. He caught himself on a tree and tensed, shoulders bunched. The woman turned away, headed for the Volkswagen. The guy lunged after her, one hand closing around her shoulder.

"W-wait!"

I stooped to lay the violin on the ground, then sprinted for the pair. I reached them just as the woman turned, yanked back by the guy. She cocked a fist to slap him. I caught him first, wrapping my fingers into his collar and snatching.

I expected resistance, but he folded like a paper doll, arms flailing and knees collapsing. I released him on the way down and circled right, ready to drive my knee into his face if he reached for a concealed weapon—always a worthy concern in Florida.

He didn't reach for a weapon. He sat on the ground with a *thud*, eyes blinking, a trail of saliva dripping from one lip. I dipped my hand into my pocket and retrieved the Streamlight Macrostream I'd carried for most of that year—a handy little camp light, easily recharged with a cell phone cable. I clicked the tail switch, blasting his face with five hundred lumens and instantly blinding him. He threw up both hands to block the beam, but I'd already seen enough.

He was much older than I expected. Early sixties, perhaps. Healthy but not bulky. Gray hair disheveled, clothes stained. Gaze clouded with inebriation.

I lowered the light and looked to the woman. In stark contrast to her aggressor, she was a lot younger than I expected. Early twenties, maybe. Very cute, with strawberry blonde hair, big green eyes, and slender features. She wore cutoff denim shorts and a spaghetti strap tank top that dipped low enough to attract attention.

She looked more pissed than scared.

"You okay?" I asked.

The old guy was still on the ground. Still blinking to regain his vision. The woman ran a hand across her lip, sweeping me up and down with those big green eyes. She shrugged.

"I'm okay." Her voice said Georgia, maybe Carolina. Accents I'd grown familiar with over the past year.

I reached a hand down to grab the old guy by the collar again.

"On your feet, buddy." He didn't fight me, but he swayed as he stood. I raised the light again, not quite pointing it in his face, but ready to do so should he try anything.

"You wanna explain yourself?" I said. I didn't really care what his explanation was. I'd been a street cop just long enough to learn to *not* entangle myself in domestic squabbles. I simply needed to confirm that this was, indeed, a domestic squabble. Then I'd be on my way.

"He followed me out of the bar," the girl said. "He's a creep!"

"I'm not a cweep!" the guy slurred. His voice was laden by the effects of alcohol, but I still detected an accent from someplace far north of Georgia or Carolina. New Jersey, maybe. Philadelphia.

"I'm just wooking for my girlfriend. I just wanna t-talk."

The slurring continued, blended with a hiccup. The guy stumbled. I caught his elbow and shot the girl a sideways look. She had her arms folded now. Disgust radiated from a curled lip.

"I have no idea what he's talking about."

I sighed, still propping the guy up. Then I tilted my head and led the two of them back into the glow of the security light. The guy walked alongside me in a sloppy shuffle, not resisting, but maybe he was unable to resist. Back in front of the bar I stopped next to a bench and he crumpled onto it, his face falling into worn hands as he broke into a sob.

"I'm not tryin' to cause any twouble..."

Before I could answer, the woman—or girl—jumped in. "If you don't want trouble, you shouldn't *stalk people!*"

I held up a hand, backing her down. She kept her arms folded while I regarded the man's slumped posture. The trembling of his shoulders. The defeat in his voice.

He was wasted—no doubt about it. But something in his tone connected with me. A sort of raw desperation that felt too authentic to be fabricated by booze alone. The guy was messed up.

"You sure you don't know what he's talking about?" I asked.

The girl shook her head. Her body language had softened a little. Maybe she felt some sympathy, also. Or maybe we were all simply exhausted.

"He approached me at the bar. I thought he was just hitting on me. Then the fight happened and I took cover. When I left the bar, he was waiting. That's all I know."

I nodded, hands in my pockets while the old guy's sobs subsided. His vision was so glazed I doubted he still knew we were there. He just stared at the gravel, a little trail of drool running from the corner of his mouth.

Another Sunday night.

"Hey. You're the fiddle player, right?" the girl spoke again, and this time Georgia or Carolina was a little heavier on her voice. I glanced left to see her standing with her head cocked, a cute little smile hung on her lips. One strap of that tank top drifting over her shoulder, sudden flirtation in her eyes.

"Right." I flushed a little and looked quickly away,

kneeling next to the old guy and placing a hand on his knee. The security light falling over his face was strong enough to drive back a little of the fog in his eyes. Our gazes locked for the first time, and hot steel cut through my gut like a blast from Hank's shotgun.

The grief in the guy's face was absolute—honest, unfettered, and completely transparent. Maybe it was the alcohol, or maybe he was just one of those people who never tried to hide anything. Whatever the case, I felt like I could see straight into his soul.

And I didn't like what I found there. It was suffering. It was fear. It was a lot of desperation.

Feelings I knew all too well.

"What's your name?" I asked, keeping my voice gentle.

The old guy sniffed, scrubbing saliva from his lip. "Ralph," he mumbled.

"You bring a car, Ralph?"

He shook his head. "Taxi."

I checked my watch. It was indeed well past midnight. This far from the city getting another taxi would be tricky, to say nothing of expensive.

"You live here?" I asked.

Another shake of his head. His eyes watered, and the sobs threatened to return.

I straightened as Braydon—or maybe it was Brandon; I honestly couldn't tell the difference—appeared from the bar entrance and made a bee-line for us. The bouncer sported one black eye and a busted lip. He looked ready to pound something.

"He pay his tab?"

It wasn't a question so much as an accusation. Ralph looked from the bouncer to the girl to me, the sobs freezing over in his chest. He reached for the bench's armrest and struggled to stand. The bouncer reached him first and put a thick hand on his shoulder.

"Hey. Buddy. You pay your tab?"

I put a hand on the bouncer's arm and pushed gently.

"He's wasted, dude."

"He can't pay his tab," the girl said, feeding a stick of gum into her mouth. "The bartender came by just before the fight. His card declined."

"B-bank problems," Ralph slurred. "I'll fix it tomorrow."

"You owe us tonight," the bouncer snapped, clamping down on Ralph's shoulder. The old guy twisted and fought to wriggle away. The bouncer shook him.

I interjected between them and put two hands on the bouncer's barrel chest, shoving hard enough to knock him off balance.

"Hey! Chill out. Tell Hank I'll cover the tab, okay?"

The bouncer regained his balance, eyes blazing. Corded muscle rippled beneath his stained T-shirt, and for a moment I thought he might take a swing at me. Instead he simply muttered a curse, then turned away.

"I better not find you sleeping on that bench tomorrow, old man."

I rolled my eyes and turned back to Ralph. The girl shifted on her feet, popping gum now, and fiddling with keys. Finally ready to go, but feeling stuck in the awkwardness. As was I.

"I got him," I said. "You're good."

The girl flashed me another smile. "Nice fiddling tonight... I really liked it."

"Thanks," I said, a flash of discomfort rising in my gut. She wouldn't look away from me. She wouldn't blink, either.

"I guess I'll see you around," she said. I nodded dumbly, still avoiding her gaze. Then she set off across the parking lot, wedge shoes working her hips a little harder than God intended. She descended into the Volkswagen, and a moment later the engine hummed to life.

I turned back to Ralph, now the last sober adult left standing when the music stopped. Momentary hesitation clouded my mind, but I knew there was really only one right answer. I couldn't leave him here.

"You got a place to sleep?" I said with a sigh. "A hotel I can take you to?"

Ralph sniffed. Then shook his head. He wouldn't look up.

I checked my watch again, willing it to not to be the middle of the night. No such luck. Wiping sweat from my forehead, I glanced over one shoulder toward the bar. Brandon, Braydon, and Hank were still bustling about inside.

Ralph didn't need to be sitting on this bench when they finally locked up.

"Come on," I said. "You can sleep it off at my place."

Ralph looked up, and once again I was confronted with that open window into gut-wrenching pain. A lot of it, perhaps amplified by the inebriation, but not originated by it.

"Where?" he mumbled.

I clasped his hand and helped him up.

"This way," I said.

3

The campground I had called home for the past six months sat right alongside a sprawling lagoon, about two miles east of the Florida gulf coast, and about thirty miles northwest of downtown Tampa. It was a hodgepodge of travel trailer lots, most served by electrical terminals and fresh water, but not all. There was a lodge featuring battered vending machines that seldom worked and an ice cream machine that never worked. A little camp store sat next to it, offering canned goods, firewood, and bug spray for sale, all for less than market value. Then there was a mechanical shed populated by maintenance equipment and half a dozen antique motorcycles in various stages of restoration and repair, a fish-cleaning station, a rickety old pier that stretched out over the lagoon, and something resembling a playground following the apocalypse. A rusted merry-go-round, sagging monkey bars, and one of those metal slides that you can grill hamburgers on in mid-August.

The crown jewel of the entire property was the bar—a windowless cedar-sided building staffed by sunburnt local girls and two meat-headed twin brothers who spent as much time shooting up steroids as they did enforcing Hank's rules.

Hank himself owned the place—all of it. The campground, the broken ice cream machine, and the bar. He was a retired United States Marine who now enjoyed his twilight years living in a twenty-eight-foot Airstream propped up on blocks next to the mechanical shed. He drank a lot of beer. He told a lot of jokes.

He made a lot of people laugh, and he waived a lot of tabs. More than he should, probably. Maybe that explained the perpetual disrepair of the property.

I'd stumbled into Hank's "little corner of paradise"—his words, not mine—the previous December after wandering south out of Jacksonville, and I liked it so much I decided to park my battered 1967 GMC pickup in a lot only yards from the lagoon, and call Florida home for a while longer. The rent was cheap. Just fifteen bucks per night, and I easily made three times that playing violin at the bar, working for tips.

Hank was easy to get along with. The locals were easy to talk to. The transients in rusting Dodge vans and faded Winnebagos told funny stories and let me play with their dogs. The sunsets were beautiful, and the days undemanding.

I wouldn't call it paradise, but it was peaceful. Or it had been, anyway. Until some fool set off world war three in the middle of my violin solo.

I led Ralph through the trees along a worn path, two hundred yards to my campsite. He stumbled a lot on the way, tripping over roots and ruts that didn't exist and doing his best to ram his head into an oak tree. I kept him upright and took my time, too relaxed by the warm salt breeze to be frustrated. By the time we finally reached my little slice of Hank's paradise, Ralph was ready to drop, and I was ready to drop him. I guided him into a sagging camping chair and he collapsed without complaint. Then I ran a hand over my face and cast a quick glance around my campsite.

It was the most developed home I had enjoyed in over a year, which wasn't saying much. My truck sat parked beneath a pine tree, the tailgate dropped open and the roof of the faded aluminum camper shell laden with pine needles. Inside that bed lay my air mattress—twin sized, jammed in alongside plastic containers loaded with camping gear. Not an entirely dry place when it rained, but dryer than sleeping outside.

Surrounding the rear of the truck stood a picnic table, a park grill that leaned ten degrees away from the coast—hurricane damage, I guessed—a fire pit, and a string of lights tacked to the pine trees and plugged into the electrical terminal.

A home that was not really a home. But it was my home.

From the camping chair Ralph mumbled something. His chin rested against his chest, and he looked ready to fall face-first from the chair. I glanced momentarily at my bed, my sore muscles and tired mind longing for the familiar sag of the air mattress. Then I sighed and helped Ralph up again, heaving him across the lowered tailgate. He passed out only moments after resting his head on my pillow, and I tugged my T-shirt off and mopped sweat from my forehead before retreating toward the lagoon.

Halfway between my truck and the water I'd strung a hammock up between two pines, tight enough to provide ample support for my six-foot-two frame. The hammock was made by Wise Owl Outfitters, and this was one of their "double" models, designed for affectionate couples, I guessed. Or big guys. I won it in an arm-wrestling competition with a loud-mouthed Navy pilot who had a lot of derogatory opinions about "grounding pounding" Army guys.

He likely still had the opinions. But he didn't have his hammock.

The nylon straps groaned as I swung in, kicking my shoes off and leaving each leg bent at the knee and overhanging the hammock's sides. With my head propped on one forearm, I had a clear view of the lagoon stretching and weaving along a muddy coast, working inland to my right and toward the Gulf of Mexico on my left.

Moonlight played on the dark water. The orange eyes of a six-foot alligator gleamed from fifty yards away. A whippoorwill sang from some invisible spot high in the trees, and behind me Ralph snored.

I pulled my mosquito net up over my face and closed my eyes, trying not to think of the pain in Ralph's face as I drifted off to sleep.

4

I awoke just after sunrise to the sound of Ralph puking out of the back of my truck. The old guy had reached the tailgate, at least, but I would have been happier had he reached the lagoon.

Swinging out of my hammock, I stretched in the early morning warmth, flexing my back and neck until my spine crackled, and ignoring the sounds of guttural discharge behind me. Gentle sunlight broke through the trees to spill over the lagoon's quiet waters, reflecting a dozen shades of gold back into a brilliant, cloudless sky.

It was going to be a beautiful day. A very hot day.

Shuffling to the battered ice chest situated next to the picnic table, I fished a bottle of water out of a lake of melted ice and twisted the cap off. Then I finally turned to Ralph.

"Sleep well?"

The old guy turned bloodshot eyes on me, scrubbing the back of one hand across soiled lips. He looked embarrassed, and that reassured me. Memories of the confrontation from the night before replayed in my mind, and now that I was freshly recharged and better equipped to unpack them, it occurred to me that Ralph could well be the creep the girl accused him of being.

The flush of his cheeks and nervous twitch of his eyes cast a vote in favor of a foolish drunk instead.

Ralph accepted the bottle and swished water in his mouth before spitting it over the pool of bile. I kicked gravel over the mess, then returned to the picnic table and twisted the gas knob on my camping stove.

I had a morning routine pretty well hammered out, and I fell into it without thought. Coffee first, brewed on the stove, rich and black. Then came the eggs and toast, smeared with apple butter and heaped on a metal camping plate. Once in a while I enjoyed a side of bacon, but with all the ice melted in my ice chest, there was no way to keep it cold. I opted for a can of baked beans and sausage instead, using the can opener on my Victorinox Locksmith to work the metal lid off. The knife had been with me since Afghanistan, save for a short stint inside the evidence locker of a north Florida sheriff's department—another story. It almost required an act of congress to get it back, and now the Swiss-made multi-tool worked overtime to sustain my new lifestyle.

Full-time camper, or perhaps full-time vagrant. Take your pick.

I cracked twice my normal quantity of eggs into a stainless-steel skillet and went to work scrambling them while the beans heated in a little pot. Ralph shuffled off to a tree to relieve himself, then took a seat on the far side of the picnic table and accepted a cup of coffee with a sheepish smile. I whistled softly as I finished the eggs—the tune was my solo from the night before. The one I'd been interrupted from by the bar fight. My nose still hurt and my head pounded a little, but all things considered I was confident I had given a good account of myself as a former ground pounder. Too bad the Navy pilot wasn't around to see it. I figured I'd finish the solo next time and enjoy the increased tips from a crowd full of guilty souls.

"Salt and pepper?" I asked.

"Salt."

I passed him a plastic shaker and a plate full of breakfast. Ralph interlaced his fingers and bowed his head. His lips moved in a silent prayer, then he picked up my metal spoon while I took the fork. I only had one of each.

We ate in silence for ten minutes, Ralph stealing glances now and then across the campsite, back toward the bar. He finished his coffee and returned to the water bottle, fidgeting with the label and shifting on his seat. He didn't look nervous so much as preoccupied, as though he were present in body only.

Maybe he was simply hung over.

I finished my beans and restrained a burp. Then I poured more coffee. The caffeine had already entered my bloodstream, and I was feeling good. The fistfight from the night before had been strangely exhilarating. I hadn't engaged in a physical encounter in some months... Maybe I missed the action.

"Feel free to explain yourself at any time," I said, slurping coffee.

Ralph pivoted back toward me as though he'd forgotten I was sitting there. He squinted gray eyes, coffee cup cradled in his hands. I noticed that he'd stopped fidgeting, but he didn't look calm. He looked uncertain, and very tired, and a lot strained. The bloodshot eyes had worsened since breakfast. He chewed one corner of his lip.

I rotated a hand palm-up, raising both eyebrows. Ralph dropped his gaze.

"I'm...sorry about last night. Had a few too many."

The east coast accent I had detected before was stronger now. My previous estimations of Jersey or Philadelphia refined into something a little closer to New York City.

"Lots of people had a few too many," I said. "That doesn't explain groping a random woman."

Ralph's gaze snapped up. "I didn't grope her! I was just...I just wanted to talk to her."

"Uhuh." I half believed him, but I kept my tone suspicious. In truth, I'd only ever seen him touch her arm, and nothing about his harassment appeared sexual so much as general. But I could tell he was ashamed of himself, and I wasn't above using that to my advantage.

Ralph's gaze dropped to his now-empty plate. His chin dropped with it.

"I'm sorry I imposed. Thanks for the bed. I'll pay you."

I laughed. "You couldn't even pay for your beer."

He reddened, and a flash of guilt washed through my gut. I saw the pain in his eyes again, that haunting sort of desperation. His lips tightened, and I thought he might cry. I softened my tone.

"You said you were looking for your girlfriend?"

Ralph didn't answer. His lower lip trembled.

I set my coffee cup down. "Okay. Why don't you just tell me where you're from?"

"Newark."

"Born and raised?"

Another nod.

"Go, Giants."

That brought the hint of a smile.

"What do you do in Newark?"

He shrugged. "Work in the paint plant."

"You done that for long?"

"Thirty-two years." The smile was real this time. Proud.

"Good for you. What brings a paint mixer from Newark to a beach bar outside of Tampa?"

It was the blade question—the question that I knew would cut to the heart of the matter at hand. Ralph stiffened a little, but he didn't fold this time.

"I'm looking for my girlfriend."

I was ready to press for specifics, but I didn't have to. Ralph's lip trembled again, and a tear slipped down one cheek. Then he broke like a collapsing dam, and the details gushed out. It turned out he wasn't a paint mixer—not anymore. Now he worked in the paint plant's marketing division. He attended trade shows and shook hands. After his wife of thirty years had passed away on his fifty-eighth birthday, he needed a change. He liked being on the road, meeting new people and not being home alone in a house full of memories.

It was a story I could easily resonate with, but I didn't say so. Ralph was barely holding himself together, and didn't need to hear the long, brutal tale of my own heartbreak. I kept our coffee mugs full while the story wandered through promotions and irrelevant details about the paint industry before finally landing in Tampa...six months prior.

"I met her at a trade show," Ralph said. The smile returned to his lips, accompanied by a lovesick glow in his tired gray eyes. "She's a model. She works the shows, you know. Like when they have pretty girls handing out pens and spinning the game wheels so you win prizes?"

I grunted like I understood, but I know even less about

trade shows than I know about paint. Spinning wheels and collecting free pens isn't the kind of thing you do as an Army Ranger, or a homicide detective. Even so, I couldn't help but feel a trickle of uncertainty creeping into the back of my mind. The terms "model" and "girls" didn't mesh with the image of a mature woman Ralph's age.

"What's her name?" I asked.

"Camilla." The smile widened. "Isn't that pretty? She's Cuban."

I thought of the Cuban guy from the night before who busted my nose, and I grimaced before I could help myself. Ralph flinched, indignation passing across his face. He dug into his pocket.

"You don't believe me? I got a picture right here."

Sure enough, he produced a strip of photographs from his pocket, a little creased and bent, printed in black and white. It was one of those photo booth strips, like you might find in a shopping mall or at a carnival. The ones where kids climb in and pay five bucks to make silly faces with their girlfriends.

Ralph extended the strip, and I surveyed it. There was a Cuban woman, alright. And she was indeed beautiful. Gorgeous, in fact. Smooth, dark skin, dark eyes, and curled hair. A killer smile. Twenty, maybe twenty-five years Ralph's junior, she wore a black sequin dress that left little to the imagination, and she sat curled up on Ralph's lap inside the booth.

I squinted, caught off-guard by the dichotomy of what I saw. Ralph looked better in the photographs than he did sitting before me now, with a clean haircut and a scrubbed face, but everything about his style hadn't been updated since the turn of the century. He wore a tweed suit, an oversized tie, and a pocket protector. Yes, a pocket protector.

I glanced up, raising one eyebrow. Ralph flushed again.

"I know what you're thinking. Why would a girl like that be with a guy like me, right?"

"That's not what I'm thinking."

Not exactly.

Ralph reclaimed the photo strip. "I can't explain it. We met at the show and I told a joke and she laughed. We started chatting. We went to the bar for drinks. I got tipsy. I asked for her number as a joke. She gave me her Instagram handle. We started messaging. We..."

His lip trembled. His eyes watered. He sniffed hard and looked away. The pain returned to his eyes and was reflected in my gut, and I regretted my instinctual judgments. Who was I to question his romance? Love is difficult to find, and even harder to keep. I'd learned that the hardest way possible.

"I believe you," I said simply.

Ralph scrubbed his nose and nodded a couple times, seeming to collect himself.

"Look. I know you've already done a lot, but...I could really use a ride into town. I'm having trouble with my bank card. I can't pay for another cab. I just have to get to the bank and straighten it out."

I sipped coffee, my mind spinning through a half dozen further questions I wanted to ask. Questions about how Ralph had misplaced his girlfriend, or why he'd turned up at a random campsite bar in the middle of nowhere looking for her.

But none of that really mattered, I decided. Ralph could be lying to me, or he could be telling the honest truth.

Regardless, I was in no position to question either his love for this woman or the nature of his current predicament.

Love makes us do crazy things. I was in no position to judge.

"Sure," I said. "I can give you a ride."

5

I t took a little effort to get the GMC started. I hadn't left the campsite in nearly two weeks, and the engine needed some choking and coaxing before rumbling to life. The front left tire also required inflating—it had picked up a nail somewhere along the way and now had a slow leak, but Hank had an air compressor that sort of worked. At least enough to get us back on the road.

Ralph piled in on the bench seat next to a pile of dirty clothes, and we were off down the busted campsite road, beeping the horn and lifting a hand to a couple of morning beer drinkers gathered around a breakfast campfire.

Life at a campsite—not for everyone, but it suited me just fine.

The nearest town was a suburb of Tampa, a place called Harper Springs. Twenty-five thousand people, most of them New England transplants come to Florida for the warm winters and much warmer summers, with enough restaurants and retail to find anything you needed but maybe not everything you wanted. Ralph banked with a large financial institution which had a branch in town, and we rumbled along with the windows down, the engine purring at an accelerated RPM due to a rich fuel mixture. The carburetor was in need of a cleaning and a tune...something I should have found plenty of time to address between the beers and the late nights playing violin at the bar.

Somehow, I hadn't.

The brakes squealed as I eased to a stop at the bank. Ralph shook my hand awkwardly, thanking me for the bed and breakfast and again offering to pay me. I waved him off and wished him well, avoiding his gaze. I still didn't want to face the pain in his eyes. One year and six months had worked magic on my shattered heart, healing a lot of the pain and nursing my mind back to a semblance of normalcy, but I was coming to think that you never really heal.

Not after losing somebody like Mia.

"See you around, Ralph."

He climbed out and the heavy door slammed. I watched while he entered the bank, shuffling along, looking a little homeless. He needed a shower and a change of clothes. I thought again about Camilla, the beautiful Cuban woman in the photo strip, and the investigator's instincts programed into my brain clicked automatically into gear, asking questions. Pulling at loose threads. Wondering...

Then I pushed it all away, shutting those instincts down with practiced lethality. Because Ralph's problems were Ralph's problems, and I had enough of my own to solve, beginning with a front left tire that was already going flat again.

I bumped the truck a block down the street to a tire shop and squealed to a stop in an empty bay. A grizzled old mechanic came out to admire the truck and inquire about my needs. I requested a fix-a-flat, then added an oil change on reflection. It had been a while.

Leaving the truck in his greasy hands I returned to the street, basking in the sunlight and thinking about groceries. I needed a new toothbrush. More eggs and bacon. Maybe some bell peppers to make omelets with...

My train of thought was derailed by Ralph appearing at the bank door and stumbling down the steps. He looked flustered and shouted something back at the door. A man in a suit appeared, waving him away and calling inaudible threats. Ralph lifted a finger, then he reached the sidewalk. He turned to face the street, a hangdog expression dragging on his face like a ton of bricks. Then he crumpled to the steps, knees drawn to his chest, and sobbed.

The knife of pain returned to my gut, as hot and sharp as ever, but I didn't move to cross the street. Instead I took two steps back, into the shade cast by the tire shop, and leaned against the wall someplace where Ralph was unlikely to see me. My own journey of grief and recovery had been a long one, and painful. In fact, in some ways, I was still on it. Whatever misery would drive a person to sob on the steps of a bank, I knew what it felt like to lose all sense of shame. To crumble in broad daylight.

I would give him a minute. Let him collect himself and resume his composure. Then maybe I would return to the bank...

Ralph was on his feet now, scrubbing his face. He glared at the bank and pocketed his hands. Looked both ways down the street, maybe searching for me. Maybe at a loss as to where to go next. Then he turned right and took the sidewalk in a frustrated shuffle.

He was angry now. I could see it in his march. The tense

bulge of his shoulders. The way his jaw clenched and ground, almost like he was chewing gum, but he hadn't been chewing gum when I dropped him off. He was on a warpath.

I scratched a cheek and reevaluated my plans to involve myself, but I didn't have long to think. Ralph had made it barely halfway down the block when the next players appeared—a pair of dark-skinned guys dressed in jeans and open-collared shirts. I recognized one of them the instant he appeared from the front of a barber shop, a fresh haircut gleaming with gel under the blazing Florida sun.

It was the Cuban I had tangled with the night before— the one who had busted my nose. He was accompanied by a similar looking guy two inches taller, also sporting a fresh haircut. They were both sliding sunglasses on as they reached the sidewalk, the shorter guy flipping car keys while the taller unwrapped a stick of gum.

Ralph saw them also, and his reaction was instantaneous. His shoulders heaved like a boxer's bracing for an attack, and the grinding of his jaw locked into an ugly frown. He shouted something, and both Cubans pivoted toward him.

In an instant the confrontation in Ralph's gaze was matched by a shout and jabbing index finger from the guy who busted my nose. It wasn't the reaction Ralph expected. He stopped, uncertainty flashing across his face. He took a step back.

The Cubans lunged for him, and Ralph broke into a run, turning right instead of left, selecting an alleyway that ran between the barbershop and an adjacent furniture store. Tall piles of cardboard boxes lined the alleyway, and I supposed he thought he could lose himself amongst them.

He would have been better off making a dash into the

open street and risking the traffic. There was zero chance he could outrun the young, healthy Cubans, and removed from public attention inside the alleyway, it wasn't difficult to guess what would happen when they caught him. I could already see in their faces that both men were out for blood.

Propelling myself off the wall, I glanced quickly both ways before jogging into the street. The Cubans faded into the alley as Ralph crashed amid the furniture boxes, stumbling through a mud puddle and nearly collapsing. He made it to the back of the barbershop and turned left, no doubt hoping to circle behind it. Something blocked his path, and he slid to a halt. He looked back, panic clouding his face. The Cubans threw boxes aside, charging ahead like bulldogs. They were five paces behind him, and I was twenty-five behind them.

A flash of dull pain ran through my face, reminding me of the unprovoked right hook I had sustained, and a flash of my own indignation ignited in my gut. I broke into a sprint, reaching the entrance of the alley just as the Cubans reached Ralph. One of them threw him against the wall of the barbershop while the other landed a right hook into his gut. Ralph groaned and doubled over. They were shouting at him, but the blood pounding in my ears drowned out their voices. I slid between the boxes and zeroed in on the guy who was doing the pounding—the shorter of the two, my dance partner from the previous night.

"Hey, jackass!"

The Cuban turned, dark eyes blazing. He saw me coming and pivoted automatically to address the new threat.

He was much too slow. This wasn't a bar fight any longer —it was a street brawl. I don't play games in a street brawl.

I caught him on the jaw hard enough to realign teeth,

sending his head snapping back against his shoulder blades. The force of the blow sent a shockwave of pain ripping up my arm, but I didn't care. I pivoted automatically to the second guy just as brass knuckles appeared out of nowhere, yellow metal glimmering in the sunlight. He swept his arm back like an ax, maybe thinking he would knock my head off.

It was a dumb move. There was no need for me to close, within striking distance of his fist. Legs are longer than arms, and his fighting stance offered ample access to the family jewels.

I struck with my left shin, straight between his legs, all the way to downtown. Hard shinbone collided with unprotected groin, and the guy collapsed like a house of cards.

I let him fall and turned back to the first guy, ready for an encore dance. My focus was locked on his nose now, and I was thinking about doing a lot more than just busting it. Maybe I'd flatten it—shatter every bone, wreck the cartilage. Make him a mouth breather for the rest of his life.

But the Cuban didn't advance. He stood three yards back, well out of reach, blood streaming from his smashed lower lip. There was a nice welt on his jaw, compliments of my right hook. Maybe enough to knock some sense into him.

"You want some more?" I snapped.

He looked to his companion. The taller Cuban had also stumbled back, still clinging to his brass knuckles but very much removed from the fight. He shuddered, heaving like a cow giving birth while Ralph stood by in disbelieving silence.

The first guy wiped his lip, regarding me with cutting black eyes. Not defying me. He appeared to actually be thinking, which was an improvement. Instead of addressing me, he turned back to Ralph, jabbing with a trembling finger.

"You leave our sister *alone*. I see you again, I'll dump you in the bay!"

His voice trembled with a heavy accent and a lot of emotion, but the message was clear. He spat blood and cast me a glower, then snapped a line of Spanish to the second man—his brother, I guessed—and the two of them left the alley. One with his head up, the other still shielding his crotch as he staggered and gasped. I watched until they faded from view, then pivoted slowly to Ralph. Both eyebrows up. Not asking anymore.

Ralph dropped his gaze, wilting like a desert flower. I spoke the obvious.

"You've got some explaining to do."

6

Ralph accompanied me without complaint another block down the street, beyond the barbershop, to a coffee shop. The Cubans were long gone and my truck stood on a rack at the tire place, so I figured we had some time. I purchased us both coffee, then selected a booth in a quiet corner and waited for Ralph to speak up. When he finally did, it wasn't what I wanted to hear.

"It's not what you think."

"I don't know what I think," I said. "Except that maybe you lied to me, and I invited you into my home, so now I'm pissed."

"I didn't lie," Ralph said, looking up quickly. He appeared older than he had that same morning. More tired, more hopeless. I still saw the pain in his eyes, but I no longer trusted it. I waited.

Ralph looked back to his coffee and rotated the cup. Tears bubbled into his eyes.

"Man up," I said. "I've seen enough tears. If you don't want to tell me the truth, I'm happy to leave you here."

Ralph wiped his eyes. He collected himself through a long slurp and a deep breath.

"I didn't lie," he said. "I met Camilla just like I said. We hit it off."

"Are those two guys her brothers?" I asked.

Ralph shrugged. "They say so."

"So what's their problem?"

A hesitation. Another swallow. "They...they think I'm stalking her."

"And why would they think that?"

The panic returned to his creased face. "I have no idea."

There was an earnestness to his disposition that I might have found convincing, but I was a long way from being convinced.

"Explain. From the top."

Ralph relaxed in the booth. He seemed to focus. Then the story unfolded, right from the beginning.

"I met Camilla at the trade show. I...I thought she was beautiful. Obviously. So after she gave me her Instagram, I messaged her. I never expected her to message back, but she did. We started talking. I had to go back to Jersey. We kept talking. It was...it worked, you know?"

The tears returned. His lip trembled. I squinted hard, evaluating whether I believed him. Nothing in his face spoke to deception, but there were still the questions on the table. Questions about the Cuban guys, and why Ralph had harassed the woman at the bar.

"What next?" I kept my voice direct, almost clinical.

"Camilla has a lot going on," Ralph said. "She's Cuban, like I said. She's got a lot of family still in Cuba. It's bad down there. I mean, I've read the news articles. It's like a third world country. So much poverty, and the government is abusive. They're trying to get out, but it's expensive. So..."

My stomach descended into knots. I suddenly wanted to punch Ralph in the nose.

"Don't say you gave her money."

Ralph shrugged.

"How much?" The question came out as a disbelieving demand. Ralph didn't answer.

"*How much*, Ralph?"

His voice descended into a dry whisper, barely audible. "Everything."

The weight on my shoulders redoubled. I pushed my coffee away, unsure whether to be disgusted or overwhelmed by pity. I'd seen this before, as a homicide detective for the Phoenix Police Department. There was an old woman living by herself. She had a retirement account, and an internet connection. She met a guy online—an American soldier, he claimed, stranded overseas. He needed money to get home. It never occurred to the old lady that the DOD would never leave a service member stranded that way, so she helped out.

And kept helping out. And kept helping out.

He drained her retirement account and left her with nothing, then he vanished. When she couldn't pay rent, her back was against the wall. There was no family. Nobody to turn to. She was in poor health.

So she swallowed a bottle full of sleeping pills. I responded to the scene per department policy to check for suspicious circumstances, but there were none. Just a very bad end to a very sad story.

"She strung you along, Ralph," I said. "I've seen this before. It's a scam."

Ralph shook his head. "No. This isn't like that. We're in love. We really get along. We've even talked about getting married!"

"And that doesn't seem wildly unlikely to you?"

The words streamed out before I could stop them. They hit Ralph hard, and he recoiled in the booth, indignation illuminating his face.

But he didn't leave. He fought back the emotion and kept going.

"I know how it looks," he said. "But it's *not* like that. I've dated before, okay? Lots of times. I was married for thirty years. When...when I lost my wife..."

Now the emotion came in a wave. He choked. He fought through it.

"I've been alone for almost a *decade*, okay? I know how to be alone. I'm okay with it. But when I met Camilla..."

His hands shook. He wrapped them around the coffee cup and dropped his face. He clamped his eyes closed, but a tear slipped out anyway.

The knives in my stomach sank a little deeper. I sat in perfect silence, no longer thinking about Ralph, or even the old woman in Phoenix. His last words had raked through me harder than he could ever have imagined.

I know how to be alone.

They were words I could have said myself. Words I *had* said to myself, many times over the past six months. Words of reassurance. Words of confidence that I didn't really feel. Dishonest words that I desperately wanted to be true.

I had reached peace with the loss of my fiancée. It wasn't something I could change. But I hadn't reached peace with being alone, and part of me wondered if I ever would.

Looking at Ralph now, I knew his pain like it was my

own. It was enough to erase the frustration in my mind and leave only the sympathy. A metric ton of it.

"Why did you come to Tampa?" I said, more gently this time.

Ralph nodded a couple times, ready to return to his narrative.

"Right...Tampa. I knew she lived here. I mean, mostly. She spends a lot of time flying back and forth to Havana. That's part of what the money was for. But recently...she disappeared. She stopped answering my messages. She wasn't posting on Instagram anymore. I got scared. Really scared. So I...came down here."

"To find her?"

"Yeah..."

"And how in the world did that lead you to a beach bar an hour outside of town?"

Ralph shifted uncomfortably. He swallowed. I put the pieces together.

"You trailed that woman there, didn't you? The woman you were harassing?"

Ralph shook his head quickly. "No, not trailed. She invited me. She said we could meet there."

"Why?"

"She works with Camilla," Ralph said. "At a modeling agency. I went down to their corporate office looking for Camilla, and I met Sophie there instead. That's the woman from last night. She texted me later and suggested we meet at the bar. It's like a secret spot for her. So I got a taxi, but when I got to the bar she wouldn't talk about Camilla. She just kept asking me to buy her drinks. I went along with it for a while hoping she would tell me where Camilla was. I was getting drunk. Then there was the bar fight and..."

He trailed off. I sat back in the booth and drained my coffee. I thought again of the woman—or girl, really—at the bar. The revealing top. The loose look.

Sophie was a player, I figured. The female version of a player, anyway. Working an obvious idiot from out of town. Just like Camilla had.

"She was toying with you, Ralph," I said. "They both were."

There was no judgement in my tone. Just resigned disappointment.

Ralph shook his head again. "No. I'm *telling you*. This is real. I know it like I've never known anything. Maybe you've never experienced love, but if you had, you'd *know*. It's as real...as real as my wife."

He choked up again. Again I felt the knives in my gut, thinking of Mia. Thinking of loss. Thinking of being alone, and what that loneliness could drive a man to become.

Oh, I'd experienced love, alright. And I'd experienced heartbreak. It was a vortex and a spiral that had led me to do all kinds of things I wasn't proud of. Most of them involved late nights and too many six-packs. It wasn't as embarrassing as handing over my life savings to a sunkissed Cuban girl on Instagram...but was it really so different?

"Are you out of money?" I knew I would regret the question before I even voiced it, but I couldn't stop myself. I simply couldn't get up and leave him there.

"My account is in the negative," Ralph said. "The bank is supposed to let me overdraft but...they cut me off."

"And work?" I asked.

He shrugged. "I'm on leave. I have a lot of vacation."

I looked out the window, thinking quickly. Unraveling the puzzle.

There wasn't a doubt in my mind that Camilla had robbed Ralph blind. Whether those Cuban guys were really her brothers or just a couple of street thugs she hired to run Ralph off, the fact that they turned up at the bar said something. Somebody must have sent them there, and I didn't think it was Sophie. She was playing her own game.

No, Camilla had sent them. To send a message, maybe. To run Ralph off, because his behavior had gotten out of hand. He was in Tampa now, not Jersey. He wouldn't leave her alone.

The best case scenario for Ralph at this point would be to lick his wounds and head home. I wasn't aware of any legal recourse available to recover money that was freely given, even if it was given under dishonest circumstances. He should simply let this go. Move on with life.

But one look in his eyes, and I knew that was never going to happen. The only way he'd ever let this go was if he knew for *sure*. If he found Camilla. If undeniable, overwhelming proof of her corruption landed in his lap.

And that left me caught in the middle.

"I'm going to help you," I said.

Ralph's gaze snapped up. "Really?"

The hope in his voice cut straight to my heart. I simply nodded.

"I was a cop. I'm pretty good at finding people. I'll see what I can do."

He reached across the table and took my hand before I could stop him. He squeezed and blinked away tears. He didn't say a word.

He didn't have to.

7

I recovered my pickup from the tire shop and dropped Ralph off at a local dive motel, paying two nights' rent on his behalf. Whatever the nature of his situation at the bank, it was clear that he was destitute, and a hundred bucks plus a little cash for food felt like a cheap price to pay to have him not sleeping in my truck while I sorted this mess out.

"Take a shower," I said. "You smell like a dumpster."

Ralph smiled a little at that, sheepishly accepting the motel key. Then I was back in my truck, pointed toward the campsite.

After giving my head a little time to clear, it occurred to me that it was a terrible coincidence for the Cuban brothers to appear twice in Ralph's vicinity in so short a period. The one I had tangled with the night prior seemed heavily invested in the bar fight, and that made me wonder if he had, in fact, started it.

Whatever the case, the Cuban brothers seemed my first and most obvious lead in locating Camilla, and I happened to know that Hank kept a camera hidden behind the bar, filming the goings-on at the counter in the event that somebody should sue him.

For a guy who prided himself in appearing poor, Hank was proactive about protecting his interests. The camera was one half of that protection—the shotgun beneath the counter the other half.

I parked the GMC in front of the bar and found Hank working alone inside—repairing a busted table with salvaged drywall screws and wood glue. Cigarette smoke gathered around his head in a cloud, and an icy bottle of Coors Light rested on the floor next to half a dozen of its emptied siblings. His shirtless chest was slick with sweat, tangled gray and black hair obscuring the Semper Fidelis tattoo on his shoulder.

"Rough morning, Hank?"

The grizzled old campsite owner dragged on his cigarette, then ground it out against the floor with a curse.

"Freaking rednecks. Every one of them is paying a premium tonight, mark my words. I had to replace a chair."

I surveyed the mottled assortment of cast-off chairs collected from closing schools and out-of-business restaurants all around the region. More than a few of them looked ready for retirement even before the bar fight, but I didn't say so.

"You run back the tape?" I asked, jabbing my thumb over my shoulder toward the invisible camera. Hank had never actually mentioned it to me before, but he didn't seem surprised that I knew where it was.

"Naw..." He lit another cigarette. "What's the point? Ain't like I can prosecute nobody."

"I'd like to have a look," I said.

"How come?"

"Some other thing. That old guy who hung around last night. He's in some trouble."

"You getting involved?"

"Trying not to."

Hank snorted and reached for the wood glue. "People like you."

"Excuse me?"

"People like you! Just can't help but stick your neck out. Camera's in the office. Help yourself."

I left Hank to his work, thinking he was probably right about the neck-sticking, but there was little point in worrying about that now. I found the office unlocked and waded past a heap of empty beer bottles to a desk laden with an outdated computer, a lot of unpaid bills, and one dusty digital security camera mounted to the wall with its lens poking through a hole. A wire ran from the camera to the computer, and I went to work tracking down the footage from the previous night.

There was a lot of it. Apparently, the camera ran on an endless loop, overwriting what had been recorded the previous week, and leaving me with a perpetual 168 hours of tape to scan. Backtracking across hours of Hank's repair efforts, I almost missed the bar fight altogether. It only lasted a total of four minutes—much quicker than it felt like at the time. I started the playback with a grainy shot of the bar featuring a couple of the sunburnt local girls serving beers to a tight crowd of sweaty rednecks. I saw myself on the stage and was pleased to note that four months of regular pushups and lagoon swims were bearing some fruit. I'd shed ten pounds of beer weight and restored a little of my old muscle.

I didn't look half bad.

Returning my attention to the bar, I located Ralph almost immediately. He sat two stools to the left of the camera's point of focus, sipping beer and talking up the pretty girl from the night before. Sophie. She stirred a cosmo with a cocktail straw and feigned interest in whatever he was saying —the video was silent. Ralph seemed earnest about something, and the hallmarks of inebriation were already evident. He'd put back more than a few of those beers. Sophie looked a little tipsy herself.

I played the video at double speed, scratching a cheek as the interaction continued. Ralph became more insistent, and Sophie more irritated. At one point she made as if to get up, and he put a hand on her arm. That garnered the attention of the bartender, who lifted her hand to draw Braydon or Brandon from the door.

The steroid-charged bouncer crew never had the chance to respond, however. The Cuban brothers responded first. I'd only seen the shorter of the two during the fight, but apparently both men were present at the bar. They appeared from the right-hand side of the screen, the short one toting a beer bottle, the tall one empty handed. They walked straight for Ralph, and the shorter one put a hand on his shoulder, yanking him back.

The interaction was brief. The confrontation immediate. Ralph returned the shove with more speed and aggression than I would have expected given his apparent level of inebriation. The Cuban was caught off-guard and stumbled backward into a big guy on a stool. That guy fell, spilling beer on his girl. The girl shouted and threw her hands up.

And the rest was history. The second Cuban got a punch in, Ralph hit the floor, the redneck returned to his feet to avenge his beer-soaked female. Then everybody was punching, just like that. The fight spilled into the crowd of tables gathered around the stage. Somebody threw a chair. Bottles crashed against the stage. The bar stool hurtled past my head like a Patriot missile.

It was chaos, just as I remembered it.

I paused the video and gave myself a moment to reflect. I wasn't overly surprised to find Ralph at the nucleus of the fight, but I was a little surprised to observe how intentionally the Cubans had interjected themselves into the scene. Almost as if they had been waiting for an opportunity to confront the old man.

Almost as if they had been watching him.

I recalled the beer the first Cuban had been drinking, and rewound the tape again. My second scan took longer—a full twenty minutes of watching in double time. I located the first point the Cubans arrived at the bar, which was immediately after Ralph arrived. Sophie was already there. The Cubans ordered beer and paid. Not in cash, but with a card. And it wasn't a tab, because the sunburnt bartender handed them a receipt.

I froze the camera and made note of the time stamp. Then I called through the open door back into the bar.

"Hey, Hank! Where are last night's receipts?"

"Huh?"

"The receipts! From last night."

"Oh...uh. Top right drawer. Why?"

I ignored the question and tugged the drawer open. It was every bit as messy and overloaded as I expected, with faded and crumpled receipt paper spilling out over the floor. Fortunately, the most recent receipts were located on top, and it took me only a few more minutes to match a ten-dollar tab—two four-dollar beers, plus a two-dollar tip—to the time stamp on the camera.

The charge was processed against a credit card. *Emilio Cruz*, signed as a squiggly mark. But that wasn't all. The credit card was a business card, not personal. The business was listed as *Havana Seafood Restaurant*.

I clicked away from the camera and pulled up a web page. A quick web search produced an address only seven miles away, on the south side of Harper Springs.

Bingo.

8
---

ay in central Florida isn't for everyone. I'd
enjoyed the mild winter and balmy spring,
often walking shirtless around my campsite
and almost never wearing shoes, but summer felt like
another beast entirely. Even with the windows of my pickup
rolled down and a gentle breeze wafting through the cabin, I
felt like I was trapped in an oven. The rotating digital sign on
a bank I passed marked the temperature at ninety-six
degrees, and the humidity felt thick enough to cut with a
knife.

Maybe, after I found Camilla and proved her to be a
fraud, it would be time to contemplate new scenery. Something a little farther north, perhaps in the mountains. Something cooler.

Since leaving Phoenix eighteen months prior, it had
almost never crossed my mind to return, and I was now
confident that I was uninterested in a continued career in
law enforcement. For that matter, I was pretty sure I was
uninterested in any sort of career. It turned out that money

was easy enough to come by when you only needed a little of it. With a house on wheels and my beer habit in check, playing for tips more than covered my expenses, and I still had nearly thirty-five grand hidden in a lock box beneath the GMC's bench seat—proceeds from my late fiancée's retirement account, her last gift to me. It was enough to keep me wandering around almost indefinitely.

Thoughts of my financial situation and future temporary addresses faded as I cranked up the radio. With plenty of time on my hands and a borrowed box of Hank's rusty tools, I'd finally managed to work out the bugs in the audio system. Jimmy Buffet sang about fast boats to China and mangos in Paris, lyrics that reminded me I hadn't eaten in hours. My stomach growled, and I wondered what sort of food a Cuban seafood restaurant served.

Something fresh, I hoped. Maybe something blackened, with sweet iced tea to wash it down. Assuming they would serve me.

I reached my destination an hour past noon and parked at the edge of a crowded gravel lot. The restaurant sat within line of sight to the Gulf of Mexico, salt breeze on the air, a baking midday sun pounding down on faded lapboard siding and a rusting metal roof. The sign hung between palm trees, suspended on chains. Printed first in Spanish, second in English, all the letters peeling.

Havana Seafood Restaurant. Fresh Seafood Caught and Cooked Daily!

The place had an overall appearance of disrepair, but none of that disrepair seemed to have any impact on the restaurant's patronage. As I pushed through the front door I was greeted by a clamor of voices and cutlery clanging on plates, a segmented dining room packed with low square tables and a mottled mix of preppy Clearwater types and down-home Floridians. Caramel-skinned servers rushed amid the tables, trays held over their heads, sweat gleaming on their forearms. The hostess station was empty. Lunch hour was in full swing.

I seated myself in a booth at the back corner of the restaurant, sliding in with a clear view of both the kitchen and the door. It was five minutes before the first server stopped by—a very cute Latina girl in a tank top. She cradled a tray of empty dishes and looked a little winded, but she flashed me a smile as warm as the Caribbean sun.

"What can I get you, sweetie?"

Her accent said Puerto Rico. I liked it.

"Sweet tea with lemon," I said. "And a menu."

She winked and hurried off. I relaxed into the booth, keeping an eye out for either of my friends from the alley next to the barbershop. Rewinding the interaction in my mind, I found myself wondering how a couple of busy restaurant owners found time to grab haircuts only a few hours prior to a lunch rush this significant. I assumed it was a setup, at the time, but now I wondered if it was just more of Ralph's magnificent bad luck.

It made me feel sorry for him, again.

The Latina girl returned with my iced tea and introduced herself as Rosa. I scanned the menu quickly before ordering the Cuban-style paella with a filet of redfish.

"You got it. Anything else?"

"Yes, actually. Is Emilio in?"

Rosa didn't seem surprised by the request. "He's in back. Can I tell him who's asking?"

"Ralph," I said.

"I'll tell him."

I squeezed the lemon over my tea and enjoyed a long pull of rich, cool refreshment. It was strong, but not over-sweetened. I thought I might drink a few refills.

Emilio didn't keep me waiting—and neither did his brother. Both Cubans appeared through the swinging double doors that led to the kitchen, the shorter wearing a server's apron tied around his waist, the taller dressed in a chef's jacket. Their faces spoke to murderous intentions as they swept the crowd, but when Rosa pointed me out, those inflections of violence flickered into confusion.

I lifted a hand and offered a relaxed smile. The Cubans marched my way, not returning either friendly gesture. They reached my table and fanned out, standing close enough to block my view of the restaurant, but not speaking. The shorter guy—Emilio I assumed, based on Hank's security recording—glared down at me, his nose still swollen and now turning dark purple.

The bigger guy chewed gum, looking somehow even more enraged. I recalled his busted testicles and elected to forgive his lack of hospitality.

"I ordered the paella," I said. "Just wanted to make sure nobody spit in it."

"You need to *leave*," Emilio said.

"Why?" I feigned shock. "I just got here."

"This is a place of *business*," Emilio said. "We're don't want any drama."

"Neither do I," I said. "I just want some paella. And a short conversation."

The big guy gritted his teeth. I noted one hand clenching into a fist, and I allowed my gaze to freeze over. Offering him a warning. Advising him not to let me bust his nuts a second time.

"I'm not here for trouble," I said. "I just want to talk."

Emilio cast a quick glance over his shoulder, across the crowded restaurant full of innocent customers. Repeat customers, probably. People he didn't want to embarrass himself in front of.

He muttered something in Spanish. The big guy snorted. Emilio snapped a further line of Spanish, more insistent this time. He shoved his brother in the arm, pointing to the kitchen.

The big guy fumed, teeth grinding. But he went, skulking slowly to the double doors and casting a lot of irate glances over his shoulder. Emilio waited a beat, then slid into the seat opposite me. His hands rested palm-down on the table-top, and I noted busted knuckles.

From the bar fight, no doubt. From whacking my nose, maybe.

"Jorge," Emilio said, his tone semi-apologetic. "My little brother. He's a little slow in the head. A little protective."

And a little sore in the crotch.

I thought it, I didn't say it. No point in poking the bear.

"He's got a mean right hook," I said.

Emilio didn't blink. His face remained perfectly flat, but I could see in his eyes that wheels were turning. He was thinking quickly. Evaluating me, maybe estimating me.

"What do you want?" Emilio said at last, his tone as flat as his expression.

"I want to talk to your sister," I said. "I want to talk to Camilla."

Rosa brought me a refill just as I completed my demand,

and Emilio didn't so much as glance at her. As soon as the waitress departed, he spoke.

"I don't know what you think you're involved in, but you're hitching your horse to the wrong wagon. That is a very sick old man. He's harassed my sister for months. He won't leave her alone. Now he's here, and if I see him again, I'll make good on my promise. They find bodies in the bay all the time. A fool from New Jersey would be nothing special."

"Except this fool from New Jersey claims that your sister stole money from him," I said. "A lot of money."

Emilio snorted. "And you believe that? My sister is a model—she runs an active Instagram account. Lots of pretty pictures, many of them quite sensual. I don't judge how she makes her money, and trust me when I tell you that she makes plenty of it. She doesn't need to steal from anybody."

I rotated my straw amid the ice, not breaking eye contact. Estimating Emilio's claims at face value, because that's all I had to go on. The Cuban certainly didn't feel like he was lying. He didn't blink or avoid my gaze, and his body language remained perfectly calm. Almost troublingly so.

Part of me believed him. Certainly, it was a reasonable story. I don't know much about social media, but I know about models, and I know about sensual pictures. It was easy enough to believe that a creepy old man could form an attachment. Become obsessive.

Fly all the way to Florida to harass somebody.

And yet...

I couldn't get past a gut feeling about Ralph. His haunted eyes and trembling hands had been genuine. He didn't look lust-sick, he looked love-sick.

"I saw a picture of your sister," I said. "She's very beautiful."

Emilio nodded. No comment.

"A woman like her posting pictures like that must garner a lot of attention."

"There are many creeps in this world," Emilio said.

"That there are. And I'd break the legs of any one of them. But I can't help but wonder if sometimes, just maybe, they're led on. You know...*send me a few dollars, and maybe you'll get another kind of picture.*"

That finally broke Emilio. His face flushed, and he rose from the booth. I remained seated and calm as his hands closed into fists. Before he could speak, Rosa appeared with the paella redfish. It steamed from a shallow bowl. She set it down, took one glance at Emilio, and scurried off.

Emilio spoke through his teeth. "Enjoy your fish, fiddler. I was up at four a.m. to catch it."

He stormed back to the kitchen without another word, blasting through the double doors. I watched him go, still playing with the straw in my tea.

Not quite sold.

9

The paella was delicious, and the redfish even better. It certainly tasted fresh. Back in my truck I deliberated only a moment before navigating toward downtown Tampa. While eating I had used my phone to conduct a little research of my own into Camilla Cruz, and it hadn't taken me long to find a website portfolio featuring a number of her photo shoots, along with references to her place of employment.

Queen City Modeling Agency. Tampa, Florida.

I didn't bother to investigate the agency or dig into Camilla's Instagram account. I didn't have an Instagram account of my own and I wasn't interested in acquiring one. Maybe if I hit a wall at the modeling agency, I could reevaluate that lead. For now, I was more interested in what Emilio had said—and perhaps more importantly, what he had *not* said.

He hadn't denied my insinuation that Camilla could be milking creeps on the internet for extra cash. He'd been offended, certainly. But sometimes people are most offended by the raw truth.

Regardless, I was no more interested in judging Camilla's activities or choices of income generation than Emilio was. I only wanted to prove her as the fraud I suspected her to be, or else prove Ralph as a fraud, and then wash my hands of this mess. Think about a next destination. Think about someplace cooler.

Queen City Modeling Agency was headquartered on the tenth floor of a Tampa high rise situated right in the heart of downtown. It took me some time to find parking. I dusted my faded T-shirt off as I stepped out of the truck and swept my gaze across my equally faded jeans and battered tennis shoes. It wasn't a great look, and it made me wonder what my story would be. Something convincing, ideally, but not overly complex.

I was a private client, I decided. I had need of a model for a specialized photoshoot. Maybe I owned a new local brewery and wanted a pretty girl to hand out fliers or pose for advertising. Maybe I'd seen Camilla's Instagram, and I liked what I saw.

It was a weak pitch, but with luck it would be enough to locate Camilla. A quick conversation should put this matter to bed and get me back to my campsite in time to tune up my violin for the evening bar crowd.

It wasn't like I had much else to do.

The receptionist directed me to an elevator, which led me to a frosted glass door with Queen City's logo printed in gold ink—the initials of the company running in a circle around the silhouette of a woman's body. All curves and long hair.

Well. That certainly communicates a brand.

Pushing inside, I was immediately greeted by a storm of noise and activity. For some reason I expected a segmented maze of offices fronted by a quiet receptionist's desk. Maybe a fake tree in one corner, and a stack of magazines on a low table. Like a dentist's office.

The receptionist's desk was there, occupied by a cute twenty-something blonde in a neon green blouse, but the area beyond was wide open across the bulk of the floor, with only one office situated in a rear corner.

The center of the room was packed with flurrying activity—people, cameras, backdrops and lighting rigs. Tables full of clothes and two dozen young women dressed in everything from ball gowns to cowgirl outfits to bikinis. Photographers moved like bees buzzing next to a hive, squatting and snapping pictures, calling for different poses or more lighting while stylists adjusted makeup and hair pieces.

It looked like absolute chaos to my untrained eye, and it immediately put me on edge. There was a sort of cubical standing in the middle of the room where the models buzzed in and out, changing clothes. It wasn't quite tall enough to shield everything, and I caught more than a flash as I surveyed the room.

"Can I help you, sir?"

I turned a flushed face on the receptionist. She'd just hung up the phone and flashed me one of those crystal-white smiles you see in toothpaste commercials. I fumbled for words, still thrown off balance by the display of skin.

"I'm...looking for somebody."

"Who are you looking for?" The receptionist remained unfazed, still beaming that lambent smile. It was enough to shake me back to the present.

"Camilla," I said. "Camilla Cruz."

That broke the smile. Just for a second—a brief flinch of the lips and flash of the eyes. A glimpse of concern, maybe. Or personal distaste. I couldn't be sure—it was gone as fast as it came, and the toothpaste grin resumed.

"May I ask who's inquiring?"

"Emmitt Smith," I said.

It wasn't the best pseudonym to choose, but I always default to famous football players when I'm thinking quickly, and I doubted very seriously whether a room full of giggling young models would have any clue about the NFL's all-time leading rusher.

The blonde returned to the phone. I stood with my hands in my pockets, trying not to glance toward the cubical. Camera flashes made me squint as the receptionist mumbled into her phone, turning her head away.

I thought it was odd. I thought the entire thing was odd. I wasn't sure what the daily machinations of a modeling agency should look like, but this felt...a little unhinged. A little chaotic.

Vaguely fast and loose.

The blonde hung up the phone and beamed the smile again. "Our CEO will be right with you, Mr. Smith. Can I get you a refreshment?"

"No, thanks." I resumed my awkward stance, fixating on a worn patch of carpet. I couldn't recall feeling so out of place since that one time I wound up spending two weeks aboard USS *America*, one of the Navy's amphibious assault ships. It was an uncomfortable environment for any Army Ranger, but it didn't hold a candle to this.

"Hey, I know you!"

The voice cut through the clamor from just beyond the

receptionist's desk. My gaze flicked up to find the girl from the bar leaning against a chair, fiddling with the strap of a high-heeled shoe. Sophie.

Her strawberry blonde hair was held back in loose curls, falling over bare shoulders. She wore a sequin mermaid dress hugging her legs down to the ankles and making it difficult to affix the shoes. Sophie didn't seem to mind.

"Hey," I mumbled, unsure what else to say. I thought I probably looked like an idiot, and that was starting to piss me off.

A photographer snapped his fingers nearby and a stylist scurried in to help Sophie with the shoes. She straightened, sweeping hair behind one ear.

"Cologne ads," she said with a grin. "Seafarer musk... makes the women flip out. Don't you want to buy?"

Not even a little.

I offered Sophie a tight smile. She remained unfazed.

"You gonna be playing tonight?" she asked. "I was thinking of coming by. Maybe I could buy you a beer! You know...to thank you for last night."

Last night. My mind spun back to the confrontation between Ralph and Sophie. I hadn't interpreted my own actions as heroic so much as instinctual, but one look in Sophie's glimmering eyes and it was clear that she had. Suddenly, I wasn't sure what to say. I stalled, hoping for an exit. I was saved by the bell when a third woman appeared, taller than Sophie and walking with her chin held up. Late forties or early fifties. Rich, dark hair that looked dyed. The tell-tale traces of a face lift, and a snug-fitting black business dress that highlighted...well.

Other cosmetic adjustments.

"Mr. Smith?"

The woman projected confidence as she cut Sophie off without so much as a glance, extending a hand. I took it and was rewarded with a gentle squeeze and an elegant shake.

"Yes," I said.

"Ava Sullivan, president and CEO of Queen City Modeling Agency. A pleasure to meet you."

"Likewise," I said.

Ava interlaced her fingers over a slim-line waist, remaining straight-backed and poised like a statue. Bright blue eyes contrasted the dark hair perfectly, tasteful makeup accentuating high cheekbones and a pleasant mouth.

She was beautiful—in her day, she had likely been stunning. Maybe a model in her own right.

"Amber said you were looking for Miss Cruz?" Ava said.

"Right," I said.

"May I ask why?"

My mind switched gears back to my cover story. "I own a little brewery up in Harper Springs. Our grand opening is next month. I ran across some of Camilla's work and thought she might be perfect for some ads we want to run."

Ava beamed. "Camilla is one of our best. What's the name of your brewery?"

My mind hit a block wall.

"Uhm...Harper Springs Brewers." I shrugged apologetically. "Our beer is more creative than our name."

Ava laughed—a gentle melody that felt as practiced and calibrated as her appearance. "Well, I'm sure we can help, Mr. Smith. Won't you join me in my office?"

I followed Ava across the crowded room, skirting the cubical as one of the models pulled a dress over her head with no regard for anybody watching. Ava spoke clipped directions to a photographer here or a stylist there as she wove toward the lone office, directing a model to lift her chin or an assistant to adjust lighting. I got the vibe that if this was a circus, Ava was the ringmaster, and very comfortable in her role.

The office was built of glass walls, populated by a matching desk and a tasteful number of award plaques and potted plants. No clutter. No personal photographs. Ava extended a hand toward a chair in front of the desk, then seated herself with the grace of British royalty as the door swung closed automatically. The bustle of the modeling floor faded, and Ava's smile widened.

"I do apologize for the chaos," Ava said. "We've got a big trade show coming up this week—the Tampa Auto Exchange. A large client. We're having to cram our regular photoshoots."

"It's no problem."

Ava folded her hands in her lap, still smiling, still looking as poised as a plastic doll...plus a few carefully disguised wrinkles.

"So," she said. "Camilla?"

"Yes. I was hoping to speak with her. Get a feel for her personality. We may want to cut some video ads."

"Camilla is great on camera," Ava said. "Unfortunately, she's not available this morning. She's been a little under the weather. It might be a while before she returns. Maybe if you told me what your objectives are, I could match you with a similar model. I've got another Cuban girl, if that's what you're looking for."

I thought quickly. Hesitated. "I was pretty impressed with Camilla. I don't mind waiting a few weeks to shoot our commercials. Maybe I could connect with her over the phone?"

Ava didn't answer. She didn't blink. And she didn't stop smiling.

"Are you a long-time Cowboys fan, Mr. Smith?"

"I'm sorry?"

"I'm from New York, myself. My father was a Giants fan. I saw Emmitt Smith smash through our D-line twice a year for over a decade. Not a lot of fun, really. But I could understand a fan borrowing his name."

The room dropped a couple degrees in temperature. I remained calm, not looking away. Ava kept her chin up, hands in her lap. That form-fitting dress rising and falling with each calm breath.

"I was more of a fan when he played for Arizona," I said.

"The twilight years. Such a cursed franchise. They always wind up with the washouts."

I said nothing. Ava stood, and I felt obliged to follow suit. She produced a business card and extended it over the table.

"Give me a call if you're serious about any ads. I'm sure we could find a girl around here someplace who suits you."

I glanced at the card. It was thick and ivory in color. Ava's name was printed in scrolling blue ink.

President and CEO.

I flipped the card over and took a pen from her desk. I wrote my number down and handed it back.

"Have Camilla call me. I'd really love to speak with her."

Ava took the card, and the smile cooled a little. Just like the room.

"Have a great day, Mr. Smith."

10

I returned to my truck and turned north for Harper Springs, both frustrated and intrigued by my interactions with Ava. It felt obvious that she was covering for Camilla, but that by itself was no indicator of conspiracy. With a room full of half-naked women in their prime, I could only imagine that Ava managed a daily deluge of creeps posing as prospective clients.

My use of an obvious pseudonym couldn't have helped.

By the time I reached Hank's backwater campground I had barely an hour to spare before I was due to perform at the bar. I used the time to shower in the grimy bathhouse a hundred yards from my campsite, then shoveled down a ham sandwich as the sun descended over the lagoon. The whippoorwill had returned to a nearby tree, and pelicans dove over the glimmering water to snag their own dinner.

It was serenity at its finest, just as it had been for six months. But with Ralph and Camilla on my mind, I couldn't help but feel that the charm of my little sanctuary had been tarnished, and that irritated me. I'd told Ralph that I was good at finding people, and that's true, but it's also true that even my most refined skillsets are quickly dulled by a lack of motivation. I've never been the kind of person who can put his heart into something that his heart doesn't believe in, and I was starting to doubt Ralph.

Or maybe the situation in general.

Whatever the case, I resigned myself to perform my musical duties at the bar, get a good night's rest, and then invest myself one further day into locating Camilla. If I hit another wall, I would call it quits and advise Ralph to return to his paint factory.

That seemed a fair effort, all things considered.

Cradling the violin, I walked to the bar and offered Hank a two-finger salute. Most of the band was there, a few of them a little battered and bruised from the previous night's mayhem, but none of them said anything to me about their share of the tips. Maybe Hank had already informed them not to expect anything.

Maybe he hadn't needed to.

We picked up where we left off, swinging through Charlie Daniels before I recommended a stint of Jimmy Buffett—I still had "Last Mango in Paris" stuck in my head. The bar filled out nicely, many of the faces bruised and sheepish, ducking their heads whenever Hank walked by, and tipping the sunburnt bar girls a little more generously than usual.

The band bucket filled with cash also, and frosty bottles kept sliding down the counter. By nine p.m. I knew it was going to be a good night. Our guitarist announced a break, and I toweled sweat from my forehead, thinking it was time for a drink of my own. I was halfway to the bar when a familiar voice rang above the clamor.

"Hey, hot stuff!"

I turned to find Sophie seated at a table near the back wall, reclined with one leg crossed over the other, wearing skinny jeans and a tank top. The strawberry blonde hair was held back in a ponytail, and while much of her mermaid makeup remained, she looked overall a lot more comfortable than she had six hours previously.

Sophie shot me a wink, a Coors Light sweating in one hand while another rested on the table next to her, cap already removed.

"Ready for that beer?" she shouted.

I hesitated for only a moment before scraping back a chair and taking a seat. Sophie swigged from the bottle like a woman well accustomed to light beer, glossed lips shimmering with foam. I tipped my bottle toward her before taking a sip.

"Thanks."

Sophie shrugged as if it was nothing, picking at her bottle's label. She had an odd sort of nervous energy about her—as though she were perfectly at home in a grungy dive bar like this, but also self-conscious about her every move. A little on edge about something, perhaps.

I gave her body language only momentary evaluation before relegating it to a mental bin full of things I'll never understand about women and thought instead about Ralph. About the previous night. About the encounter, and Sophie's place in it.

I'd been so fixated on contacting Camilla directly that I hadn't even considered the fact that Ralph's initial line of investigation was a solid one. Sophie seemed like a girl who would talk. With the beer rotating in one hand and a buzzed gleam in her eye, I thought she might just talk to me.

"So where you from?" Sophie asked. A silly little grin crept onto her lips, looking a little too natural to be a factor in her self-conscious poise. Another battleground between composure and relaxation.

"Arizona," I said. "And you?"

"Charleston." She said it with pride. "You ever been?"

I shook my head. "I'd like to."

"It's beautiful. Real classy Old South."

"What brings you to Tampa?"

I already knew the answer, but it's always easiest to get people talking with simple questions.

"Work! You saw today. I model for TV commercials... magazine ads. You know. Silly stuff."

She said it with a sheepish little shrug that felt as sincere as the grin. It made me sad, for some reason. I couldn't put my finger on why.

"You play for long?" she asked.

"Huh?"

"The fiddle."

"Oh. Right. Yeah...a few years. Picked it up in the Army."

"Oh yeah?"

Sophie propped one elbow on the table, resting her chin in her palm and turning glimmering green eyes on me. There was more inebriation in her gaze than I'd seen barely three minutes prior.

More unfettered interest, also. It made me uncomfortable.

"So...about last night," I said.

"What about it?"

"That thing with the old guy. With Ralph."

"Oh."

The grin faded a little. Disinterest clouded her gaze. I pressed ahead.

"He says he's looking for his girlfriend. I guess you work together?"

Sophie retracted into her seat, swallowing two big gulps from the bottle. She wiped her mouth with the back of one hand, smearing lip gloss.

She was drunker than I thought.

"What about it?" The charm had melted from her voice. Sophie now sounded vaguely irritated.

"Do you know where she is?" I asked.

"Who?"

"Camilla Cruz."

Sophie snorted. Eyeballed me with a slight squint, as though she thought I was up to something and wanted me to know it.

"Is that what this is about?"

"What?"

"You coming over here to chat."

"You invited me."

Sophie swigged beer and looked away. She shrugged and inspected her nails. "I don't know where Camilla is. I heard she's sick."

"That's what Ava said."

"So there you have it."

I cocked my head, evaluating. Sophie huffed a little, rolling her shoulders back to maximize the flattering benefits of her tank top.

She was toying with me, I thought. Having fun. And I also thought she was lying.

Before I could think of a way to regain control of the conversation, my guitarist returned to the stage and hit a riff on his six-string. The crowd unleashed a drunken cheer, and I fished a ten out of my pocket.

"Next round's on me," I said. "Enjoy the music."

Sophie grunted a disinterested thanks, biting a fingernail and refusing to make eye contact. I tried not to roll my eyes as I returned to the stage, hopping into place just in time to join the band for "Havana Daydreamin'", another Buffet song. It felt ironically apropos to Ralph's current fixation with a Cuban girl.

Women. I watched Sophie at the table in the back, drinking and pretending not to watch me. Still playing games. It would have irritated me, a decade prior, but I've outgrown twenty-something cat-and-mouse dances between the sexes. At our next break I would return to the table and cut straight to business.

But I never got the chance. The guy appeared halfway through our set, standing just inside the doorway for five seconds while he surveyed the entire crowd. Then he made a bee-line for Sophie's table, and she sat up when she saw him coming.

He was short. Wore black jeans and a jet-black T-shirt, untucked and a little looser than it needed to be. Reddish blond hair, not unlike Sophie's, but there was no relation between the two. He was burly and thick, his features wide and blunt. Altogether unlike Sophie's angular cheekbones and pleasing mouth.

He sat down like he was familiar with her. He laid a tattooed arm on the tabletop. Sophie sat rigid, her face cold and expressionless, her mouth moving in only subdued whispers to answer his jabbing questions. I couldn't hear a thing over the noise of my own music, but the body language was clear.

He would say something. She would shoot back a clipped reply. Then repeat. The sunburnt barmaid came by to offer him a drink and was immediately dismissed.

A boot toed my leg, and my head snapped right. My guitarist raised both eyebrows in a "what are you doing?" expression. My mind snapped back to the present and I looked down to the violin. It was only then that I realized I had been playing my solo on repeat.

Nobody in the drunken crowd seemed to have noticed. I fell back into the chorus with practiced ease, and the guitarist sang. The drummer pounded.

When I looked toward the back of the room again, the man was gone. Sophie was gone. The table stood unoccupied, my ten-dollar bill pinned beneath a beer bottle. I looked out for their return through the rest of the set, but even as the bar wound down and the crowd thinned out, Sophie never appeared. When I finally packed up, cashed out, and ventured into the parking lot, her red Volkswagen Beetle was nowhere in sight.

Running a hand over my face, I let my shoulders sag as exhaustion crushed down on me. It had been a week, already. I was still sore from the bar fight and frustrated by repeatedly fruitless conversations.

I was done for the day. I cradled the violin under one arm and turned for my campsite, content to forget Ralph's problems for the night.

11

The chirp of songbirds woke me the next morning long before the sun could. I rolled over in the back of my truck and scrubbed sleep out of my eyes, peering through the open tailgate to the black waters of the lagoon. The sky had just begun to turn gray in the east, clouds parting behind the trees as early bird pelicans now dove for breakfast.

It was the morning melody of coastal Florida, and the charm was enough to wash away the ache in my back left by a leaking air mattress. I scrambled over the tailgate and gave myself a moment to stretch in the stillness, working out the kinks in my neck. There had been nothing wrong with my air mattress before I lent it to Ralph. The old guy must have slept with nails in his pockets.

I rustled up coffee, making note of my depleted breakfast supplies, then sat at the picnic table and opened the plastic sandwich bag that I'd kept at the bottom of my backpack for most of the previous year. Only one item was housed inside.

A small Bible, bound in worn brown leather, with my fiancée's name engraved in elegant script.

Mia Hayes.

The Bible was bookmarked midway through, my lone photo of Mia pinned in front of the 37th Psalm. I took a moment to gaze at her glowing face, running a thumb gently over the creased paper.

I felt the sadness deep in my gut, just the way I'd felt it for eighteen months. But my eyes didn't blur. My stomach didn't twist into knots. I just smiled, placed the photo on the table, and read for a while.

I've never been religious. In fact, I was nearly an adult before anybody ever asked me if I knew who Jesus was—a question I'm still not sure how to answer. When I met Mia and she mentioned her faith, I thought it would be a turnoff. I'd had run-ins with religious zealots aplenty by then, many of them armed with AK-47s and hellbent on blowing my head off.

But Mia was different. She was real. I couldn't put my finger on it, but there was an authenticity to her belief separate of any pretense or insecurity. Simple identity, expressed by faith in a higher power who loved her. Who wanted better things for her.

And for me, she used to say. I never could wrap my head around that bit, and the moment she slipped away right before my eyes I thought her faith must have been a sham. What sort of God would throw one of His own to the wolves that way?

I wasn't sure, but the further the memories of Mia's death

faded into my mind, the more I wondered. Curiosity was getting the better of me. I felt drawn to that little book by an unidentifiable sort of hunger.

I read the Psalms because I remembered Mia liked the Psalms. It seemed a safe place to start.

By the time the sun had crested the horizon, I was five chapters in, and my stomach growled. I returned the photo to the pages, the Bible to the plastic bag, and the bag to my backpack. Then I tossed all of the above onto the floorboard of my truck and started for town. I figured I would begin with some groceries, then swing by Ralph's motel for an early morning chat. I had questions—more than a few of which would probe the integrity of Ralph's own story. I was going to make one more attempt to locate Camilla before giving Ralph the advice I probably should have given him from the start.

Let it go. Head back to New Jersey. Sell some paint. Face the music I'd had to face myself over the past year. It wasn't easy, and my personal circumstances were quite different from his, but the end result was the same. He had to move on.

The GMC rolled along backroads into Harper Springs with "Take it Easy" by Eagles rumbling through the speakers. It was one of my favorite tracks and helped to ease the tension in my mind as I navigated for the nearest grocery story. It sat two blocks from Ralph's motel, and it hadn't opened yet, but I didn't care because I was already distracted by the flash of blue lights from the motel parking lot. I swerved back onto the two-lane and punched the gas, leaning forward beneath the roofline of the old pickup for a better view. Long before I reached the aging neon sign that overhung the entrance, the flash of emergency lights had gathered into a fireworks show of blinking blue joined by glimmers of amber and bright red. Four Harper Springs police cruisers sat in the lot, parked at odd angles with their doors hanging open, cops in royal blue uniforms swarming the steps running up to the second floor.

There was an ambulance, also. Back doors open, a lone paramedic standing with arms crossed, jaw working on a wad of gum. A handful of motel occupants and the manager watched from open doors and parted blinds, all fixated on the same room the cops were focused on—an open door on the second floor, about halfway to the end of the motel wing. Gold numbers mounted on the closed doors to either side read 21 and 23.

The middle was 22, and it was a number I remembered. It was Ralph's room.

I spun the truck into the lot, sliding to a stop next to a police cruiser and cutting my motor. A wash of Florida sunshine spilled over my face as I piled out. One officer looked my way but didn't leave the base of the steps. As I watched, the cops gathered around the door of room 22 parted, and paramedics appeared. They carried an orange gurney between them, cradling it with care through the door and onto the walkway. There was a body stretched across the gurney, semi-obscured by an EMS blanket.

And the body didn't move.

My heart thumped and I took two steps closer to the steps. One of the cops cut me off, holding up a hand.

"Stand back, sir."

"Who is it?" I said, pointing to the gurney.

"Just stand back!"

The cop turned away. I waited, watching as the paramedics started down the steps. My stomach tightened. I craned my neck for a glimpse of the partially obscured face. I couldn't make it out.

Then movement caught my eye—from the open door of room 22. More cops appeared, marching straight-backed with heavy hands resting on the shoulders of a detainee. The detainee was Ralph. He was handcuffed and barefoot, his eyes bloodshot and wild, his hair tangled and sweaty. Tears ran down his face, and he stumbled on the threshold. My heart skipped in momentary confusion, and my gaze snapped back to the gurney. It had reached the rear of the ambulance now, and a puff of Florida breeze tugged on the EMS blanket. The light, reflective material lifted a little, and sunlight spilled over the face.

It was Camilla. I recognized her in an instant from the photo strips Ralph had shown me, and just as quickly I knew she was dead. Her eyes were frozen open, her lips parted, death clouding over her face like a thunderstorm. Deep gashes tore across one cheek and her forehead, dried blood caked amid swollen red skin.

The gurney slid into the ambulance and the doors smacked shut. Ralph stumbled down the steps, hauled along by the cops. One glance at their stone-cold faces, and I knew the story. Or at least their version of it. Ralph reached the parking lot and they thrust him toward a car. I stepped forward, but the cop at the base of the stairway stiff-armed me like a running back hurtling past a safety.

"Stand *back*, sir. I won't ask you again."

I didn't fight. Ralph reached the car and finally saw me. Wild eyes locked with mine, and a wave of terror washed between us. But not just terror. Pain, also. Deep, heartfelt, agonizing pain.

"I didn't do it," Ralph choked. "I swear I didn't do it."

Then the cops shoved him into the back seat, and the door closed. While I stood in the parking lot tires spun, and Ralph was whisked away.

12

T he remaining cops would tell me nothing. Stiff-Arm shot me a look cold enough to freeze vodka, placing a beefy hand over his sidearm. I abandoned the motel at that stage and returned to my truck. A quick search on my phone produced the location of the Harper Springs police station, barely three miles away. I made the drive while fixating on the haunted look in Ralph's eye as he was shoved into the cop car.

The fear. And the loss.

It registered perfectly alongside the heartbreak I'd detected in my initial meeting with Ralph, and that created a conflict. The heartbreak was fixated on Camilla, as was the loss. Two emotions birthed out of love, or at least obsession, which flew in the face of whatever demon passion could bring a man to kill somebody.

It wasn't impossible, but my gut told me it didn't make sense as I piloted the GMC into the police station's parking lot and cut the engine. The heavy door slammed like a tank hatch, just loud enough to jar my mind back into reason.

I stopped. Caught my breath and cleared my head.

Slow now, Mason. Be calm.

I pushed through the glass door into the lobby. A desk sergeant waited there—a sleepy middle-aged woman with a giant cup of coffee steaming in one hand. She breathed on it as I approached, barely looking up.

"Can I help you, sir?"

"Yeah. You just arrested a guy—Ralph..."

I'd forgotten his last name. She waited, cocking one eyebrow.

"I'd like to speak with him," I said.

The sergeant directed her attention to her computer. She did some clicking and typing. She blew on her coffee again and took a tentative sip. Then she grunted.

"Are you an attorney?" she asked.

"No."

"Then I'm afraid you'll have to wait for visiting hours."

"Which are?"

"This afternoon. Assuming he's been processed and cleared interrogation. You can call to check if you like."

She jabbed a card at me. I ignored it.

"I'd like to speak with your captain, please."

That brought on a sarcastic smile. "My captain?"

"Or chief. Whatever you have here."

The desk sergeant held my gaze and slurped. Then she slowly lifted a telephone headset and punched a button.

"Mack? Yeah...there's a fella here wants to see you. He's... what's your name?"

"Mason Sharpe."

"And you are?"

I hesitated. Then I decided to fudge a little.

"Homicide. Phoenix PD."

It used to be true. The sergeant cocked an eyebrow and repeated the title. Then she hung up.

"It'll be a minute. You can have a seat."

Back to the blowing on the coffee. I retreated to the empty lobby and located a sagging chair encased in cracking vinyl. There were sports car magazines and saltwater fishing circulars, but I ignored them. I drummed one finger on the arm of the chair and retraced my steps back to the motel. To the body. To Ralph.

What had happened? I'd left Ralph for not even twenty-four hours. I'd left him at that motel, which meant Camilla had come to him. Willingly, I presumed. Unless she was already staying there. And then?

The investigator in me jumped to logical assumptions. Ralph had killed her. Guessing by the cuts and welts on her face, it seemed she had been belted over the head with some sharp and hefty object. Blunt force trauma. Lights out.

But I still couldn't buy it. It was that gut feeling again, paired with the pain in Ralph's face. It just didn't feel right.

I waited an hour before "Mack" appeared. Lieutenant Trent Kellerman. How they got *Mack* out of that was beyond me, but he introduced himself as such and shook my hand. He looked all business—average height, in excellent shape, with a clean and crisp uniform. A few years my junior. Maybe twenty-five. A pencil black mustache and matching eyes.

"You're a detective with the Phoenix PD? Phoenix, Arizona?"

"Right."

"Mind if I see some identification?"

I expected that request and decided to switch back to honesty. It was always the best policy.

"I'm a former detective. I only claimed the title so you'd talk to me."

Mack grunted, but he didn't seem irritated. He looked like a man who understood. He was a cop, after all. Seasoned investigators often appreciate a pragmatic approach.

"What can I do for you, Mr. Sharpe?"

"I'd like to speak with your detainee. The old guy you brought in from the motel."

Mack squinted. I thought he might decline me the way the desk sergeant had, but instead he probed for details. Because he was smart.

"What's your connection with him?"

That was a more complicated question to answer than it should have been. I thought quickly.

"I met him recently," I said, remaining intentionally vague.

"You're a friend?"

"I wouldn't say that. He asked me to help him find somebody. A woman."

"The woman we carted out on a stretcher?" Mack raised both eyebrows. I shrugged, suddenly realizing that I was feeding the police information that might easily serve to further incriminate Ralph. Which might be justified.

Or maybe not.

I didn't do it. I heard Ralph's insistent plea in my mind again and felt the sting of it. The sincerity in his voice. The desperation.

"Why don't you join me in my office, and we'll have a little chat?" Mack suggested.

I shook my head. "No. I want to speak to Ralph. I'm not giving a witness statement until I do."

Mack snorted. "I shouldn't have to tell another cop that withholding information is a crime."

I indulged in a brief smile. "And I shouldn't have to tell another cop that withholding information is a difficult crime to prove."

That brought the flicker of a smirk to Mack's lips, but he didn't surrender immediately.

"I can't grant you an interview. He's under interrogation. He's only entitled to speak to an attorney."

"He's entitled to a phone call," I said.

"So give me your number. Maybe he'll call you."

I shook my head. "No. Put me in a room with him. Five minutes. Tell him that qualifies as his phone call."

Mack considered. I waited.

"Then you'll talk?" he asked.

I shrugged. "Maybe. Depends on what he says."

Another long pause. A keen light ignited in Mack's eyes. A bit of calculation. An idea, maybe.

I thought I knew what the idea was.

"Three minutes," he said. "Then you're out of here."

13

They put me in a boxy little room with stark white walls and a two-way mirror. There was a camera in one corner, but I could tell by the dusty lens that it didn't work and hadn't worked in some time.

I took a seat behind the lone metal table, and they marched Ralph in a few minutes later. He was cuffed, hand and foot, and already dressed in a dingy white jailhouse jumpsuit matched with foam flip-flops. He descended into a heap in the opposing chair, choking on a sob, cheeks glistening with tears. The tangled mass of gray hair clinging to his scalp was slick with sweat, and his chest rose and fell in jerky waves.

He was a wreck.

"Mack says three minutes," Ralph's escort declared.

"Thanks. Turn the camera off, please." I said it with a smile, and the escort chuckled. The door closed, and I turned to Ralph.

"Talk quickly," I said. "What happened?"

Ralph's hands shook, and he looked to the camera.

"It's broken," I said.

"They could be listening," Ralph said.

"They're absolutely listening. It's the only reason they let me talk to you. I'm not an attorney and you're not covered under any sort of confidentiality privilege. This is by far their easiest method of interrogating you."

Ralph swallowed hard. He looked to the two-way mirror.

"You were a cop?" he asked.

"Yes."

"And you think I should talk to them?"

"That's up to you."

"But they say you shouldn't talk to cops."

"They're right."

Another heavy gasp. A tear splashed against the stainless steel. He gripped the edge of the table to steady his hand.

"Make up your mind," I said. "You're running out of time."

He looked back to me. "You can help me?"

"That depends on what you did."

"I didn't do *anything*. I swear!"

"Okay. So tell me what happened."

Ralph collected himself. His hand steadied a little. He inhaled slowly. Then he spoke, voice lower than before. I assumed Mack and his buddies could still hear. There was probably a microphone planted in the lamp hanging just over the table.

"I was at the motel. Right where you left me."

"Okay."

"I...I was messaging Camilla on Instagram. Like we used to."

"And?"

"And she messaged back."

Ralph's eyes bubbled with tears. His voice rasped. He was losing it.

"Get it together," I said calmly.

Ralph scrubbed his face with the back of one hand. "She said she'd been in Cuba. She lost her phone. That's why she went missing for so long. But...she was back in Tampa. She was really excited that I was down here."

His voice broke again, words tumbling over each other into a stream. I just listened.

"She said she wanted to see me. I offered to go to her place. She said she'd come to me, instead. So...I gave her the address. She took a cab. She...she..."

Ralph slumped over, sobs racking his body. I waited it out, not the least bit concerned about the clock. There was zero chance Mack would cut our conversation short. He'd let us talk all morning if we wanted. The three-minute thing was just a ploy to maybe fool us from knowing that he would be listening.

But I wasn't fooled—I'd been a cop before.

Ralph scrubbed his face again. He seemed to bottle everything up someplace deep in his heaving chest. His wrinkled old face glistened with tears and sweat. He started again.

"We hung out in my motel room. We had some wine."

"Did you have sex?" It was a relevant question. Intercourse would have left all manner of biological evidence. Ralph was almost certainly pinned to the scene of the crime by virtue of his presence when the police arrived, but any sort of DNA could be used to establish a broader timeline. Just one more nail in the coffin.

Ralph nodded, a sad sort of smile crossing his lips. "Yes... first time."

My gut tightened. I lowered my voice. "What *happened?*"

Ralph returned to the present. He focused.

"After we were finished...we were just hanging out, you know. Cuddling. I thought I would do something special for her. Get us some dessert."

"And?" I asked.

He faced me. His lip shook. "I walked down the street to the grocery store. When I returned...she...she..."

"Was dead," I finished.

The sobs returned. I leaned back in my seat and crossed my arms, observing the body language. Reading the tone of each racking gasp. The slump of the shoulders, the tremble of the hands.

The tongue can lie. The body has a harder time disguising the truth. All the signs I now saw were convincing ones, but I'd learned the hard way to not be so easily sold.

"Ralph."

He kept crying, bent over the table.

"Look at me." I kept my tone calm. Ralph looked up.

"Did you kill her?" I asked.

Ralph would be a fool to say yes, even if it was true. Something in my gut told me he was just simple enough a soul to not know that. He blinked back tears, chin trembling. Breath rasping. But he shook his head.

"No. I couldn't have. I *love her.*"

I nodded slowly, noting his present tense use of the word *love*. Because in his heart, he still couldn't accept that she was really gone. I had some idea what that felt like.

"Help me," Ralph whispered. "Please. I don't have anybody. They're going to lock me up. They're going to—"

The door opened, cutting Ralph off. Mack stepped in. "Time's up, Sharpe."

I shot him an "Are you kidding me?" look. He made a show of checking his watch, but he closed the door. I leaned close to Ralph and lowered my voice.

"I need something, Ralph. You gotta give me something to work with."

Ralph blinked hard. His gaze darted. He sniffed and scrubbed his nose. Then a light clicked on behind his eyes.

"Our messages," he said. "They're all on Instagram."

"Lower your voice," I said.

Ralph settled into a whisper. "If you saw those, you'd know I couldn't have killed her. You'd know I love her!"

I thought about that. Thought about what Ralph had told me about the money—about a family in Cuba struggling to reach the land of the free.

I doubted very seriously whether any testament of undying affection expressed over instant messages could prove Ralph's innocence, but the Instagram messages weren't a bad idea. They might prove something else.

They might prove Camilla's guilt.

"I need your username and password," I said.

Ralph sat up. His lips parted, and I held up a hand.

"Don't tell me. They're listening."

He squinted. Chewed his lip. Then he whispered again.

"The username is my email address. It's my name, Ralph Roberts, plus the company I work for. You remember?"

I nodded. "And the password?"

The door opened behind us. Mack and one of his beat cops appeared, marching to put hands on Ralph's arms.

"You already know," Ralph said with a sad smile. "You said it yourself, right after we met."

I frowned. "What?"

"Remember? When I told you where I was from?"

"That's enough, Sharpe," Mack said. "You gotta go."

They hauled Ralph out, rushing him along so that his feet dragged. Mack remained in the room, arms crossed, giving me the iron stare.

"Well?" he said.

"Well what?" I replied. "You were listening."

"What's the password?" Mack said.

I stood, scraping my chair back over the concrete. Mind spinning.

"I have no idea," I said. It was the truth—at least for the moment.

"You better not be lying to me, Sharpe. If there's evidence on that Instagram account—"

"Then you'll find it with a warrant," I said. "I'm sure there's a judge around here, someplace."

I turned for the door.

"We had a deal," Mack said. "Don't make my job harder than it has to be."

I stopped. Put my hands in my pockets and thought about Ralph. About the story his lips told, and whether his body validated it. I looked back to Mack.

"There was a broken wine bottle, right?"

He frowned. "What?"

"Camilla's face was cut and bruised. She was hit with something sharp and hard. Enough blunt force trauma to kill her while shredding her face. I'm betting you found broken glass on the floor. Ralph said they were drinking wine."

Mack's mouth closed. His face set into a hard line. I knew I'd hit on the truth, but maybe not all of it. My mind ascended quickly to the next natural step. I thought back to the bar fight, and how a person holds a glass bottle when they use it as a weapon.

They grip it by the neck. They strike with the base. And they leave fingerprints.

"You didn't find the bottle neck, did you?"

"What are you trying to say, Sharpe?"

"I'm saying...what if you've got the wrong guy?"

Mack snorted. "You really think so?"

"Smashing a bottle over somebody's face is a crime of rage, Mack. Doesn't take a genius to know that. Hiding the bottle neck is an act of contemplated concealment. Does that guy seem like a contemplative genius to you? He can barely remember his own name right now. And who called the police, anyway? It was him, right? So, he was smart enough to hide the bottle neck but dumb enough to hang around and be pinned for the murder?"

Mack closed the distance between us. His tone dropped. "When there's a cold body and a hot-blooded lover leaning over it...it ain't rocket science."

I thought about that. Generally, Mack was correct. Good police work isn't rocket science...not usually.

But with Ralph, I couldn't buy it. Something was wrong. It felt like I was missing the forest for the trees.

I turned for the hallway, Mack calling after me as I reached the door for the lobby.

"Don't go far, Sharpe. I may have questions for you."

Hot Florida sunshine spilled over my face as I stepped outside the police station. I squinted into the sunrise and flexed my neck. I smelled salt breeze and baking asphalt. My stomach growled but I barely noticed.

I was still thinking about Ralph when the Dodge Ramcharger rocketed around the block and appeared in the police station's parking lot with a squeal of oversized mud tires. Heat waves shimmered off the hood and sun rays obscured my vision of the windshield, but I didn't have to wonder about the occupants for long. Both front doors rocketed open, and the Cruz brothers hit the concrete, Emilio from the driver's side, Jorge from the passenger's. They orbited the front of the jacked-up SUV and fast-marched not toward the police station, but toward me.

"*You!*" Emilio shouted, jabbing a finger. His face was puffy and red, his eyes bloodshot. Jorge was actively crying, his big chest rising and falling as he stopped halfway between the Ramcharger and me, lips trembling, fists clenched.

Something glimmered in his right hand—something familiar. It was the brass knuckles he'd wielded against Ralph in the alley next to the barber shop. I took half a step back, falling into a fighting stance, and raised a hand.

"Just calm down—"

"I *told you* the old man was a creep!" Emilio screamed. "You egged him on!"

Emilio marched onward. Jorge orbited to my left, stepping quickly around me and headed for my truck. Before I could stop him he reached the driver's side window, arm ratcheting back like a cocked artillery piece.

"You better not—" My warning was cut short as brass knuckles crashed through the pickup's window as though it were made of tissue paper. Glass exploded over the seat and Jorge roared.

Then Emilio was on me. I don't know if he planned to swing, or if he was thinking at all. I didn't give him the chance to decide—I met his jaw with my right elbow, twisting at the hips and driving with enough force to knock him off balance. Emilio flailed and tumbled. Then Jorge was on me. His long legs carried him from the truck straight to my position in another two strides. Brass knuckles flashed in the sunrise. I ducked the first blow and went for his gut, striking with a right hook that should have driven the wind right out of him.

It didn't—I wasn't even sure if he felt it. My knuckles collided with a brick wall and Jorge didn't so much as grunt. He brought his closed right fist down over my back like a sledgehammer, and I choked.

Emilio was back on his feet, lunging toward my unprotected flank. I dropped to my knees and rolled left, landing back on my feet outside Jorge's grip as the big man pivoted with his brass knuckles.

"My sister!" Jorge sobbed. "*My sister!*"

He swung again. I sidestepped this time and went for his face, clipping upward fast and sudden, catching him on the jaw. The blow hurt my hand as badly as his face, but it was enough to knock him off balance and give me time to address Emilio. I pivoted right just as a metallic snap rang across the parking lot, sharp and sudden.

Emilio held a switchblade, teeth gritted, rage overcoming his face. The double-edged blade gleamed. He fell into a fighting stance.

Then Mack and his beat cops exploded through the front door of the police station, pepper spray and tasers brandished.

"*Emilio!*" Mack shouted. "Put it down!"

Emilio didn't move, the blade still extended toward my chest. Jorge held his jaw and slumped against the Ramcharger, sobbing.

I lowered my fists, still throbbing from Jorge's blow to my back.

Tears ran down Emilio's cheek. He lowered the knife and hit the switch. The blade disappeared, but he held my gaze.

All that pain and anger boiling like a hurricane, just behind glassy brown eyes.

"I told you," Emilio rasped.

I said nothing, and the Cruz brothers turned for the police station.

14

My driver's side window was obliterated. I cleared cubes of glass from the bench seat before abandoning the police station in favor of the same coffee shop Ralph and I had shared drinks at following the last deployment of Jorge's brass knuckles.

My back hurt. My knees ached from hitting the gravel. My nose still burned from Emilio's punch the night of the barfight. I was winded and pissed. But most of my mental energy had already moved beyond the parking lot brawl and back to Ralph—and his story.

By the time the barista brought me a medium roast in an oversized cup, I had Ralph's email address figured out. His name, maybe with a period in-between *Ralph* and *Roberts*, with his company name as the web address after the @ symbol.

The password was trickier, but when I finally retraced our conversation in my mind and recalled that throwaway line following his declaration of his home state, it all came together.

He had said he was from New Jersey, and I had said "Go, Giants."

Surely it's not that obvious.

But it was. I downloaded the Instagram app and logged in on the third attempt. The G's were capitalized. There was no period between his names in the email address. The rest was just as it appeared.

Ralph's account featured a slew of selfies and sunsets, many of them blurry, none of them particularly aesthetically pleasing, but the captions were enthusiastic. He wrote about happiness. About peace and knowing yourself. The overall vibe was exceptionally positive, with the most recent photograph posted only four days prior. It was another selfie, Ralph sitting in an airplane seat, grinning ear to ear, with the woman next to him leaning away to avoid the camera.

The caption read:

Off to see the love of my life! Smooth flights and clear skies.

There was a little red heart emoji between the sentences. A few hashtags about love and life and being willing to leave everything behind. Nobody had liked or commented on the post. Not many people seemed to follow Ralph at all.

Not many...but one name stuck out. Camilla Cruz, Instagram model.

A quick survey of her page produced an altogether different aesthetic. The sunsets were there, as were the selfies, but they were filtered and edited. Calibrated and snapped from the most flattering angles. Camilla was featured in all of them, and she was every bit as beautiful as she'd looked in the picture Ralph showed me. A mid-twenties Cuban-American girl with a lithe body equipped with just the right curves. Tanned skin. Deep, dreamy eyes.

She was stunning, and evidently knew it. There was little modesty to the photos, physical or otherwise. The captions were quippy and confident, loaded with new age proverbs and sarcastic one-liners.

She was a kid, but she clearly didn't know it, and neither did Ralph. I switched away from the photos and reluctantly opened the instant messenger box, already suspecting what I would find. I wasn't wrong about the content, but the sheer volume of messages took me off-guard.

There were thousands of them. I scrolled and scrolled to wind back the calendar to the day Ralph and Camilla met, sliding past hundreds of wordy proclamations of adoration from Ralph and selective affirmation from Camilla. There were emojis. There were pictures—most of them from Camilla. Every bit as filtered and carefully calibrated as before but featuring...well. A lot less clothing.

There was sexting. There was lonely conversation and dreams about a future together. There were references to video calls, many of them laced with innuendo and suggestion. There were pleas for attention from Ralph and aloof dismissal from Camilla.

And there were a *lot* of references to money. Thousands and thousands of dollars' worth, far worse than I expected. Camilla had drained Ralph while never directly declaring any sort of exchange of attention for money. She spun a story about family stranded in Cuba. Ralph swallowed it—hook, line, and sinker. He sent her wire transfers, some of them ranging north of ten thousand dollars. He talked about tapping into his 401k and draining his savings account.

He would do anything for Camilla. Whatever it took to

get her family to the Land of the Free. Whatever it took for them to be together, and Camilla promised they would be together the moment she resolved her familial problems.

I penciled together a list of transfers in my mind and generated a total north of a hundred thousand dollars in wires, online transfers, and transactions sent by Western Union. Ralph talked about running short on funds. Camilla asked about loans, claiming that her credit was bad after maxing out her own credit cards. Ralph said he would talk to his banker.

The entire thing made me want to puke. When I reached the conclusion of the message thread I found the interaction Ralph had described. Camilla disappeared for over a week. Ralph became desperate. He messaged regularly, eventually every half hour. He flew to Tampa. He kept messaging. I could tell when he was drunk and tell when he was sleeping. The messages became slurred or sparse, respectively.

Finally, Camilla messaged back. She'd been in Cuba. She'd just returned to Tampa. She wanted to see him. Not her place, no. She'd come to his motel.

I shut the phone off and tossed it onto the table, my coffee growing cold next to my arm. Around me the coffee shop now buzzed with activity, but I barely noticed. I was thinking about Ralph and the conglomeration of thousands of messages, all boiling down into two very clear realities.

First, Ralph was desperately, madly, drunkenly in love. He'd fallen for this girl, and really believed that she loved him too.

Second, the moment Mack obtained a warrant and read these messages, Ralph was done. He'd never see the light of day again. He'd never obtain bail. He'd finish his life in prison, because it was all there. The means, the opportunity, and most importantly the *motive*. It was a prosecutor's dream.

I could hear the opening argument now. Camilla had taken everything from Ralph. She'd lied to him. She met him at his motel to break up with him. Ralph had raped her, then beaten her to death in his lovesick rage. A crime of passion—almost understandable, but still a horrific crime that demanded immediate and absolute justice. Special circumstances, even. The death penalty.

I sucked my teeth. There was a tightness in my chest that I didn't quite understand. A sort of vague desperation expressed in a singular impulsive thought: *I should delete the messages.*

It hit me so suddenly that it took me off-guard, and I stopped myself. From Ralph's end, I could erase the message history. At least on his account. The cops would need a warrant for Camilla's account to read them on her end, which might be difficult, because she was dead and nobody knew her password.

But none of that really mattered so much as the question of *why* I wanted to delete the messages. It would be a direct obstruction of justice, a crime in and of itself. And shouldn't I want justice to be carried out? Shouldn't I want Ralph behind bars?

I would...except I didn't believe he was guilty. The reality of it struck me as suddenly as the thought had, and I knew it was true deep in my bones. Not because of any particular evidence, or because I could argue with the means, opportunity, and motive.

I didn't believe Ralph was guilty because of what I'd seen in his eyes. The way his voice quivered. The story his body language told. That man, for better or worse, was madly in love with Camilla. Obsessed with her in a soulful way that only a fraction of society may ever experience.

But I'd experienced it, and I'd lost it. I knew what that felt like. I knew what it looked like. And I knew that Ralph couldn't have killed Camilla.

The only thing I didn't know was what to do about it.

15

I found a glass shop and let them inspect the truck. It would be two hundred bucks for a new crank-up window, which made me want to punch Jorge in the face all over again. Then I thought about his broken sobs, vacant eyes staring right through me as he repeated "*My sister, my sister,*" and I simply told the glass guy to make the order. It would take a few days for the window to be shipped in. Hopefully it wouldn't rain before then.

Back in my truck I sat with my phone in my lap, tapping the plastic and thinking. Not about Ralph, and not even about Camilla, but about murder. Hot-blooded, enraged murder. The kind of unbridled evil that would drive one person to break a wine bottle over another person's face.

I've killed men with my bare hands before. Once, in Afghanistan, with a jammed M4 and my ears still ringing from a grenade blast, I was stumbling through the living room of a Taliban target's home. He hit me from behind. I couldn't reach my sidearm—I couldn't even reach my knife.

We fought like cats, tumbling and rolling while gunfire exploded all around us.

I landed on top. My hands found a little metal tractor some kid had left on the floor. A toy.

I beat him to death with it. One bloody blow after the next. It was the worst fifteen seconds of my life—extrapolated into what felt like hours as I kept striking. It was hell. It was misery. Only my own desperate need for survival was enough to keep me going.

Camilla may not have been hit multiple times. She may have only been hit once, knocked unconscious and collapsing before she drowned on the blood running into her mouth. But that would have taken time. Even if Ralph had somehow become enraged enough to strike her—which didn't feel right to me, either—then he would have called for an ambulance after the first blow. By then the moment of rage would have already passed. If it hadn't, he would have kept striking.

He should have called for help, but instead he called for the police...and that wasn't right. You only call for the police when you know for sure that somebody is dead, and I couldn't imagine Ralph standing over Camilla's gasping form as death enveloped her.

No. It wasn't in him. I couldn't buy it. I couldn't make myself believe that Ralph was a killer. Even if I was somehow radically misjudging his character, I would need to prove that for myself. I would need to dig up the truth and see it with my own eyes.

I would have to investigate. It was the only remaining option.

I mashed the clutch and restarted my truck as my mind

switched gears into my old investigator's brain. I was already thinking about leads, resolved now to commit myself to the process no matter how long it took. All I needed was a place to start, and it wasn't a difficult decision to make.

I would begin with the only personal connection I knew Camilla to have outside her enraged brothers—the same connection Ralph himself had thought to investigate when he was searching for Camilla. I turned the pickup south again, back across the bay, back to the high rise in downtown Tampa. I parked on the street and took the elevator to the tenth floor.

The blonde wore a different neon blouse this time, orange instead of green. She greeted me with a lot less energy than she had the day prior. The open floor of Queen City Modeling Agency was as full of women and cameras as before, but the nervous energy was gone. All the chatter, all the giggling. The bustle was subdued, and the plastered smiles looked a little less enthusiastic.

A stack of flower bouquets resting on a table near the receptionist's desk summarized the story. News of Camilla's murder had clearly swept the building, and it had made an impact.

"Mr. Smith, right?" the receptionist asked. She sniffed a little, but the effect seemed to be contrived. Her eyes were clear enough.

"Right."

"Let me get Ms. Sullivan." The blonde reached for her phone.

"Actually, I was hoping to speak to Sophie."

The blonde squinted. "Sophie Wilson?"

I shrugged, hands in my pockets. The blonde cocked her

head over her shoulder, sweeping the room. Sophie was visible halfway across the floor, seated at a makeup bar, fussing with her strawberry hair.

"What's this regarding?"

"A personal matter," I said.

The blonde sighed and hauled herself out of her chair. She waded through the room to Sophie's side and said something to her. Sophie craned her neck to look into the lobby. I lifted a hand.

***

SOPHIE AGREED to join me for lunch without too much persuasion. I had the feeling she was eager to get out of the building. She referenced a Greek restaurant two blocks away, and I waited half an hour in a corner booth before she showed up with styled hair sprayed into a solid block that resembled a helmet. She wore jeans and a loose white blouse printed with four leaf clovers like polka dots. Her nails sparked bright green.

"More cologne ads?" I asked.

Sophie snorted, requesting water from the waiter. "Irish breath mints."

A part of me wondered what made a breath mint Irish, but a bigger part of me didn't care. There was something haunted about Sophie's gaze. The playful, semi-mischievous glint I'd noted at the bar was gone. She fidgeted a lot. She looked like she hadn't slept well.

We both ordered salads with roast lamb, and Sophie picked at her fingernails as the waiter retreated to the kitchen. She avoided my gaze, her nose a little red as she gazed out the window.

"Did you know her well?" I asked.

Sophie shrugged. "Not really. Not like some of the girls."

"How long did you work together?"

"Six months, I guess."

"She ever express any fears? Any concerns about people she knew?"

Sophie rotated away from the window, squinting at me as though she were realizing who she was talking to for the first time. The waiter brought her water and left a straw. Sophie ignored both.

"Who are you?" she said.

It was my turn to shrug. "Just a guy."

"You've got a lot of questions for a guy."

A fair point. I deliberated for a moment, unenthusiastic about showing my cards but knowing I had to give her something. Sophie's good-natured agreeability was running short.

"I wanted to ask you about the other night," I said.

"Which one?"

"The first one. The bar fight."

Sophie unwrapped her straw and jabbed it into the water. Ice rattled against a plastic cup.

"What about it?" The Carolina drawl was still there, but an undertone of frustration joined it. I chose my words carefully.

"Ralph approached you about Camilla..."

"The old guy?"

"Right."

Sophie sipped water. "Yeah? So what?"

"What exactly did he say? How did he find you?"

Another shrug. Sophie looked out the window, and I couldn't tell if she were playing hard to get or if she were simply shell-shocked. Her eyes rimmed red. She sniffed a little.

"He said he didn't do it," I said quietly.

That got her attention. Sophie's gaze snapped back to mine. "What?"

"He said he didn't kill her."

"And you believe him?" Disgust joined the disbelief in her tone.

I didn't answer.

"Look, *buddy*. I came here because I thought you were being nice. I thought you were trying to make up for the other night."

I squinted. "Make up for what?"

"For blowing me off!"

I rewound my second interaction with Sophie at the bar, replaying it at my mind. The table in the back. The extra beer...

"Wait. Did you..."

Sophie flushed. She shoved the water aside and scooted out of the booth. I followed her.

"Hey, look. I didn't mean to blow you off. I just want to know what happened—"

Sophie wheeled on me, a stiff forefinger jabbing my chest. "What *happened* is that old creep killed her! He raped her and he beat her to death. You don't know what it's like to be one of us, but guys like him are everywhere. They never leave us alone. If you're too stupid to understand that, I can't help you."

"Wait—"

She was done. Sophie whirled for the door and marched out with her chin held up, helmet hair stiff and unyielding against the Florida breeze. I stood next to the table, a little hot under the collar as I ignored the crowd of restaurant patrons staring at me with mouths half open.

The waiter returned, two salads with roast lamb riding a tray. He looked for Sophie and frowned.

"I'll take those in boxes," I said, dropping cash on the table. "To go."

16

I piled the salads into the truck next to me and turned north for the campground. It was late afternoon by the time I parked in the little gravel slot next to the lagoon. I had eaten one of the salads while driving, and I packed the second one into my cooler before changing my shirt and heading for the bar. My band wasn't scheduled to play that night, which meant there would be no tips to earn. The beer would still be cold, however, and just then I felt in need of it. I selected the same rear table where Sophie had sat the night before and asked the sunburnt waitress to bring me Coors in the bottle—plenty of it.

The alcohol helped to numb the dull ache in my brain as I kicked back with one boot in the opposing chair. Maybe it was the long day of ramming my head against the wall, or the frustration of Sophie's self-indignant refusal to be helpful. Whatever the case, I felt growing irritability bubbling just beneath the surface of my practiced calm. I don't count on anybody to make my life easy, but thus far every stroke felt like a stroke against a tidal wave.

I needed a break. Something tangible.

I cracked open my fifth beer as the bar speakers blared local country radio and the tables filled out with the dinner crowd. Hank was in the back, working the burger grill. The air hung thick with greasy kitchen smells, reminding me of Bailey's in Alabama. The Skyline diner in Atlanta. Marley's Pub in North Carolina. Places that had hallmarked my wanderings since leaving Phoenix, drifting from motels to campsites to empty parking lots on an endless quest for...what?

I wasn't sure. Peace, I guessed. Which I thought I'd found at Hank's campsite, but now the smells and clamor of a campground bar were growing old in my ears. I was feeling restless again.

And I couldn't get Ralph off my mind. I thought of him in the jail cell all alone, mourning the loss of his beloved girlfriend, and I felt none of the condemnation Sophie had reflected. I felt sad. I felt a burning sense of injustice.

I felt the truth, dancing in the shadows, just out of reach.

I drained my sixth and final beer, a solid buzz numbing the back of my skull, and left a nice tip for the waitress. Then I shot Hank a salute and ventured back out into the Florida evening. It was full dark, and the air hung thick with a blanket of humidity. A mosquito the size of a helicopter buzzed near my face and I swatted it away. The path to my campsite lay strewn with fallen sticks and pinecones, crunching beneath my boots as the buzzing in my head redoubled. I remembered Sophie's salad in my ice chest and thought I would reheat the lamb on my camp stove. With any luck, I could clean up dinner and be in bed by ten. Maybe sleep in the hammock with my mosquito net. Enjoy the stars.

I tripped over a divot in the path and caught myself on a tree, shaking my head to clear my vision. The tree wavered a little, and I questioned my decision to dump a six-pack on nothing more robust than a salad.

Back at the campsite I clicked the stove on and set my coffee pot over the flame, figuring I would sober up a little with some decaf before bedtime. The salad was a mess in the takeout box, so I gave up picking out the lamb strips and ate it cold standing next to the table.

I was halfway finished when the stick snapped behind me, cracking like a gunshot through the stillness of the campsite. My back went rigid, instantaneous instinct overcoming my inebriation as I dropped the salad and pivoted toward the disturbance.

A campsite speckled with trees and crowded with crawling critters makes all kinds of noises, but there's something perfectly distinct about a human footfall. Maybe it was the Army, or my training as a cop, or any number of would-be muggers on the streets of Phoenix that had taught me the difference. Whatever the case, I knew somebody was behind me even as I twisted and cocked an arm, ready to engage.

I *didn't* know that somebody also stood to my left, hidden by the bulk of the GMC. Even as I cocked my fist and made ready to knock the block off the guy rocketing between the pines, his face covered by a black neck gaiter, the second guy appeared in my peripheral vision from the rear of my truck, a baseball bat arcing toward my skull like a rocket.

I chose to ignore the oncoming aggressor and address the more immediate concern—that bat. Twisting right, I took the bat on my shoulder blade instead of my skull, pain exploding through my back and racing down my spine in a burst. I lost my footing and stumbled forward—straight into the arms of my initial attacker.

There was no way to avoid the next blow. It struck my jaw with the force of a trained boxer, detonating stars across my vision as I stumbled. I threw a left jab that connected with thick muscle, earning a grunt from my attacker, but little more. He grabbed my shirt and yanked me close, breath whistling between invisible teeth.

It wasn't the move I expected. I had thought he would shove me away, giving me time to make a groin shot with my right shin. There was no time for that, now. I was off balance, and the second guy was on me, grabbing my shoulder and spinning me around. I threw up an arm to shield my face, expecting the baseball bat.

The bat rocketed in, just as I expected. But instead of going for my face, he went for my stomach. The air rushed from my lungs and I doubled over, agony racking my body. My arms dropped instinctively to clutch my gut.

Then he went for my face. The bat snapped like a fishing rod, cracking me right over the crown of my head. Blackness closed in, and I toppled. Leaves and sticks crunched beneath my hips, but I couldn't feel them. The sky overhead swirled like a vortex. My stomach tightened and surged, and overwhelming pain clouded my head. I was so dizzy I couldn't tell which way was up. Consciousness evaded me, playing at the edges of my vision. I twisted and struggled to get up, but then a heavy boot landed on my chest. Pressure crushed down. The tip of the bat rammed beneath my throat as my vision started to clear.

I stared up the length of the wooden weapon, regarding the second of the two men. He also wore a neck gaiter, pulled high over his nose until it obscured everything except pitch-black eyes.

Those eyes were fixed on me, and they didn't blink.

"Anything?" the guy with the bat said.

From somewhere behind me, the first man spoke. "Nothing. Just junk."

"Great. Ditch it."

A metallic pop rang across the campground. I recognized it as the heavy latch opening on my pickup. The door groaned, and the gear shifter rattled. I gritted my teeth and twisted on the ground, fingers sinking into loamy Florida soil.

Both the bat and the boot crushed down, forcing me into the dirt and driving the air from my lungs. It was a simple hold, but an effective one. I could barely breathe. I couldn't budge.

Behind me tires ground over gravel. My pickup's engine hadn't turned over, but it didn't take a rocket scientist to know what was happening. The first guy had taken the truck out of gear. It was rolling—passing the picnic table, headed for the lagoon.

I twisted on the ground, the bat scraping against my neck as I watched the GMC's tailgate glide by. The truck gained speed as the masked man shoved against the door frame. It was moving too quickly to stop, now. It crashed right between a row of low bushes, and the masked man released it with a final shove.

The truck hit the lagoon bank and never stopped. Water crashed against the open tailgate and surged into the bed. Heavy American steel dragged the back of the truck down until water was surging through the busted driver's side window.

In mere seconds, the pickup was gone. Fully underwater, a faded chrome grill vanishing into the dark. I turned gritted teeth on the man standing over me, still gasping for enough breath to speak. Still held helpless against the ground.

"You're gonna regret that," I snarled.

The first guy returned from the truck, kneeling next to me. He hooked a finger over the top of the neck gaiter, drawing it down to expose a gently tanned face. Dark eyes. Flashing white teeth and a bold nose.

"I'm gonna make this brutally simple," he said, his voice carrying a soft Floridian drawl. "Leave the girls alone. Leave the modeling agency alone. Leave the questions alone. You turn up in Tampa again—we'll kill you. Got it?"

I never had the chance to answer. The boot crushed down. The first man stood and replaced his neck gaiter, still holding my gaze. I tensed, fingers closing around a small rock. Ready to drive it against the leg crushing down on me with all the force I could muster.

I never got the chance. The first man nodded once. The bat left my throat with a sudden flick.

Then it crashed down directly over the top of my skull, hard and fast. Everything went black.

17

I awoke to flashing red lights, with the mother of all headaches exploding through my skull like a nuclear blast. Voices crowded into my mind even before I could blink back the confusion and make sense of my surroundings. I saw trees, and I saw faces. I saw a giant of a guy in a heavy black and yellow uniform with a red hardhat on.

A fireman's hat, I realized. I was no longer lying on the ground. I now lay on a gurney. Paramedics surrounded me. The flashing lights gleamed from the top of a fire department ambulance. I still couldn't make sense of the words spoken, but I began to recognize some of the voices. They were those of several of my campsite neighbors, joined now and then by barks from Hank.

"Can you hear me, brother?" The big fireman leaned down. A paramedic clicked a flashlight on and shone it into my eyes. I tried not to squint.

"Mason? You all right?"

Hank appeared at my elbow. I relaxed into the gurney

and closed my eyes, fighting to block out that exploding pain that ripped down my spine. I thought it originated from the top of my head.

Then I remembered the bat. The two men. The boot crushing down on my chest. The snarled warning.

"You turn up in Tampa again—we'll kill you."

I sucked down a deep breath, noting an aching chest for the first time but grateful for the oxygen. The paramedic went on probing my head with two gloved fingers.

"Can you tell me what happened?" she asked.

I winced as the fingers made contact with the crown of my head. It felt like there was a lump there.

There ought to be.

"Baseball bat," I muttered.

"Say what?" Hank barked. "Who hit you?"

"I don't know." I tried to sit up. The big fireman pressed me down.

"Hold up there, cowboy. You stay put. We're gonna get you to the hospital."

That woke me up. The cloud in my head evaporated, and I forced myself into a seated position.

"No hospital. Just get me a bottle of water."

"You need to be evaluated," the paramedic said. "You could have a brain bleed."

"Yeah, okay. If I do, I'll die. I'm not paying that bill."

The paramedic folded her arms. "We're required to take you to the nearest hospital for a full evaluation."

"Not if I refuse, you aren't. Now somebody hand me a water—or better yet, a beer."

One of my campsite neighbors obliged, shoving past the fireman and thrusting a bottle between my fingers. It wasn't beer, and it wasn't cold, but it was wet. I guzzled the entire thing in one long pull and scrubbed my face with the back of one hand. The paramedic still hadn't moved. She stood with muscled arms crossed, a bodybuilder's neck protruding from a tank top. The look on her face said she was already tired of my nonsense.

"I'm fine," I said. "I haven't got any health insurance."

"You won't have any health, either, if you don't take care of yourself."

Granted.

I compromised with the paramedic and allowed her and her partner to perform a series of medical inspections on me before eventually capitulating to my demands to be released. They gave me a heavy painkiller, advised me not to drink with it, then the firefighter helped me off the gurney and guided me to the picnic table. I sat down with a wince and knocked back the pills before checking my watch.

It was nearly five a.m. I'd been unconscious almost all night.

"If that's everything," the paramedic said.

I extended my thanks, earning a derisive snort. Then the trio of first responders loaded into the ambulance and the flashing lights cut off before the heavy vehicle rolled away, leaving me awash in a flood of lantern glow and flashlight beams. In an instant I was surrounded by a buzz of curious neighbors, each of them thrusting granola bars and bags of their uncle's homemade venison jerky into my lap as hefty hands rubbed my back and concerned voices asked if I needed anything.

It was all very warm and genuine, but I knew why everybody was really there. It was the same reason that had drawn them out of bed in the first place—the same unifying motivator that brings vacationing city dwellers and laid-back full-timers together like bees circling a hive.

Curiosity.

"What happened?" That was Hank. His raspy, perpetually irritated voice cut through the noise, and everybody went silent almost immediately. Eager to hear the story.

I touched my head with two fingers, probing gently. The knot on my skull gave meaning to the term *goose egg*. It was certainly large enough to qualify, and that was actually a good sign. It meant the swelling was extending away from my brain, and not pressing into it.

I likely still had a concussion.

"Baseball bat," I said again.

"From who?" A Canadian accent carried the breathless question just loud enough for everybody to hear. I squinted, rewinding my mind again. Remembering the broken stick, the sudden appearance of the twin shadowy figures. The masked faces. The crack of the bat against my head.

And then...

"I don't know," I said. "Bigfoot, I guess."

It was a weak joke, but it earned a ripple of laughs. Somebody smacked my back again, and the murmur of voices resumed. I looked up to catch Hank's gray eyes and noted that he wasn't blinking. He just stared, arms crossed.

Then somebody else spoke a question that jarred loose another layer of memories.

"Say, where's your truck?"

My gaze snapped left, away from the campsite, toward the lagoon. Twin tire tracks traced a path away from the lot, across soft soil and right to the water line. I could no longer see the vehicle, but in a flash I recalled the crash of water as the rear bumper made impact. The suck of blackness closing around the cab. Surging in through the busted window.

And then I thought of something else—not the truck, or the meaningless, replaceable camping gear gathered in the bed. I thought of my backpack.

And Mia's Bible.

Lunging off the picnic table, I stumbled as I approached the waterline. The crowd called after me, and flashlight beams danced across the ground. Somebody noticed the tire treads. That earned a chorus of curses and disbelieving gasps.

Digging one hand into my pocket, I found the Streamlight and mashed the switch to deliver maximum output. Then I clamped it between my teeth and advanced to the waterline.

"Mason, you can't be divin' in thar—"

I ignored the warning and launched off the bank, swandiving straight into the water. It closed over my head and I descended, casting three or four feet of illumination straight ahead as I kicked downward along a sloping, muddy lagoon floor.

I made it twenty feet and saw nothing. Returning to the surface, I gasped for air around the flashlight before flipping over and diving again. The process repeated three times, leading me farther and farther away from shore, deeper into the brackish water. Even at the midpoint of the lagoon the depth couldn't be greater than thirty feet, but that was well deeper than I could free-dive in the dark.

I needed the truck to be closer, but searching in the mucky water was like stumbling around blindfolded. The flashlight was almost no help, and with each passing second my heart thundered harder as thoughts of Mia's precious Bible pounded in my head.

It was wrapped inside a plastic bag. It *should* be fine. But if not...

I finally found the truck on my sixth dive. It had rolled forty feet away from shore, the white cab resting fully ten feet beneath the surface. The LED gleamed off the chrome grill as I kicked to the driver's side window and hooked my arm through the open hole.

Another thought crossed my mind—a sudden panic that maybe the Bible or even the entire backpack had left the truck during its descent into the water. My heart thumped and my head turned dizzy. I twisted face-down and pointed the light into the cab.

Bits of trash and empty soda bottles bobbed just beneath the ceiling where a pocket of air was still trapped. A salt-water catfish detected my sweeping arm and darted head-first into the passenger side window, ramming his ugly face into the glass and thrashing.

I ignored it all and swept my hands over the bench seat. The brackish water was thick with silt. I couldn't see beneath the dash. I pulled my body deeper into the cab as oxygen evaporated from my lungs. The pounding in my head was slower, now. My vision blurred and water surged into my throat around the flashlight. I almost choked.

Then I touched the backpack. It lay semi-pinned beneath the seat. I wrapped my fingers around one strap and snatched it free. As I writhed backward I cut my arm on a jagged shard of glass left by Jorge and his brass knuckles.

Escaping the cab, I rocketed straight for the surface, dragging the backpack behind me. I broke through with a desperate gasp for air, sucking down salty water and oxygen like a pearl diver only seconds away from drowning.

The campsite neighbors all waited for me at the bank, dragging me up with more curses and pontifications about my obvious desire to commit suicide. I spat the flashlight out and caught it in one hand. I took the backpack to the picnic table and tore the zipper open. I dumped the contents out.

Toiletries. A spare T-shirt. Socks. A lighter and some paracord. A knife sharpener.

And the plastic bag.

I knew the moment I touched it that somehow water had leaked inside. I heard the squish of wet plastic and damp pages. I pulled it out and a drizzle of the lagoon escaped the semi-open mouth.

Two inches of water clouded the bottom, the Bible floating amid them.

My vision blurred and my stomach twisted into knots as I drew the Bible out. My fingers trembled a little, and nobody spoke. The crowd around the table was suddenly deathly quiet.

I flipped the Bible open to the Psalms, where Mia's photograph served as a bookmark. My last picture of her.

It was water stained, the color draining from the bottom and spilling across wet Bible pages. I choked, a hot tear sliding down my cheek. My fingers turned rigid. I breathed through my teeth.

Hank appeared next to me, putting a gentle hand on my arm. He spoke softly.

"Mason. Who was it?"

"Dead men," I said, softly. "They were dead men walking."

18

I spent the next two hours gently separating the pages
of Mia's Bible, wiping away excess water and blowing
on each one to help them dry. Whatever paper Bible
pages are made of, it's reasonably water resistant, but it still
wrinkled as it dried and a few passages blurred with
brackish grime.

It made me angrier than I've felt about anything except
Mia's murder. It made me want to throat-punch somebody.

It made me want to do some bashing with a bat of
my own.

When the sun came up and the campground awoke,
several of the old-timers backed their heavy-duty pickup
trucks near to the water and we set about retrieving my truck
from the lagoon. Hank produced a tangled mess of chains,
ropes, and tow straps, and we linked them all together until
a loop was formed, large enough to wrap around the tow
hitches of a couple one-tons before draping into the water.

Then I dove in again with a flashlight between my teeth
and hooked the loop to the pickup's frame. The GMC rose

from the lagoon like a forgotten artifact of the Civil War, water gushing from every orifice and muddy gunk clinging to the tires. Much of my camping gear had floated free of the open tailgate and was now lost. What remained was water damaged beyond recognition. Only the air mattress—which remained pinned beneath the camper shell—was relatively unharmed.

I mashed the latch and hauled the driver's side door open, unleashing a deluge of murky water occupied by two more saltwater cats and a turtle. They all flopped around on the mud until I managed to scoop them back into the lagoon with my foot.

My bench seat was soaked, the windshield obscured by grit. The gauge cluster was gunky and unusable, and the lock box I had hidden beneath my seat was completely flooded, saturating the stacks of hundred-dollar bills stashed there.

Worst of all, one of the jerkwads from the night before had thought to remove my gas cap, allowing gallons of filthy water to surge into the metal tank.

Amazing.

"Count your blessings, son," one of the old-timers spoke around a wad of tobacco. "Drain her out and tune her up and she'll run as good as ever. If it were my truck it woulda been totaled."

He jabbed a finger toward the shiny new F-350 idling near the bank. I couldn't resist a muttered retort.

"Well, it isn't your truck, is it?"

The old-timers drifted off, and Hank lent me his box of rusty tools. I went to work under the hood, pulling fuel lines and dissembling the carburetor to drain out the water. The entire engine bay was a gunky mess, with slime and bits of ocean debris sticking to every surface. Even the headlight fixtures had flooded, shorting out some old wiring. Of course, the radio I had invested so many hours into repairing was now completely destroyed.

By noon I was sweaty and covered in grease, but hours of work remained. I still had to drain the fuel tank, rebuild the carburetor, and likely replace the battery before I could even turn it over and see if it would start. Those repairs would likely constitute only the beginning of my troubles. The GMC had been fully submerged for no less than six hours. There could be water in the block for all I knew.

Stepping back from the hood, I scrubbed a forearm across my face to displace rivers of sweat and wiped my hands on a now-destroyed T-shirt. I hadn't spoken to anyone or so much as stopped to take a drink in nearly an hour. The painkillers the bodybuilder paramedic had given me were doing their job at managing the ache in my skull, but did little for my mental state. The tension boiling just beneath my skin had built into a steady bonfire, now hotter even than the blazing Florida sun.

Every time I thought of the Bible spread out in the bed of the truck to dry, I imagined myself with a baseball bat. I envisioned a pair of targets.

"Any luck?" Hank appeared from behind, shuffling across the gravel with a pair of ice-cold water bottles cradled under one arm. I tossed a wrench into the tool box with an irritated flick of my wrist and didn't answer. Hank passed me one of the bottles and I cracked it open, draining it in a protracted pull.

It wasn't enough to kill the fire, but it restored a little of my perspective.

"Gotta drain the tank," I said. "And find a battery. Then we'll see."

Hank nodded slowly, suppressing a belch. "You need a ride?"

"Probably. At some point."

"Come here."

Hank led the way across the campsite, calling greetings to several of the long-time occupants and flatly ignoring an overnight visitor from Michigan who was busy griping about the midnight disturbance.

"Yankees," Hank growled. He led the way into the little shop built next to the campground office, flicking a switch to spill flickering light across the contents. Workbenches stood scattered with rusting tools and motorcycle components while two Honda Shadows and a Harley-Davidson Road King rested on racks in various stages of disrepair. Puddles of oil and an open gas can flooded the air with all the best smells of a mechanical shed, while the metal walls did their best to block out the continued squawking of the displeased Michigander.

Hank slurped water and led the way around the Harley to the back of the shed, where a canvas tarpaulin lay draped over a fourth bike, only its tires exposed. Hank tilted his head, and I moved to help him remove the tarp. It rippled off with an explosion of dust, and Hank hacked before he drained his bottle.

Standing beneath the tarp was a Yamaha V-Max—a vintage model, maybe mid-eighties. Jet black with chrome trim, slimline saddlebags, and a pair of tail pipes large enough to lose my arms in. Racing tires were adorned with raised white letters, and a gleaming four-cylinder block was matched to silver brake rotors.

It was an absolute beast in every sense of the word. I'd seen V-Maxes before, in Phoenix. But that was years ago.

"Twelve-hundred CC's," Hank said proudly. "A hundred and forty-five ponies. Maxes out at nearly one-fifty...or so I've heard." He shot me a mischievous grin. "I bought her fresh out of college. First wife said she'd leave me if I didn't sell it... I guess you can see who stuck around."

He leaned behind the bike and pulled a keyring from a nail in the wall. "You ride?"

I stood with my hands in my pockets, admiring the smooth curves of the bike. It looked like a jungle cat—like a ball of muscle, all bunched together and ready to explode.

"Yeah," I said, a grin of my own tugging at my lips. "I ride."

Hank flipped me the keys. "Shiny side up, greasy side down. Don't have too much fun."

19

The V-Max roared to life as though it hadn't sat parked under that tarpaulin for a decade. Raw, throaty notes exploded from the tailpipe and the throttle glided beneath my right hand as the tachometer spiked.

The odometer read thirty-two thousand miles. The speedometer ran all the way to 155. Every polished chrome part and waxed black body panel gleamed in the early afternoon sunshine.

"What about a helmet?" I called over one shoulder.

Hank appeared from the mechanic's shed, his empty water bottle replaced by a fresh Coors Light. "No helmet law in Florida. Grow a pair!"

I kicked off the rough campsite gravel and turned toward the exit, giving the bike a little gas. The Yamaha lurched with an animal howl, and a full grin finally erupted across my face as I pointed the bike south, toward Harper Springs. When I gave the beast its head, the back tire tore into the pavement and the front tire lifted half an inch off the roadbed, hot Florida wind tearing at my unprotected hair. The monster rumbling between my legs felt like a long-caged beast of the underworld, finally unleashed. The bike didn't stop pulling even as I neared ninety—the guttural roar of the exhaust blending perfectly with the wind, driving back the aches and pains in my body and flooding my lungs with more than salt air.

It tasted like freedom.

When I reached the city I cruised straight onto the highway, turning for Tampa. Not only because my first lead of the day lay in Tampa, but because I'd been told not to return by the thug with the baseball bat, and such an abridgment of liberty couldn't be allowed to stand. I had discovered since leaving Phoenix that the world is full of dirtbags who want to tell a free person where they can and can't go. Call it a masochistic desire for trouble, or just a stubborn streak a mile wide, but I don't respond well to such micromanagement.

And that said nothing of the rage boiling deep in my chest at the thought of Mia's Bible. I'd obtained only a momentary glimpse of one man's face as he drew down his neck gaiter and threatened me, but that glimpse was enough. Even in a metropolis the size of Tampa, it wouldn't be difficult to find these pricks.

I simply drove straight to the one place I knew they wanted me to steer clear of—Queen City Modeling Agency. The Yamaha slid into a parallel-parking space a great deal more naturally than the GMC, and I took the elevator to the tenth floor. The cute blonde had switched to a yellow blouse now, so neon it reminded me of a highlighter. She greeted me with a forced smile, looking not so much surprised as vaguely irritated by my repeat appearance.

"Can I help you?" There wasn't any enthusiasm in her voice.

"Nope. I'm all good." I pushed right past her desk and onto the bustling floor, sidestepping a photographer and a trio of girls dressed as cats before steering for the lone office. Ava's office.

"Sir! Wait! You can't go back there."

I ignored the receptionist and pushed the door open. Ava sat behind her gleaming glass desk, a phone cradled against one ear, a pen in one hand. The office was as stark as before, save for the addition of a thick, padded envelope resting next to the computer.

Ava sat up a little as I entered, her gaze darting toward reception. The blonde raised a hand apologetically. The door closed automatically as before, and I took a seat.

I figured I'd earned that much.

Ava hung up the phone and cleared her throat. She swept those dark, piercing eyes over my disheveled clothing, and cocked an eyebrow.

"Oh, please excuse me," I said. "It's been a rough night."

Ava looked through the office's glass walls toward the modeling agency's front door, this time not for the reception-ist. She pursed her lips but didn't speak. I thought it was odd.

"You know why I'm here," I said.

Ava finally faced me. "Actually, I don't. But this really isn't a great time. Why don't you give me a call?"

"Because I can't read your body language over the phone, and I'm growing tired of being lied to."

"Excuse me?"

"Camilla. I'm here to talk about Camilla."

That threw Ava off a little. She winced. Her gaze flicked right. I noted black bags beneath her dark eyes, carefully concealed with an expert application of makeup but still noticeable. Her clothes were as fancy as before, but a touch wrinkled. Her hair a little out of place.

Maybe I wasn't the only one who'd had a rough night.

"Mr. Smith, this really isn't the time—"

"I read her Instagram messages with her alleged killer. Your little protégée cheated the man out of north of a hundred grand. Unless, of course, she *actually* has family in Cuba desperately trying to flee. I heard they do that on homemade rafts sometimes. Can't imagine a raft costing a hundred G's."

Ava's lips tightened. She stood and walked to the glass door, flicking the door lock and again glancing toward the lobby. When she returned to her chair she checked her watch. Hesitated once more, then said, "I've got five minutes. Cut to the point."

"The point is, Camilla strung Ralph along."

"Ralph being Ralph Roberts? Her killer?"

"Her alleged killer."

"And you say she cheated him?"

"Out of a hundred grand. Give or take."

"Sounds like homicidal motivation to me."

"You'd think, wouldn't you? Except, back to my body language thing. I read Ralph's, and that guy is desperately in love with Camilla. He's wrecked about her death. He says he didn't do it."

Ava snorted. "And you believe him?"

"I believe you've been lying to me about Camilla. I believe there's something sketchy going on with your business. I believe that last night two guys with a baseball bat jumped me at my campsite and knocked a decade off my life while pushing my truck into the lagoon. Oh, and by the way..."

I leaned toward the desk, lowering my voice to a dry snarl. "My dead fiancée's *Bible* was in that truck."

Ava flinched, but she didn't look away. She sat rigid in the desk chair.

"I'm very sorry," she said, at last.

"Don't be sorry. Be honest."

"About?"

"About Camilla, for a start."

Another long moment. Her lips tightened a little. Then Ava reached into the credenza running behind her desk and produced a bottle of New Amsterdam vodka, and two glasses. She poured a measure into each, then pushed one across the table. I ignored it as she took a long sip from the other, noting a slight tremor in her fingers.

The tremor faded as the liquor landed in her stomach.

"I'm sorry about the Bible," Ava said at last. "Whatever crazy ideas you have about me, you must know I had nothing to do with that."

"It's a marvelous coincidence."

"Those happen sometimes. Like when a beautiful young woman is bludgeoned to death, and a creepy old guy from another part of the country is standing over her body."

"By that logic you're guilty as sin."

Ava snorted. "Look. I don't know what you're hoping to find. A pound of flesh, maybe. But if you want to know about Camilla..."

Ava trailed off. I lifted both eyebrows. She sighed, heavily.

"I don't enjoy speaking ill of the dead."

"Humor me."

"Camilla was...troubled. Deeply. She's worked for my firm from almost the start, and she's done well. She's made a lot of money. She's got a knack for the work."

"But?"

"But sometimes girls in this industry...lose perspective."

"Perspective on what?"

"On where the money comes from."

"And where does it come from?"

"From their looks, frankly. From their bodies."

"You're telling me she didn't take care of herself."

"No, quite the opposite. Camilla maintained excellent physical form. She just started to think that maybe her charm played a bigger factor than her appearance, and that maybe there was more money to be made beyond the camera."

"I'm not good with riddles. You're going to need to elaborate."

Another sigh. "Camilla was a philanderer. Is that clear enough for you?"

"You're telling me she turned tricks."

"No. Not in that way. But you must understand that in this business a girl like Camilla would encounter a lot of very wealthy people. Many of them men. Many of those men traveling away from home. Away from their families. Away from their wives..."

Ava trailed off. I got the picture.

"She extorted them."

Ava shrugged. "I can't prove that."

"But you know it."

Ava drained the glass. "What my girls do off the clock is their business. I'm nobody's judge. All I know is that Camilla had difficulty remaining professional, and reports were getting back to me. From photographers, stylists, business partners. It was becoming a problem."

"And?"

"And...I was going to have to let her go."

"Soon?"

"Today, actually. Of course, it didn't work out that way."

"Did she have any idea?"

"No. I hadn't told anyone. Camilla is popular with the girls. Letting her go was going to make waves. You can see how distressed they all are after...well...Camilla left us."

I glanced across the floor. The hustle and bustle of snapping cameras and swishing models continued as it had the first day, but there was a definite cloud in the room. Not as many laughs. Only practiced, camera-ready smiles.

"I don't know what was happening in Camilla's life," Ava said. "But I can guess. And my guess says she got in over her head. She got greedy. She pushed too hard. Somebody pushed back."

"Ralph Roberts?" I asked.

Ava didn't answer. Her eyes told the truth.

"That's a nice story," I said. "But it doesn't explain why two jackasses with a baseball bat would pound the snot out of me for poking around."

"This is the South, Mr. Smith. People appreciate their privacy."

"People appreciate their privacy all over the world, but they only turn violent when something is at stake. I could be forgiven for wondering."

Ava checked her watch, then glanced to the door. I followed her gaze to see another man standing in the lobby. He was tall and wore black jeans and a black T-shirt, tight over a muscled chest. His complexion was dark, his hair clipped short next to his scalp.

He eyeballed Ava with an irritated twist of his lips.

"You have to go now," Ava said. "I'm sorry about what happened to you. I really know nothing about it. If you want a nickel's worth of free advice from somebody who knows Tampa, I would let the cops do the police work. Like I said before...people like their privacy."

I stood. Ava didn't extend a hand. I measured her stare, then headed for the door, leaving the glass of New Amsterdam untouched. I passed the muscled guy in the black T-shirt on my way out. He made eye contact with me, and something glinted across his gaze. Then he was gone, and I was back down the elevator and back astride the Yamaha. I sat with my finger hovering over the electric start button, pondering my conversation with Ava. Evaluating her body language the way I had evaluated Ralph's.

She was telling the truth. That's what my gut said. But something in the back of my mind still bothered me. I sat relaxed on the bike, my gaze drifting down the broad downtown street to the Tampa convention center where a digital billboard advertised an auto auction kicking off the next day —the Tampa Auto Exchange, the event Ava had mentioned that her girls were preparing for. I pictured all the twenty-something beauties posing next to antique cars, smiling and passing out fliers. Just the way Ralph had described Camilla when he first met her at the paint convention.

A relatively ordinary scenario. A perfectly legitimate business. So why had Ava seemed so agitated? So preoccupied with people and their privacy?

My gaze flicked back to the bottom of the high rise as the muscled guy with the black T-shirt reappeared. I watched him walk to the passenger side of an idling Mercury Grand Marquis and climb in. There was something pinned beneath his left arm—something orangish yellow, thick, and papery.

A padded envelope. Unmarked. Packed with something. I'd seen it before, and the moment the memory registered, another memory joined it. The way he had looked at me. That flash of recognition in his eyes.

The Mercury pulled away from the curb, engine rumbling, and I made a quick decision. I clamped down on the clutch and hit the starter button.

Then my foot dropped the shifter into first gear, and I followed the Mercury.

I kept pace with the Mercury almost without effort. Whoever was behind the wheel drove hard, but a V8 engine burdened by several thousand pounds of body and cargo is no match for twelve-hundred CCs packed between two narrow tires. With each slow turn of the heavy sedan I kept pace, rarely rising above third gear as I guided the bike in and out of traffic. I left enough buffer between myself and my target to avoid detection, but I also had the feeling that the occupants of the Mercury weren't particularly concerned about a tail. They drove with impunity, blowing through lights as they turned red and parking in fire lanes at each stop.

And there were a lot of stops. The black sedan pulled in front of one business after another, ranging from restaurants to hair salons to hardware stores. All local places, not franchises. Mom-and-pop type joints, scattered from downtown to the suburbs and forming a trail through the city. At each stop the driver remained behind the wheel while the muscled guy with the tight T-shirt and the cropped black hair went inside.

Each time he returned with something pinned beneath his arm—envelopes usually. Wrapped-up grocery sacks sometimes. All of them thick.

By the time the Mercury turned back for the heart of the city I had a pretty clear idea what was going on. It was a protection racket. The guys I was following were street thugs, possibly members of some branch of local organized crime. In exchange for their "protection"—likely protection from themselves—they were extorting regular payments from a variety of local businesses. This must be the pickup route.

Ava and her modeling agency were on the list.

It wasn't a new idea. Organized crime had been practicing this sort of petty theft for as long as crime had been organized. In fact, if anything, I was a little surprised to see the scheme still in play. This was a modern city, populated by modern cops. Shaking down business owners was a bold move, especially in a state with more firearms than alligators. Hank couldn't be the only one who kept a shotgun under the counter.

What was I missing here?

Likely nothing related to Camilla's death and my late-night mugging, but I hadn't liked the look of the guy who passed me as I left Ava's modeling agency. There was a glint in his eyes. A sort of recognition.

As though he knew who I was.

So I kept trailing the Mercury from one pickup to the next, watching as the sun dipped toward Mexico. I waited two blocks away while the sedan ran through a drive-through and both men enjoyed an afternoon snack. Then I wound the bike out a little to keep pace with them on the highway, weaving through traffic on the return route to Tampa. They still hadn't made me, and I hung back far enough to remain unnoticed as the Mercury rumbled into an older part of the city, north and east of downtown. I knew it was old because of the architecture alone. It reminded me a little of New Orleans, with double- and triple-stacked verandas running along the faces of aged brick buildings. Wrought iron railings, and ornate wooden doors fitted with wavering old glass.

As I turned onto 7th Avenue, two giant brick columns situated on either side of the street supported a metal arch than ran one side to the other, giant black letters welded to its face that read *Ybor City*. Beyond the arch a plaque welcomed me to "one of America's 10 Great Streets", and I noted that all the street signs had also changed. They were brown now, printed with the name "Ybor City" along with alternative street names written in Spanish beneath.

It was like stepping into another world—again reminding me of New Orleans. All the old buildings, the decorative script, the narrower streets. I slowed the Yamaha as the Mercury made a right-hand turn off 7th Avenue. Something in my gut warned me not to follow directly, and I cruised past instead.

The Mercury was parked against the curb, half a block removed from the main drag. The guy with the tight black T-shirt and the close-cropped hair stood on the sidewalk, a bulky duffel bag slung from one arm. As the Yamaha growled past, the driver stepped out as well, stretching in the sunlight. His face turned, just enough for me to catch a profile.

My heart skipped, and I twisted the throttle. Before he could face me head-on I was gone, taking the next right and circling the block. I parked the Yamaha in front of a trendy coffee shop built into another one of the old buildings, and approached the corner on foot instead.

When I reached the turn, I stole a cautious look down the alley, now facing the Mercury.

It remained parked right where I left it. Both the driver and the guy in the T-shirt were gone, and there was only one building they could have entered—a four-story brick affair with bars over the windows and a neon sign reflecting the sunlight.

Club Bolita.

The door was heavy steel, painted black. It was closed, but a guy lounged on the steps with his hands cupped around the tip of a cigarette. Smoke drifted around his face as the tobacco caught fire. I didn't recognize the face—but I knew I recognized the driver. It had been a split-second visual, but sometimes a split second is enough, especially when matched with an adrenaline-soaked memory now branded into my brain.

The driver was the man from the campsite the night before. The guy who drew down his neck gaiter to threaten me. The guy who had made it "brutally simple".

The dead man walking.

21

It wasn't difficult to ascertain the nature of *Club Bolita*. The barista at the trendy coffee shop was only too happy to gush about her favorite hangout spot.

"Great music! Good drinks. You can always find a hookup there."

"Even on a weeknight?" I asked.

"Sure. They're open every night."

I took my coffee and returned to the street, checking the time before I stole one more glance at the entrance of Club Bolita. The Mercury remained, as did the guy with the cigarette. The only other sign visible anywhere near the door was a simple white sticker that read:

Must Be 21 To Enter.

All else was grungy brick and peeling black paint, which I assumed to be an intentional thing. This was a historic district, and these days it's a trend to make even the most produced establishments look like holes in the wall. Places "where the locals go". The real McCoy.

This might well be one such place. A great spot for drinks, music, and hookups if the barista was to be believed. But I've enjoyed my share of clubs during my Army days, and I never knew any sort of trendy, popular establishment which opened seven nights a week. That was a dive bar move, not an exclusive club move.

Unless, of course...Club Bolita was more than a club.

I took the Yamaha out of Ybor City and far enough into uptown to ensure that I wouldn't be detected. I located a chain burger joint and ate my first meal of the day, ravenously packing down a half-pounder with blue cheese crumbles and a side of fries, washed down by a milkshake and three glasses of water. It was a lot of calories, but calories make energy, and I planned on needing some energy. Thoughts of Ralph, Camilla, and even Ava's modeling agency had all taken a back seat in my mind to the more enraging reality of the two guys in the Mercury, at least one of whom had been an active participant in my mugging and the damage to Mia's Bible. The other guy—the muscled guy in the T-shirt—could well have been my second mugger. I couldn't be sure because he'd never lowered his neck gaiter. Even if he was, I wasn't surprised that he hadn't engaged with me at Ava's office.

He couldn't tip his hand, after all. Criminal or otherwise, he had to play things smart. I imagined he and his buddy were already scheming up an encore plan to return to the campsite and make good on their promise to kill me.

Only, they would never make it that far.

I let the burger digest while I picked at a slice of chocolate cake and watched the sun slip toward the gulf. I figured a place like Club Bolita, if it were in fact a bumping participant in Tampa nightlife, wouldn't get swinging until well after dark. Maybe nine o'clock at the earliest. To be safe, I would wait until ten, which gave me another three hours to kill. The waitress came by regularly at first to refill my water, but when she realized I wasn't leaving and I had already left a cash tip, she let me be. There were plenty of empty booths available for new customers.

At nine p.m. the restaurant was closing and I saw the waitress talking with the manager, glancing over one shoulder toward my table. I left before they could address me, returning to the Yamaha and firing up the big engine. It purred like a jungle cat, warming quickly between my legs. I liked the feel of it, and I'd already forgotten about needing a helmet. I enjoyed the city air in my hair as I rumbled back onto a four-lane and leaned toward Ybor City.

I took my time. I parked three blocks away and dropped enough quarters into the meter to keep the bike safe all night. Just in case.

Then I strolled toward Club Bolita with my hands in my pockets. Not in a hurry. Letting the clock drip toward ten p.m. before I passed the trendy little coffee shop and turned down the alleyway.

The neon sign was lit now. Red and green, like Christmas. The Mercury was gone. A muscled guy wearing a black tank top stood outside the door, slouched against the wall, apparently unoccupied. There was no line, but from beyond the thick door I thought I detected the pound of club music.

It made my head ache, or maybe that was the goose egg still rising from my scalp. Whatever medication the body-builder paramedic had given me was long gone, and I was losing count of all the aches and pains inflicted on me by Ralph's tumultuous predicament.

The best option now was to simply ignore them.

I approached the door as casually as any semi-bored tourist out for a weeknight lark. The bouncer saw me coming and straightened a little. He crossed his arms, but there was no gleam of recognition in his eyes the way I had seen with the muscled guy at Queen City Modeling Agency. This guy was both darker and heavier. He looked bored.

He did not look happy to see me.

"You guys open?" I asked.

The guy only grunted. I reached for the door.

"Cover charge, bub."

I looked for a sign. There wasn't one. "Are you serious?"

"You got a girl in your pocket?"

"No."

"You got a girl in your shoe?"

"No..."

"Then there's a cover charge."

I thought about busting his skull against the brick, but his wasn't the skull I was here to bust. I simply reached for my wallet.

"How much?"

"Twenty."

I passed him a bill and watched it disappear into his own pocket. He grunted.

"Have fun."

The door groaned on old hinges. The blare of club music intensified to a blast, igniting blazing pain in my head that shot all the way down my spine. I almost turned around, but already the door was swinging closed and I was blinking to adjust to the dim lights.

Strobes flashed from the ceiling—white, and lime green. The air hung thick with cigarette smoke and the faint smell of sweat. Stretching across aged hardwood to the back wall, an open dance floor was ringed by high-top tables and metal-legged stools. Many of the tables were empty, but thirty or so occupants gathered around a few or sat along the face of the bar counter, which ran along the back wall. I couldn't make out details amid the flash of the strobes, but all the people looked young.

Younger than me, anyway, and I was barely thirty-one. They wore trendy dresses and jeans with untucked shirts. Guys talking to girls, girls pretending to ignore them.

And the music pounding all the while. Way too loud.

"What do you want?" The bartender had to shout as I approached. She didn't offer a smile.

"Coors," I said.

"Huh?"

"Coors Light!"

She produced a bottle from beneath the counter and popped the top off. I passed her a ten-dollar bill and received no change.

Figures.

The beer wasn't quite cold, and it fizzed in my throat. I watched the mirror stretching behind the bar to survey the faces gathered around me. A guy and a girl making out in one corner. A pair of girls sitting alone at a high-top, steeling glances at the frat boys eyeballing them from the bar. A drunk chick dancing by herself between the tables, just about one whiff of vodka away from passing out.

It all made me tired just looking at it. I'd had my run in the clubs. I'd had my fun. But all those loud, late nights tasted stale from the moment I met Mia, because there's fun, and then there's real passion. The first is a cheap substitute for the second, no matter the alcohol content.

I rocked the beer back, still gazing into the mirror and estimating that I wouldn't reach the bottom of the bottle before one of my neck-gaiter friends made an appearance. I was right.

They arrived in a trio, one walking in from my right, another from my left, and the third from straight behind. Big guys—the driver of the Mercury, his buddy who made the pickups, and some new jackass with greasy long hair plastered back across a round head.

They were short, I noticed. I hadn't noticed that at the campsite, but then again, I'd been on my ass. They were muscled, but not in the lean and lethal way of a trained warrior. More in the steroid-induced, inflated way. Like Braydon and Brandon, Hank's useless bouncers. Their faces gleamed a little. Their eyes were dark.

If I had to pick an ethnicity, I would say Italian. But in a country as blended as America, who knew?

The driver was the first to make a move. He dropped a hand on the bar six inches left on my arm and shot me a glare cold enough to freeze Florida sunshine. I grinned.

"Hey. I know you."

He didn't return the grin. He didn't so much as blink.

"Time to go," he said.

I rocked the bottle back. Took a long and luxurious pull. Then I wiped my mouth.

"I don't think so."

"Oh yeah?"

"Yeah. Actually, I'm glad you're here. My beer is warm. I think I'd like to see the manager."

The driver said nothing. He exchanged a glance with his

two inflated partners. I was watching them all in the mirror and knew they weren't yet close enough to touch me. Their clothes were too tight to conceal any weapons. They'd only brought their fists.

Rookie mistake.

"You're not talking to anybody," the driver said. "You're going. *Now.*"

"Is that right?" I asked.

His hand closed into a fist. "That's right."

"Can't I finish my beer?"

His lips twitched. A hard white line. "*Hurry.*"

I rocked the bottle back, draining the last few drops. Savoring every one.

Then I flipped the bottle, grabbed it by the neck, and broke it straight over his head.

22

Glass exploded. Beer foam rained down his face, and the guy's eyes rolled back. He wasn't dead—I hadn't hit him *that* hard—but he was out of the fight, and it happened so fast that neither of his buddies knew what to do. As the driver hit the floor I was already spinning on the rotating stool, both legs rocketing up to catch each approaching combatant in the gut with rabbit kicks. They weren't power kicks, but they were sudden and unexpected and knocked them both off-guard.

Next I was on my feet, pivoting straight for the left-hand guy because he had the bad fortune of standing perfectly within range of my right fist. Long before he could recover his breath or even think about shielding his face, my knuckles made impact. Nasal bones shattered. Blood sprayed, all punctuated by the pound of the club music. He staggered back with a scream, and then the third man finally seemed to awake to the fact that he was under attack and launched himself at me like a linebacker. One shoulder lowered toward my arm, his teeth gritted. He rammed past the stool and clipped my arm as I sidestepped him.

A twist on my right heel brought my left foot into range. I cocked. I kicked. I made impact between his legs. He shouted and tumbled.

Number two wasn't done. He wanted more, bloody nose and all. Back on his feet, he dug into his pocket and produced a gleaming pair of brass knuckles. Fat fingers struggled to wriggle into them as he heaved and blasted snot my way. His eyes were alight with battle rage, blood still gushing from his lips. I supposed he'd attended whatever underground dojo Emilio's younger brother trained in, and probably thought himself very gangster for the brass knuckles.

He should have brought a gun instead. I drove my heel into the ankle of the groin-kicked third man, leaning until bone shattered, then I casually scooped up a bar stool and grabbed it by the legs.

The guy with the brass knuckles hesitated, eyes turning wide. The seat of the stool rocketed toward him much like the Patriot missile that had ruined my violin solo, and he ducked just the way I knew he would.

So I kicked him in the face. Teeth crunched and I let go of the stool, allowing it to sail across the room and crash into a table. Girls were screaming now. Martini glasses shattered as they struck the floor. The lights and music continued, but I wasn't paying attention to any of it. I grabbed the toppling guy by the collar, allowing his body to fall while his neck and shoulders remained suspended over the hardwood. He choked and flailed with the brass knuckles, swinging for my right knee.

I took the blow with barely a grunt, then used my right

hand to grab his face. My thumb found his eye. I pressed until a shriek erupted from his bloodied mouth. Crimson sprayed across my T-shirt, and I pressed harder. It was an old T-shirt. Walmart sells them in packs of five for eight bucks.

The guy forgot about his brass knuckles and kicked both legs, fighting to break free. I shot my knee into his gut, hard enough to drive the air out. If I'd had a bat close to hand, I would have beat him over the head with it. Instead, I shouted loud enough to be heard over the music.

"Who sent you to mug me?"

No answer. Just a howl. He might be blind in one eye by now, but that was his own fault. Nobody made him shove my truck into the water.

Nobody made him drown Mia's last photo amid the Florida muck.

"I can't hear you!" I shouted. I jabbed again. Another scream. His boot thrashed against the floor. I turned to check the driver and found him still unconscious. Maybe I'd hit him harder than I thought. The third guy was also on the floor, his leg busted, one hand wrapped around his balls.

I pressed again with my thumb. "You better talk!"

The club was almost empty now. A couple guys with cell phones filmed us from a dark corner. All the girls were gone. The bouncer appeared between the strobes and shot a quick glance across the three fallen muscle heads. Then he took a step back, fumbling with a phone.

Calling the cops, no doubt. Or backup. Either way, it was time to wrap up.

I released pressure on the eye and hauled the guy up by the collar, smacking him across the face. "You think it's fun to jump people in campgrounds? You like to push trucks into the water?"

He choked and gargled. "Please. I was just doing my job!"

"Who sent you?"

"The b-b—"

He never finished. A door exploded open behind the bar, and two more guys appeared. They were smaller than the muscle masses I had pounded, and better dressed. They both wore nice shirts and snug slacks.

I made eye contact, and one guy marched down the counter, beelining for the cocktail sink.

Shotgun.

I remembered Hank and his Mossberg, and I dropped my victim with a disgusted shove. He hit the floor and I pivoted toward the counter, kicking stools out of the way. The well-dressed man headed for the sink accelerated, his gaze snapping toward an invisible spot beneath the bar. I placed both hands on the counter, prepared to flip across it and do to him what I'd already done to his thugs.

I never got the chance. A metallic click rang in my ears from not far away, and cold steel pressed into my neck. I flinched but didn't turn. A heavy voice spoke slowly.

"Don't freaking *budge.*"

It was the bouncer. He hadn't gone for the cops. He'd circled behind me somehow, and now he had a gun pressed to my skull.

I relaxed against the bar. The well-dressed man stopped in front of me and dipped a hand beneath the counter. A Remington Tac-14 appeared in a rush, a shortened little 12-gauge with a birdshead grip. He pumped a shell into the chamber with a quick flick of his wrists, then the muzzle settled over my chest.

I kept calm, both hands on the counter. Someplace behind me the other well-dressed man drove the remainder of the club's patrons through the front door. The music cut off, but the strobes continued. I stared the man with the Tac-14 in the eye and didn't budge. The bouncer kept the pistol pressed against my skull.

Stalemate. Unless somebody decided to make it checkmate and blow my brains out. I knew they wouldn't for a variety of reasons, not the least of which was the illegal nature of whatever was *really* happening in this club. Shooting me now would draw cops.

They didn't want cops in a place like this.

"*Who are you?*"

The guy with the Tac-14 spoke. He seemed to be in charge, but he wasn't the boss. Maybe a lieutenant. A secondary. A son.

"The guy you took for granted," I said.

He flinched. Curled his lip a little. But he didn't speak. He just considered.

"I should shoot you," he said at last.

"Probably. But you won't, and we both know that. So let's skip to the next part."

"The next part?"

"The boss," I said. "Take me to your boss."

23

Slick Hair obliged after only momentary consideration. He tilted his head to the bouncer, and my hands were wrenched behind my back. Steel handcuffs clicked into place. A posse of two further bouncers went to work resurrecting the fallen inflatable guys.

Then I was marched at gunpoint around the bar, to the back of the room, and through a door. A hallway followed. Slick Hair led the way, the Tac-14 still riding in one hand. The bouncer kept his gun pressed against my skull, and I remained relaxed.

They might kill me—or they might try. But it wouldn't be here, at the heart of their little criminal empire, and it wouldn't happen before I met the boss, regardless. So there was nothing to worry about.

A short stairway led upward. Another inflatable guy stood with his arms crossed at the door. Slick Hair motioned him aside, and the door opened.

The room beyond was pretty much exactly what I

expected it to be. Large, with a hardwood floor and raw brick walls. Probably original walls. There was an area rug and a lot of leather furniture. A wet bar and a table, which was laden with American currency wrapped in paper bands. I recognized the same duffel bag on the floor that the muscled guy in the black T-shirt had used on his collection run.

In the back of the room a heavy, ornate desk sat. Oversized and overloaded with papers and a laptop computer. A big leather office chair stood behind it. In the chair sat a big guy with a barrel chest. Not a muscled, inflatable, steroid junky like the men I had disassembled downstairs. This guy was the genuine article, the product of hundreds of hours beneath a bench press. I judged him to be in his late fifties, and in excellent overall condition. Graying black hair and dark eyes. A sort of olive complexion. Black slacks and a button-down shirt that was only buttoned halfway, allowing a clear view of muscled pecks and too much chest hair.

He stared at me without comment as the bouncer shoved me forward. I stopped a few feet in front of the desk. Behind me the door closed. Slick Hair stood alongside, the Tac-14 at the ready. The bouncer took a step back, but I could feel his gun trained on my back. Everybody was very quiet.

Then the big guy behind the desk smiled, and the smile was joined by a dry chuckle. He reached across the desk for a decanter, pouring two glasses of amber liquor and pushing one across the desk toward me.

"Won't you sit down, Mr. Sharpe?"

I wasn't surprised to hear my name. Anybody who knew enough about me to deploy goons to my campsite could reasonably be expected to know my name. I stood motionless while one of the inflatable guys pushed a chair against my thighs. The boss said something in a language that wasn't English—I thought it might be Italian—and my captor unlocked one wrist and transferred my arms to the front of my body. The cuffs clicked down again, a little tighter than necessary, and the drink was pressed into my hand.

The boss lifted his glass, and I lifted mine. We both drank. It was bourbon of some kind, very rich and flavorful. I'm not a big liquor guy, but this stuff was good. I nodded my appreciation.

Slick Hair snarled off a string of the same language the boss had used. Now I was confident it was Italian. I could tell by the cadence and unique use of vowels. Despite not being able to understand a word of it, it was quite pleasant to listen to.

Apart from present circumstances, anyway.

The boss listened without taking his eyes off me. He grunted.

"My son tells me you have badly beaten three of my men. Is this true?"

"I was returning a favor," I said.

Another subdued smirk passed across the boss's face. He relaxed into his chair. "Who are you, Mr. Sharpe?"

I shrugged. "Just a guy."

"A guy. Yes. But not always. At some point, you were clearly something else."

I didn't answer. The boss nodded knowingly. He swirled the bourbon in his glass.

"Do you know who I am?" he asked.

"I can guess," I said.

"So guess."

I took another sip of my own, not because I needed it, but because a free drink is a free drink.

"I'm gonna say Mafia," I said. "Italian Mafia, Tampa branch. I believe they call you the Tampa Mob. That should explain how you're all bilingual despite being multi-generational Americans. I hear tradition is a big thing in your world."

The boss cocked his eyebrows. He looked at his son and grunted. Slick Hair didn't respond—apparently, he wasn't so impressed.

"You are familiar with Tampa?" the boss asked.

"I like to read."

"Your reading has served you well. I am Giovanni De Luca. The man with the shotgun aimed at your gut is my son, Marco. Everyone else...works for me."

"Pleased to make your acquaintance," I said. "Mind telling me why two of your employees jumped me at my campsite and beat me into unconsciousness last night?"

De Luca took a deep swallow and grimaced as the bourbon went down. "Can you guess?"

I could indeed guess, and I had. But I was tired of doing all the work.

"Let's say not," I said.

"Well. You followed my men today."

I wasn't expecting that. I remained calm.

"You saw them on their pickup route," De Luca continued. "You saw them collect from our clients."

"Clients?" I played innocent.

"Security clients," De Luca clarified. "That's one of my businesses. Providing private security."

Sure it is. And when your clients don't pay, you're in the arson business.

I thought it, I didn't say it. There was no point.

"Our clients depend on us to manage whatever unforeseeable security concerns may interrupt their affairs," De Luca continued. "For instance, let's say a stranger from out of town were to turn up. Let's say that stranger were to harass the employees of a local modeling firm. To stalk the girls. Show up at the office, uninvited. Draw unwanted attention. In this case, security services would be rendered. Such a stranger would be encouraged to leave town."

"Hard to leave town with my truck underwater." I spoke through gritted teeth. The bourbon was gone, and it had done little to calm me down.

De Luca laughed. He shrugged with his bulky shoulders, turning both palms upward. "What can I say? My employees are enthusiastic."

I returned the bourbon glass to the desktop with a thump, leaving a wet ring atop a stack of paperwork. I didn't care.

"There was something in my truck that was very important to me," I said. "Something that *didn't* need to get wet."

Maybe it was the tone of my voice, or a glint in my eye. Whatever the case, the sincerity of my complaint melted the smile from De Luca's chunky lips. He grew still. I didn't so much as twitch.

De Luca lowered his glass. He placed both forearms on the desk and tapped one heavy finger against the table top. I wasn't sure if he were about to laugh or to tell Marco to blast my skull open with the Tac-14. When his lips finally parted, it was neither.

"My family has lived in Tampa for a very long time. The De Lucas are one of the last pure-blooded Italian lines remaining in the city. Our heritage is...very colorful. Tracing all the way back to the early twentieth century, to the very founding of Ybor City. Back when Tampa was a rum runners' paradise. Have you read of it?"

I shrugged. De Luca nodded.

"Things are not as they once were, Mr. Sharpe. In the decades of my father, you would already be rotting in the bay, and when your crab-torn body washed ashore, the police would throw it right back. Because understandings were in place. Today...things are more complicated. More civilized. My business practices must remain more subtle."

"There's nothing subtle about a baseball bat to the head," I snapped. I couldn't help it.

"You are correct. Perhaps that was the wrong tack. But what is done is done. Just like what was done to my men downstairs cannot be taken back. Mistakes happen. Which is why, in the interest of good business, I am willing to offer you a deal my father would never have offered."

"I'm listening," I said.

"I will look the other way on my wounded men. I will pour you another drink, and Marco will carry you back to your campsite. In exchange, you will accept my apology for the misunderstanding with the bat and the damaged personal items. You will collect your things, and you will *leave* Tampa. Permanently."

I considered briefly. It wasn't a complex offer, but it was missing something.

"Will you tell me who killed Camilla Cruz?"

De Luca squinted, then glanced at his son. Marco spoke in Italian. De Luca grunted.

"The Cuban girl?"

"Right."

"I heard it was an old man. A friend of yours, it seems."

A sarcastic lilt joined De Luca's Italian-Floridian drawl. I wasn't buying it.

"I think things are more complicated," I said, parroting De Luca's phrase. The Mob boss's smile faded.

"You should take the deal," he said. "You won't enjoy the alternative."

"You should tell me the truth about Camilla," I said. "You *really* won't enjoy the alternative."

De Luca flinched. His face flushed red. His hands pressed palms-down against the desktop.

"You're making a very serious mistake, Mr. Sharpe."

I actually laughed. Not only because I didn't believe him, but also because the irony of the situation had overcome me.

"You know what's funny, big man? Before your goons gave my truck a bath, *drowning my late fiancée's Bible*, I couldn't care less about your pure-blooded line of deadbeats."

De Luca flushed. I leaned forward, my voice dropping a notch.

"But I really hate bullies, and now you've made this personal. So don't blame me for what happens next. You say your business is complicated? I'm about to make it *real simple*."

De Luca's teeth ground. He ran a thick tongue over thicker lips. Then he jerked his head. I didn't fight as the inflatable thugs appeared—to once again cuff my hands behind my back. I didn't fight as they yanked me to my feet while De Luca fished through a deep desk drawer. He produced a canvas sack, about the size of a grocery bag, but worn by age. Something rattled from inside.

"Do you know what *bolita* is?" De Luca asked.

I knew he was about to tell me, so I said nothing. De

Luca shook the bag, and the contents clacked and rolled inside.

"It is the Spanish word for *little ball*. The Cubans brought it to Tampa. A form of gambling, back in the old days. One hundred wooden balls in a bag, and every ball has a number. Typically, this game is played with money, but tonight I'm thinking of a greater wager."

Another shake of the bag. He dipped a hand in. "Pick a number, Mr. Sharpe."

"Seven," I said. It was the number of De Luca's inflatable thugs I had encountered since meeting Ralph—Marco and his Tac-14 included.

And I was going to wreck them all.

De Luca shuffled through the bag. He fished out a small brown ball with a red numeral engraved into one side. Two digits, not one.

De Luca grimaced. "Forty-three. What a shame. At least the gators will dine well. You look like a hefty meal!"

The inflatable thugs dragged me backwards, but I didn't fight. A black bag descended over my head, blocking out my view. De Luca couldn't see my smile as they ratcheted me toward the door. I didn't bother to voice the thought coursing through my head in a thunderclap.

Not a threat. Just a promise.

You'll be the meal.

24

I was manhandled back down the stairs, through another hall, and out a back door. I thought it was a back door, anyway. I couldn't be sure with the bag over my head, but regardless, I wasn't concerned.

I've been kidnapped before. More than once, actually. As a veteran hostage I'd established a certain expectation for what happens. First, they tie you up. They blind you, usually. They don't worry about your ears because ears are relatively harmless. Then they drag you into a car, because wherever they snatched you is probably an unsuitable place for murder. But cars mean public roads, and public roads feature cops, and cops respond to things like bound people with bags over their heads. So they don't put you in the back seat, they put you in the trunk.

It's all very scary the first time, and almost as scary the second time. But after a while, it's just plain annoying. De Luca's inflatable thugs dragged me across rough concrete and removed everything from my pockets—phone, wallet, motorcycle keys, Streamlight, and Victorinox Locksmith.

Then they wadded me into the trunk of a large sedan, right on schedule. My hands were still cuffed behind my back, which I suppose they thought was a great hinderance to my combat ability. Perhaps it would have been, but I'd done this before.

And I'd made preparations accordingly.

As soon as the trunk slammed closed I went to work on my belt. I didn't worry about the bag over my head, or the cramps tightening in my thighs. Those damages would be repaid with interest. Instead, I traced my fingers along the underside of the belt's nylon edge, pressing a fingernail along the heavy-duty stitching until I located the little Velcro compartment hidden just beneath my spine.

The work was meticulous, and frustrating, because whoever was driving had never learned how to brake or accelerate smoothly. The car surged a lot, rocking on creaking hinges and jumping over bumps hard enough to send my hooded head smacking into the underside of the trunk.

It hurt, but I focused on the belt, wiggling a finger between the hooks and loops of the Velcro to open that hidden pocket. The harsh edge of one handcuff bit into my wrist as I tugged at the belt, shooting pain up my arms. My shoulders began to cramp.

I didn't rush. One mistake here could turn the next half hour from a sure victory into a fatal defeat. I remembered De Luca's mention of the alligators and wondered if he had been serious.

Possibly. Probably not. A man in De Luca's position was more interested in preserving his business interests than enforcing terror. Bodies had a way of being found, even if alligators had their way with them first. Whatever cops De

Luca had bought off would be difficult to manage amid a homicide investigation.

More than likely, the two inflatable thugs driving me out of town were planning to simply break a few bones and leave me in a ditch. Maybe let me think I had escaped.

Too bad they'd never get that far.

The pocket of the belt finally opened with a little *shrick* of tearing Velcro. I cupped my hands and wiggled my hips, jarring the belt.

The universal handcuff key concealed within the pocket dropped right into my palm, landing without a sound. I spun it with my fingers, sat up a little, and fished for the keyhole.

By the time I was free of both the cuffs and the hood over my head, I figured we had journeyed at least twenty minutes outside of Ybor City. The inside of the trunk was just as dark without the hood as it had been with it, but it was a lot easier to breathe. I sucked down a lung-full of sour air, tainted by grease and body odor, then tossed the handcuffs on the floor and took a moment to replace the key in my belt.

Just in case.

At last I was ready to fish around and figure out which way was up, and what other useful items might lie around me. The jolting of harsh brakes and acceleration had lessened somewhat, while the hum of tires intensified. I thought we were probably on a highway, which confirmed my suspicions about a ride well outside of Tampa.

Maybe we were headed to a gator pond. It was still a possibility.

Without the Streamlight to illuminate my prison, I was left to dig around the floor of the trunk with my bare hands, tossing aside smelly clothes and an even smellier pair of boots. I had a feeling I was trapped inside the same Mercury

Grand Marquis I had trailed all afternoon. Maybe my captors were my muggers from the campsite. That would be convenient.

I found nothing useful until at last I located a duffel bag jammed in one corner of the trunk. It was heavy, and clunked a little as I shifted it. A tool bag, I thought. I took my time locating the zipper, eager to not make any unnecessary noise.

The muscles in my back and bunched legs were beginning to tighten. My headache had returned, also, a steady orchestra of pain radiating from the goose egg on my scalp. I ignored it all as my hand dipped into the tool bag, touching oily metal and rubbery wires. Jumper cables, maybe, and wrenches. I searched until I felt cylindrical plastic, and my heart skipped.

Jackpot.

It was a flashlight. Not a good one—nothing like my Streamlight, but it cast a sufficiently bright yellow beam to reveal the parameters of my confinement and illuminate the rest of the tool bag.

Wrenches, just as I thought. Jumper cables. A pair of pliers. A two-pound ball-peen hammer. And...what was that?

I wriggled the plastic case from the bottom of the bag and rotated it in my hand. It was about the size of a large book, bright orange in color. A warning label curled at the edges on the bottom side. A black plastic clasp held the case closed.

I opened it and couldn't resist a grin. It was a 12-gauge flare gun, single shot, with three flares resting in the foam next to it—not an odd accessory for any resident who lived so close to the coast and might own a boat. I lifted the gun from the foam and opened the chamber, inspecting for any damage.

The tool looked brand new, and a flare fit right into place. I snapped the breach closed and flexed the hammer a little. The spring tension was excellent.

Well. This could be fun.

I took the hammer from the bag, also, then I rotated my hips until I faced the rear of the car—hammer in my strong hand, flare gun pointed with my left. There would be no time to reload, not with two guys bearing down on me. I would need to be quick.

The tires hummed on for another half hour. We were way outside of Tampa now, and we weren't on an interstate. The rush of passing cars was infrequent, and they all passed against our direction of travel. It was a two-lane, probably. Maybe a state highway, which put our speed at fifty to sixty miles per hour. I could probably find a screwdriver in the tool bag and force the trunk open, but that would mean I would need to jump from a moving car onto hard asphalt. That wouldn't be pleasant, and it would also destroy my element of surprise.

Most importantly of all, it would require me to walk back to Tampa. I wasn't interested in walking.

So I waited, almost relaxed in the trunk, and suddenly craving the melodic voice of the great blues legend B. B. King. The inflatable guys in the front of the car weren't listening to music, and they weren't talking. I wondered if the steroids had left them enough brain cells to support a conversation, or if they could still feel pain.

For their own sakes, I hoped so.

At last the car turned off the road and rumbled a while longer across gravel. I suddenly wondered about cabins alone in the woods. Places where other gangsters waited, or maybe toothless swamp people with pet alligators chilling under single-wide trailers. Maybe I would have been better off jumping from a moving car after all, but it was too late to worry about additional targets. The car ground to a stop in the gravel, and the engine cut off. I didn't hear any other traffic. I didn't hear any other voices.

Only the whisper of wind amid trees, and the unfamiliar call of a local bird.

I eased the hammer back on the flare gun and waited. The inflatable guys climbed out, shoes crunching across the gravel. Keys rattled, then ground into the lock of the trunk. I rested a finger on the trigger of the flare gun and tightened my grip on the hammer.

One, two. A lightning-quick plan of attack. Tangos down.

The trunk lid swung open, and the cargo light blazed into my face. I hadn't thought to disconnect it, and temporary disorientation flooded my mind.

But only for a moment. The first guy was there, leaned over the trunk with both hands resting on the lid. The second guy stood just behind him, a handgun hanging at his side, his puffy steroid chest fully exposed to the muzzle of my flare gun.

I grinned. "Hi there."

I pulled the trigger and swung with the hammer at the same moment. The flare gun popped, spitting white-hot fire from the muzzle and straight into the chest of the guy in the back. The two-pound ball-peen swung with all the force my cramped shoulders could muster, rocketing straight into the groin of the guy who stood with his hands on trunk lid.

Then everything happened at once. Flames erupted to my left, and the guy with the handgun dropped it, shrieking and thrashing. The guy leaning over me screamed and doubled over, just as I hoped he would. The top of his skull rocketed toward me like a bowling ball.

That bowling ball met the face of my hammer—not hard enough to kill him, just hard enough to make him forget he'd been born. He went limp even as his partner proceeded to breakdance over the gravel, ripping at his clothes and thrashing to put out the flames. The flare had apparently lodged itself someplace beneath his shirt and was still spraying sulfurous fire across his gut.

I almost felt sorry for him as I shoved the limp body off me and pried my way out of the trunk. By the time I reached my feet he'd managed to extricate himself from his shirt and continued to thrash on the ground. The flare had been extinguished. He screamed on repeat, like a broken record. I used the tail of my shirt to wipe my fingerprints from flare gun before tossing it back into the trunk, then I took the hammer and joined my thrashing target on the roadbed.

We were out in the county someplace far from civilization. I knew, because the forest surrounding us was illuminated by a three-quarter moon, bright enough to cast shadows without any city light to pollute the sky. Surveying the woods, I saw no other roads. No houses or signs of people.

It was the perfect place to ditch somebody.

I knelt next to my thrashing victim and rolled him over, pinning one shoulder down with the hammer. He sobbed. I inspected his chest.

It was bad—second degree burns, at the least. Worse than I expected, but I didn't regret pressing the trigger. He was still alive, and that was more than he deserved, especially considering who he was.

It was the driver from earlier that day, and the man who had exposed his face while mugging me at the campground. Mr. "brutally simple" himself.

"Stop sniveling," I snarled.

I popped him in the side of the skull with the hammer. He shook.

"You were gonna kill me. The least you can do is talk."

"We...we weren't gonna kill you!"

"You said so at the campground."

"Just threats, man." His eyes watered. He shook all over.

"Okay. How about you prove it?"

"How?" His voice choked with saliva.

"Tell me who killed Camilla Cruz—who *really* killed her. You?"

"No!" Hands clawed at the gravel. I applied enough pressure to his scalded shoulder to erase any ideas he might have about slinging dirt in my face.

"Who killed her, then?" I said.

"I don't know... I don't know! The old guy?"

I jabbed with the hammer. He screeched.

"Try again," I said.

He choked. Cried. Spoke in Italian. I recognized the word "mama".

"Your mama isn't coming, and if you ever want to see her again, you'd be well advised to talk."

"I don't know!" he roared. "Okay? I don't know. I don't know who killed the girl!"

More sobbing. More shaking. More tears.

I believed him—someplace in my gut, his words rang true.

"You got a phone?" I asked.

"Pocket," he gasped. I found it. He looked into the screen

long enough to unlock it. I left it unlocked and slid it into my pocket. Then I turned back to my prisoner.

"Listen carefully—I'm only going to say this once. I'm not a murderer, and this no longer feels like self-defense. So you get to walk out of here. But there are conditions."

Hope ignited in his eyes, quickly muted by the pain. "W-what?"

"You tell your boss that the job was done. Or that I escaped and ran from here. Whatever you want, I don't care. But he *does not* come after me again. Am I clear? If he does, I'm coming for you first. And then it will be self-defense. Do you understand?"

An enthusiastic nod. "Whatever you say."

"Great. Sleep well."

I popped him in the side of the head with the hammer— just hard enough to switch the lights out. The guy went limp, and I scrubbed the fingerprints off the hammer before returning it to the trunk.

Then I took the keys from the trunk lid and rolled the driver's seat back before climbing in. The Mercury fired right up. I drove back the way we had come until I identified a street sign, then I used the captured cell phone to dial 911. I reported the location of the unconscious gangsters. I didn't give my name.

I slung the phone through the open window and cranked up the radio instead. Then I used my phone to navigate back to Tampa.

25

I t was after midnight when I left De Luca's thugs in rural Florida, and it required nearly three hours to return to the campsite. According to the GPS on my phone, we'd driven south and east out of the city into some desolate patch of swampland deep in Florida's Hardee County. I had just enough cell signal to track a course northward, passing the flashing lights of an oncoming fire department ambulance on my way.

I wondered if there was a bodybuilding paramedic on board with a bottle of painkillers. I wondered if she would mandate a trip to the hospital, and an interview by the local sheriff's department.

Probably, but that didn't concern me. De Luca's thugs could hardly incriminate me without incriminating themselves. I thought it was much more likely that they would simply count their blessings and find themselves with a shocking case of temporary amnesia.

A part of me still wished I had killed them both. That had certainly been my intention after they dumped Mia's

Bible into the lagoon, but after watching Mr. Brutally Simple writhing on the ground with severe chest burns...the anger had calmed. I couldn't justify killing him, especially when I would forever link that death to the worn leather Bible that symbolized Mia's faith.

A precious faith. A faith I still didn't understand, but I wanted to. No, I wasn't a murderer, and I wasn't interested in becoming one. Hopefully the burns and bruises would be enough to buy me another couple of days to answer the nagging question of who killed Camilla Cruz, after which I would be gone anyway. Thanks to my conversation with De Luca, I was already developing next steps in my mind. But first I needed to dispose of the Mercury, and I had an excellent idea of how to go about it.

I took Highway 62 west out of Wauchula, then connected with Highway 301 north of Bradenton and wound my way closer to the bay. I found a lagoon fed by Tampa Bay just south of the community of Ruskin, running alongside Interstate 75.

I took my time wiping down all my fingerprints from the interior and exterior of the car. I collected all my stolen personal items from the back seat and called for a taxi to pick me up half a mile away.

Then I propped a rock against the Mercury's accelerator, dropped the shifter into drive, and stepped back. The car rumbled off the two-lane, down a steep hill populated by scrub brush and mangroves, and crashed nose-first into the water. Moments later a gentle current had tugged it away from shore, and fast-food debris tumbled out of the open windows as brackish water bubbled in.

The car sank completely out of sight as I crossed the bridge, hands in my pockets, headed for the taxi pickup.

Payback.

The taxi returned me to the outskirts of Ybor City, where I picked up Hank's Yamaha and rumbled north through Harper Springs to the campsite. It was after three a.m. when I reached my truck. A few of my transient neighbors stuck their heads from camper doors, shouting drunkenly for me to shut the bike off. I obliged, changing out of my dirty clothes before I stretched out in my hammock, relaxing my sore body.

A cool breeze engulfed me from the lagoon. I interlaced my fingers into a pillow and lay gazing up at a star-filled sky. I didn't think about Camilla, or Ralph, or even De Luca and his little sliver of a Mafia. I shelved all of that, and simply thought about Mia, and those magical nights in the Arizona desert when she lay next to me gazing at the same sky.

It was a beautiful enough memory to sooth my mind and send me right to sleep.

I SLEPT LATE, only awaking an hour before noon when the blast of the Florida sun through the pine trees overcame my exhaustion. The campsite was alive with a clatter of cookware, laughing children, and barking dogs. I rolled over to find a brand-new neighbor pulled into the slot next to me— a midwestern family, judging by their Indiana license plates, spilling out of a battered travel trailer.

The giggling of twin boys five or six years old put a smile on my face as I swung my legs out of the hammock and sat drinking in the warmth.

And thinking.

Hank appeared as my coffee pot bubbled to life, a sweaty

Coors Light clasped in one hand. He suppressed a belch and scratched his balding head. There was grease beneath his fingernails, and a wrench sticking out of his back pocket.

"What's broke?" I asked, knocking pine needles out of a metal coffee cup.

"Nothin', for a change. I was just tinkering on the Harley. Watching you roar off yesterday put me in the mood to get her running."

"You want the Yamaha back?"

Hank slurped beer and belched again. "Naw. I figure you'll need a few days to get the truck running…"

He trailed off, regarding the fresh bruises on my bare chest. He cocked an eyebrow.

"You know, it's a cornerstone of camping lifestyle that you don't pry into nobody's business."

"But?"

"But you make a fella wanna."

I laughed, but I didn't indulge him. I drank hot coffee and watched a great egret strutting along the glistening edge of the lagoon. I thought back to the night prior, remembering the Mercury as it disappeared beneath dark water. De Luca, and his thugs. The club, and the protection racket.

Camilla.

I barely heard Hank as he rambled about his motorcycling days, riding once from San Diego to Costa Rica during his "golden years". I was still preoccupied with the frozen face of the dead Cuban girl as she was hauled from the motel room. With the raunchy Instagram messages between her and Ralph. With my collision with De Luca, and the guys who had beat me over the head with a baseball bat.

If I'd learned anything by hunting terrorists in Afghanistan or homicidal maniacs in Phoenix, it was that truth is a living thing. The closer you drive toward it, the more ripples it sends to rock your boat. I'd felt a lot of ripples in the past day, some of them quite literal.

The thought brought my attention to Mia's Bible, which I'd pinned to the floor of the truck with the pages open. Many of them had dried. Many more were badly wrinkled. The places where Mia had made notes in the margin were now disfigured by running ink. The leather cover was blotchy with stains.

Looking at it now, I felt some anger, but mostly I felt focus. Intention. The scent in my nostrils of a target eluding me in the dark.

Something I wouldn't be able to forget until I wrapped my fingers around the truth.

"You good, Mason?"

Hank stood with his beer resting on the gut it had birthed, his head a little cocked. My mind returned from the mist of tangled thoughts, surfacing with a next step.

"I'm great," I said, finishing the coffee. "If you don't mind me using the bike, I think I'll run to town."

Hank finished his beer. He belched for a third time.

"Shiny side up," he said.

"Greasy side down," I finished. Then I reached for my shirt.

26

I returned to Harper Springs, but I wasn't headed for Ralph's motel or the police station. I headed instead for Havana Seafood Restaurant, because I was hungry. Both for lunch, and for answers.

The building was a little calmer than it had been on my last visit, but there was still a good crowd. The hostess returned me to the booth in the corner upon my request, and I sat with my back to the wall. Rosa greeted me with a cheery smile, and I ordered iced tea and a Cuban sandwich.

I barely got the words out before Emilio exploded through the swinging kitchen doors, his face engulfed in rage. He marched straight to my table with a towel snapping from one hand, shoving past Rosa and growling through his teeth.

"Leave. Now."

I played with the straw Rosa had left me, rolling it between worn fingers. Emilio steamed. The doors opened, and Jorge appeared. His thick lips worked in a confused pucker, hands closing at his sides.

"Tell your brother to mind the kitchen," I said. "You and I need to talk."

Emilio's fist landed against the table with a thump strong enough to rattle the napkin dispenser.

"My family is *grieving*," he choked, eyes rimming red. "We've been torn apart this week. Is that not enough for you to leave us in peace?"

"No," I said, simply. "Not with a killer on the loose."

Emilio's knuckles turned white. "We *know* who her killer is."

"You think you know. Part of you must wonder why I'm so convinced that you're wrong. Doesn't that part of you want answers?"

Emilio's lips tightened, but he didn't speak. Jorge remained in the kitchen doorway, lip trembling. He didn't look angry, like he had at the police station. He didn't look like a raging giant.

Now he looked very sad, and very confused. Lost, like a helpless child in a man's body. I remembered what Emilio said about Jorge being a little slow, and a needle of pain pierced my chest. I felt bad for busting Jorge's balls. I didn't want to bust them again.

"I know what it feels like to lose somebody," I said, softly. "I know how bad it hurts. And I want to help."

Emilio's eyes bubbled. He looked away, jerking his hand at Jorge. The bigger of the Cuban brothers didn't budge, and Emilio snapped in Spanish.

It was enough to drive Jorge back into the kitchen. Emilio sat across from me, brushing a hand across his face. He looked like he hadn't slept in days. He looked like he'd bottled everything up.

I had some experience with that—I knew how wearing it could be.

"What do you want?" Emilio said.

"I want to know who killed your sister."

"Why?"

A fair question.

"Because I don't think it was Ralph, and I'd rather an innocent person didn't go to prison."

"Why?"

I rotated the straw. Picked at the wrapper. Pondered.

And then I sighed.

"Because I was hurt very badly last year. I lost somebody very dear to me. I don't have a lot left to get me out of bed in the morning and...I have a hard time ignoring other people's pain. Especially when it's unjust."

Emilio considered that. Rosa brought me my tea and retreated without comment. I unwrapped the straw and took a sip.

It was every bit as excellent as before.

"Why don't you think the old man killed my sister?"

Emilio's voice had dropped to a near monotone. He stared at me, unblinking. His eyes were bloodshot, and the needle of pain returned to my chest.

"I have a few reasons," I said. "We can get to that. First, I have some questions of my own."

"About what?"

"About Camilla...and about organized crime."

Emilio didn't move. I measured the focus in his eyes and searched for any tightening of his chest, or tension in his shoulders. Tell-tale indicators of discomfort. Of prior knowledge, now concealed.

There was nothing. He remained flat, almost as though he were drugged.

"What are you talking about?" Emilio said.

"I have reason to believe your sister's business may have extended beyond modeling. Maybe into something a little less legal."

Emilio's lip twitched, and this time I detected the tension in his chest, barely perceptible but betrayed by shallower breaths.

He did know something.

"Like what?" he said.

"I'm not certain. I only know that there are parties in Florida who are invested in running me out of town, and that seems a little heavy-handed to me if all your sister did was model. Also, there's the matter of her Instagram messages with Ralph. I read them, and they confirmed his side of the story. Your sister swindled him out of better than a hundred grand. She convinced him she was desperately in love, and that she had family in Cuba who needed the money to immigrate. It's all in the messages... You can read them if you like."

Emilio finally blinked. His lips puckered, and I thought he might hit me. His fists were still clenched.

Instead, Rosa appeared to deposit my sandwich on the table, and Emilio simply looked to the window. I saw a trace of wetness in his eyes as Rosa left. He swallowed once, then spoke a single word.

"No."

I nodded, giving Emilio a moment to collect himself. He rubbed tears away, again. He cleared his throat but didn't speak.

"We don't always choose the ones we love," I said.

"Sometimes they aren't the people we think they are...or the people we wish they were."

I was speaking from observation, not experience. I grew up an orphan, without anybody to love me. Mia was probably the first person I ever loved, and she was exactly who I thought she was. No secrets there. But as a cop, I'd seen all kinds of darkness tear families apart.

I had some idea how twisted relationships could become.

"Is this conversation off the record?" Emilio asked.

"I'm not a cop," I said. "And I'm not a reporter."

"But you are investigating. And you will tell the cops what you find."

"Yes. If what I find is helpful."

Emilio swallowed. He licked his lips.

"We held a memorial for my sister last night. Sixteen people showed up. They all worked either at this restaurant or at her modeling agency. There was no family. No parents. No friends."

He faced me. "My sister's memory is carried by very few people, but what memory there is, I would not tarnish."

I let that sink in, envisioning a lonely memorial and a few dusty pictures. A soul lost in the prime of her life, with almost nobody to remember her. It was a visceral image. I thought I understood.

"I'm not here to slur your sister, Emilio. I'm only here to help."

He thought about that. Then his shoulders dropped.

"My sister was...a lot of things. Not all of them were good. I do not know of any enterprises she may have engaged in which were illegal, but..."

"You wouldn't be surprised," I finished.

Emilio shook his head.

"Did your sister associate with anybody from downtown? Any Italians?"

"What do you mean?"

Again I measured Emilio's body language, searching beyond his eyes for other signs of deceit. He appeared genuinely confused.

"Did she have any friends you think may have been shady characters?"

"I honestly wouldn't know. My sister didn't come around very often. I hadn't heard from her in nearly a month when she called to tell me about the old man. She asked Jorge and me to run him off."

"When was that?"

"Sunday."

My mind rewound to the previous Sunday night. The bar fight. How Ralph had turned up there to interview Sophie.

The convergence of three parties in one spot was interesting, to say the least. I still wondered how they all knew to find each other there. Regardless, the facts as Emilio stated them only served to underline Camilla's sleaziness. She'd told Ralph that she had been in Cuba over the previous week.

Apparently, she hadn't been. She'd been right here in Tampa, trying to think of a way to get rid of Ralph.

"To be clear, you don't have any family in Cuba?" I asked.

"Nobody we know. We're second generation American. Our parents died in a car wreck when Camilla was five. She was the baby."

"I'm very sorry."

Emilio dipped his chin once, as though he knew I meant it.

"When I was here before, you said that Camilla didn't

need to steal money from old men. That she made plenty of money on her own."

"What's your question?"

"You just said that you barely saw her. I'm wondering how you knew that she made money."

Emilio shrugged. "You know what they say. You can't hide money."

"So Camilla was flashy?"

"I guess so. Fancy clothes. An expensive car."

"How expensive?"

"I don't know. I'm not a car person. It was one of those little German cars with the engines in the back."

"A Porsche? Like a 911?"

"Right."

"New?"

"Couple years old."

I did the math in my head. I wasn't up to date on Porsche prices, but I couldn't imagine a late model 911 to retail for less than eighty grand. Maybe a hundred.

A lot of money.

"What else?"

"She recently bought a condo in Clearwater. She mentioned it to me, said Jorge and I should visit. She was just trying to butter me up to take care of Ralph."

"Camilla was like that?"

"Like what?"

"She buttered people up?"

Emilio shrugged again and avoided my gaze. I imagined he was thinking of his sister not as the woman she had become, but as the little girl he had shepherded since the untimely demise of their parents. He probably felt protective over her, which explained how zealously he'd turned out to deal with Ralph. I could only assume the pain he now felt was extraordinary. Maybe he felt responsible for her death, somehow. Like he had failed her.

It was a feeling I knew all too well, and that empathy birthed my next question before I could stop myself.

"If I find your sister's true killer, do you want to know?"

Emilio's gaze snapped up. It turned very hard, and very cold.

"Immediately," he said.

27

I took my sandwich to go and ate it while sitting astride the Yamaha. It was hot outside the restaurant, but I didn't think I could eat while Emilio was around.

The agony in his eyes was too perfect—too sincere. It cut me every bit as deep as the pain in Ralph's gaze, and it poured fuel on the fire already burning in my gut. I asked him a few additional questions about Camilla's history and lifestyle, but there wasn't much else to tell. She kept to herself, largely ignoring her brothers. Emilio thought maybe she was still in a lot of pain following the loss of their parents.

He seemed eager to give her the benefit of the doubt. It was something else I understood.

The sandwich was as good as the paella, and it brought a little life to my tired body. I wadded up the wrapper and gazed across the parking lot as cars glided by, a dozen different states represented on their license plates. Tourist season was heating up, and I could already feel the crush of several thousand additional souls descending on my quiet paradise.

I felt like I needed a break. Some crack in the seamless picture of corruption and crime that faced me. It was all a little too simple—a little too self-evident. Camilla was a model and a con-woman, swindling Ralph out of thousands and probably a few others like him, also. That could have placed her in the path of any number of murderous people willing to bludgeon her to death, but it didn't explain her association with organized crime, and for that matter, it didn't explain Ava's connection with organized crime.

I read a book once about the Italian Mafia during their heyday, back in the fifties, sixties, and seventies. Among their many carefully crafted schemes was the protection racket, a simple shakedown method whereby they would siphon profits from local businesses in exchange for not burning those businesses to the ground.

The strategy depended on fear and thrived under the blind eye of corrupt law enforcement. Perfectly logical in the context of yesteryear, but the system felt outdated and unlikely in the modern age. I couldn't help but wonder why Ava didn't simply call the police, or even the FBI. Her business was located on the tenth floor of a high rise, and De Luca couldn't be expected to bring the entire tower down. Even if he threatened to burn her home or dump her car in the bay, insurance would cover her while law enforcement ran De Luca and his inflatable thugs into the ground.

So why hadn't she called the cops?

I could think of only one logical answer—Ava was dirty herself in some way significant enough for her to avoid police interaction. Maybe De Luca knew something about her and was holding it over her head. Queen City Modeling

Agency could be more than it appeared at face value. Maybe Camilla wasn't the only corrupt model playing con games on the side.

If that were the case, it might explain why De Luca's thugs had been deployed to run me out of town. Ava might be uncomfortable with me poking around. Maybe Camilla's death had already brought the police calling, and Ava had started to panic. I could be well advised to take another look into the modeling agency.

But where?

I sat baking on the motorcycle for another ten minutes, recounting my conversations with Ava and my visits to the tenth floor of the high rise. I didn't think it would help to return. Besides making Ava skittish, I wasn't in a hurry for a rematch with De Luca. I needed some other angle...an indirect angle.

Sophie.

I remembered the Carolinian model and our last conversation at the Greek restaurant. How I'd pissed her off. She might not talk to me anymore, and she certainly wouldn't talk at work. But...

My gaze drifted across the highway to a rotating digital billboard featuring bright advertisements for car dealerships and plastic surgeons. The sun glinted off the screen, forcing me to squint as the display rotated. Something about the colorful display triggered a memory, but it took me a moment to recall it. I had to trace my way back to the previous day, sitting astride the Yamaha just as I was now. Looking at a different billboard.

The Tampa Auto Exchange.

I remembered the advertisement displayed on the side of the Tampa convention center, boasting about hundreds of classic cars for sale, beginning midway through the week. And then I remembered something else. The hustle and bustle of models and photographers on the business tower's tenth floor. How they were rushing photo shoots because they were crunched for time.

"We've got a big trade show coming up," Ava had said. *"The Tampa Auto Exchange."*

I dug my phone from my pocket and used the GPS to track a course back downtown. It was barely thirty minutes away.

I hit the starter switch.

28

I detoured to a Walmart on my way back to Tampa, perusing the men's clothing section for a fresh change of clothes. My jeans were spattered with dry blood from my bar fight at Club Bolita, and my shirt smelled badly. I added deodorant and a toothbrush to my basket and used the store bathroom to change and freshen up.

Brand new jeans, a long-sleeve button-down shirt in royal blue, and a clean undershirt—all for less than fifty bucks. I rolled the sleeves of the button-down up to my elbows and ran damp fingers through my hair. I needed a haircut, but I told myself I looked rugged more than homeless.

It was a convincing enough lie for a Walmart bathroom. I trashed my old clothes and returned to the bike.

I took my time cruising into downtown Tampa. The auto exchange was held at the convention center, which sat barely two blocks from Ava's modeling agency. It was a big building, flat-topped, with a lot of concrete and potted plants stretching out in front of the entrance. I found parking in a nearby garage and took my time approaching the main entrance. It was now late afternoon, and already a crowd was gathered to press inside. A lot of old guys with gray or balding heads, many dressed in T-shirts printed with depictions of various muscle cars. It was ten bucks to gain entry, and I exchanged cash for a wrist band. Then I stepped inside the welcome relief of commercial-grade air conditioning and listened to the clamor of excited voices echoing off a high ceiling.

It took me all of three seconds to understand the link between a modeling agency and a car auction. Ava's models were everywhere—generally dressed in tight, low-cut tank tops and shorty shorts, flexing tan legs and flashing sunbeam smiles. They stood next to polished vintage cars, posing for pictures with old guys and handing out fliers that described the car's attributes and starting bid.

Not every car featured a Queen City model, but the most popular ones certainly did. The bald and graying heads clustered around them like bees to honey, and the fliers dispensed by the dozens. There was a lot of laughing at bad jokes. A lot of practiced poses for cell phone selfies. A lot of arms draping a little too low around narrow waists.

Unbelievable.

I drifted through the crowd for the better part of the hour, hands in my pockets, not engaging with anybody. Looking out for Sophie. I found her near the rear of the expansive convention room, giggling and flirting with a pot-bellied biker dude whose braided beard reached almost to his belt buckle. Behind her glistened a 1970 Buick GSX, painted bumblebee yellow, with twin black stripes and glistening rally wheels.

It was a beautiful car, but the guy with the braided beard

seemed preoccupied with real estate south of Sophie's collar bone. He held a foaming light beer in a plastic cup, and eagerly accepted a flier for the car as Sophie bubbled along, pretending to ignore his ogling.

I remained with my hands in my pockets, actually admiring the Buick. I couldn't recall ever seeing a GSX in person before, but I used to work with an old-timer at the Phoenix PD who was a muscle car enthusiast, and I thought I recalled him mentioning one. It certainly looked like a powerhouse.

Beard Braid eventually stumbled off, leaving a temporary opening around Sophie. She lifted a compact mirror to adjust her cloud of strawberry blonde hair before refreshing her smile and turning to greet her next guest.

The smile froze over when her green eyes fell across me. She didn't move.

"Nice car," I said. "Do you come with it?"

To her credit, Sophie didn't so much as flinch. The smile remained plastered and perfect, but her eyes cooled enough to suspend Florida summer.

"Ha. Ha. Ha," she said. "Never heard that one before."

I extended my hand for a flier. Sophie passed it off in stride. The GSX would roll onto the auction floor later that evening, starting bid of thirty-five thousand. I grimaced.

"I may be a little light. Do you take credit cards?"

"Funny again," Sophie quipped. "What do you want?"

An edge crept into her voice that I probably deserved but didn't enjoy. I handed the flier back. Sophie ignored it.

"Keep it," she said without moving her lips. "My client is watching."

I kept the paper and pretended to inspect the car.

"I was hoping we could talk," I said.

"We already talked. You were a jerkwad."

"Maybe I can make up for that."

"I seriously doubt it."

I stepped to the front of the car and bent to look beneath the open hood. A General Motors GS 455 rested in the engine well, topped by a glistening air filter shroud and flawlessly clean components. The car was either never driven or freshly restored.

"I want to talk about your boss," I said.

"What about her?"

"I want to know what she's really up to."

Sophie didn't answer, but I caught her shoulders stiffening out of the corner of my eye.

Body language, telling the truth her lips denied.

"I don't know what you're talking about."

I smiled. Faced her again. "I think you do."

Sophie glanced left. I followed her line of sight to a businessman in a black suit. He was tall and wore sunglasses. The lenses weren't quite dark enough to disguise his gaze. He stared right at us.

Sophie spoke out of the corner of her mouth.

"Take a picture."

"Of what?"

"Of the car, *idiot*."

I retrieved my phone and snapped a picture of the GSX. Then I leaned next to Sophie and flipped the camera into selfie mode.

"Ralph didn't kill Camilla," I said. "And your boss is hiding something. You can help me or not, but I won't go away until I know the truth."

Sophie grinned for the camera, leaning away from me without making it look like she was leaning away from me. I snapped the picture and pocketed the phone. The businessman was still watching.

"Good luck with the auction," Sophie said cheerily. "I hope you win!"

I pocketed the flier, and Sophie turned to the next in line.

29

The auction began at seven p.m. I took a seat in the auditorium as one gleaming car after another was pushed by hand across the stage, pausing for a bit under the high-powered blast of spotlights while the auctioneer rattled off the specs and named the starting bid. A projector displayed a history of the car, alongside additional photos of its restoration or heritage. Anyone bidding sat near the front, raising little cardboard signs to match each bid.

Some of the cars sold for north of a hundred grand, Queen City models leaning against their hoods and waving to the crowds as the bids rolled in. It was overtly and unapologetically sexual, mixing voluptuous girls with polished hunks of metal, but it clearly worked. There was alcohol being served, also. Big plastic cups of it, brought exclusively by male waiters in plain black clothes.

No distraction for the predominantly male audience of semi-inebriated bidders.

I watched for an hour until the GSX rolled across the

stage. Sophie stood near it, casually resting one nail-polished hand on the hood while bids ran north of fifty grand. The GSX sold, and Sophie shot her trademark smile at the winner. He was mostly drunk. He signed the bid ticket anyway, and both Sophie and the car disappeared offstage.

"Can I get you anything, sir?" It was one of the waiters. I hadn't made a purchase all night.

"No, thanks," I said. "Is there a bar in the building?"

"First floor, down that hallway."

He pointed, and I stood. I found the bar right where he'd described it, on the far side of the convention floor where new cars were already appearing on dollies—the sales offerings for the next day, I supposed. The bar was lined by chrome stools cushioned with maroon vinyl. I wanted a beer, but I ordered a club soda with lime instead. I was already pushing the boundaries of sanity by riding the Yamaha without a helmet. No need to add alcohol to the mix.

I decided to wait an hour for Sophie, but she only left me hanging for half that time. When she appeared on the convention room floor she wore the same cut-off jean shorts and skin-tight tank top as before, the cloud of hair brushed back behind her ears. She looked very tired. She looked like she was done with life.

But that look changed when she saw me. She paused at the end of the bar, as though she weren't sure whether she was surprised or irritated. She cocked her head and gave me a long, piercing stare. I felt like she was waiting for an invitation.

"Can I buy you a drink?" I asked.

Sophie flicked a stray lock of hair away from her face. Then she shrugged.

"I guess you owe me one."

I still wasn't sure *how* I owed her one, but I didn't argue. Sophie ordered a dirty martini and took the seat next to me. I sipped on my club soda.

"I know you drink," Sophie said, placing a cell phone inside a wallet case on the counter. Her fingernails glistened red in the bar lights.

"I'm driving later," I said.

"How responsible."

There was mischief in her tone. Maybe it was her practiced behavior while flaunting herself next to the Buick, but the tone turned me off. I wasn't in the mood to play games.

"You wanna tell me about work?" I asked.

The bartender brought the martini. Sophie played with her straw.

"My, my, aren't we forward." She sipped the drink, then waved a hand dramatically in front of her face. "Wow. That's a good one."

I chugged my club soda, crunching on ice. I already detected a slight flush in Sophie's cheeks, and wondered if she was a lightweight. She certainly seemed well inebriated every time I'd seen her at Hank's bar. The investigator in me thought that could be useful, but the man in me resisted the idea of leveraging it.

Sophie looked like a kid. Twenty-one or twenty-two, trying very hard to be five years older and not quite making the sale. I wondered what sort of home life had driven a bright, beautiful young woman like her out of Carolina and into a sleazy modeling job, tolerating drunken slobs with two-foot braided beards.

There had to be a story. Maybe I would get further by playing the slow game.

"So, Charleston."

Sophie sipped the martini. The flush intensified.

"Summerville, technically. But nobody knows where that is. It's near Charleston."

"And school?"

"For a little while. I dropped out."

"How come?"

Sophie hesitated. She looked away. "I wasn't learning anything. I wanted to make money. I wanted to be an actress."

"That led to Tampa?"

The flush turned a little darker, and I thought it wasn't the alcohol. Sophie played with the straw again.

"Atlanta, actually. There's a lot of movie business there these days. But it's hard to break into. I ran out of money. A friend of a friend knew of a job opportunity. She thought I could be a model...so here I am."

She smiled innocently, but the smile didn't feel sincere. I rattled my glass in a signal for a refill. The bartender obliged.

"I knew some people who wanted to be actors," I said.

"In Atlanta?"

"In Phoenix."

"There's movie business in Arizona?"

"Some. Mostly it's just wannabes who got priced out of LA."

"Sounds like me," Sophie mumbled.

The self-pity in her voice edged closer to genuine pain, strong enough to make me wince. I decided to pivot the conversation.

"How long have you worked for Ava?"

Sophie rocked her glass back. The martini was already mostly gone, but the cloudy haze in her eyes outpaced even a strong drink. I wondered if she'd pregamed before walking up on stage.

"Not long," she said. "Like six months."

"A good job?"

"It pays well!" Artificial enthusiasm edged into her voice. I saw an opening and pounced on it.

"I imagine it must. I heard Camilla drove a Porsche."

Sophie snorted and shook her head.

"What?" I asked.

Instead of answering, Sophie raised her glass. The bartender went to work mixing a second drink.

"She didn't drive a Porsche?" I pressed.

"Oh, she drove a Porsche," Sophie said. "Had a nice apartment downtown, too. All the best clothes. Louis bags."

"Wow," I said. "Good for her."

Sophie shrugged. She drew an olive from her empty martini glass and chewed it delicately. I could feel the tension in the air. I'd hit a nerve. There was something behind her forced disengagement. Something she *wanted* to talk about.

I decided to wait it out, and once again Sophie didn't leave me hanging.

"Something paid well," she muttered.

Bingo.

"What does that mean?"

The bartender brought the second martini. Sophie went right to work on it, her shoulders loosening, hair falling over her face and being ignored. I wasn't overly comfortable with the developing dynamic. I felt a little dirty getting her drunk and probing out the truth—like I was taking advantage.

But she shouldn't be this tipsy after less than two drinks.

I'd watched the bartender mix the second one, and he'd measured the vodka. It wasn't overly strong.

"I really shouldn't say," Sophie said. A slur had slipped into her voice. The flush of her cheeks was almost absolute now.

I didn't press. I still thought she wanted to talk, and with a witness who wants to talk, the best thing you can do is shut up and listen.

Sophie faced me, toying with her straw. Gently brushing hair behind one ear. Looking sly.

"What?" I asked.

"Well. I mean. I can't prove anything."

"But?"

"But...you know. There's models. And then there's *models*."

"What does that mean?" I thought I knew what it meant but I didn't want to say it and be wrong.

"Ava...you know. She's a great businesswoman. But she has favorites. Like...elites."

"An inner circle?" I suggested.

"Exactly." Sophie dipped her head toward the straw and stabbed herself in the lip. She didn't so much as wince.

"Camilla was a member?"

Another soft snort. "Camilla was the queen."

Interesting. I pondered for a moment. The martini shrank inside its glass. The uneasy voice in the back of my head grew a little louder, warning me that I was treading into dangerous territory.

I pressed ahead with one more question.

"So I guess the inner circle got the better jobs," I said. "The higher-paying jobs."

"You'd think, right? But I mean, they did the same jobs we did. Generally. I mean, model stuff."

Her words fell over themselves, and foggy green eyes drifted across the convention room floor to survey the new cars. I decided to take the plunge.

"Did you ever feel like...you know."

"What?"

"Maybe Camilla was doing *other* kinds of modeling."

Sophie laughed. "Porn? Heck no. You clearly never knew her."

I shrugged. Sophie finished her drink with a powerful tug and pushed the glass back. The bartender shot me a sideways look, and I shook my head. He nodded once, then went to work mixing another drink on Sophie's request—reducing the vodka to barely a splash this time.

Sophie accepted the refill and didn't seem to notice the missing liquor. She swept me with a slow pass of her foggy gaze, moving past my face this time and across my shoulders. Down the length of one arm.

It was a very slow, focused progression. I twitched in sudden discomfort.

"So you're from Phoenix?"

"Originally."

"And now?"

I swallowed club soda. "Now I just...travel around. I camp a lot."

"Like van life?"

"Everybody says that." I laughed.

"That's the dream, right?"

I thought about my battered pickup truck. The worn air mattress. Mia's wrinkled Bible. The burned eggs and watery coffee.

The long nights alone.

"Yeah," I said, softly. "That's the dream."

Sophie reached a hand across the bar. One polished fingernail traced a scar on my right forearm, snaking its way from beneath the rolled-up sleeve and reaching for my wrist.

"What happened here?" she asked.

I tensed, a sudden flush of heat washing through my chest. I pulled my arm away and drained the club soda.

"Army," I said simply, sliding off the stool and reaching for my wallet. Sophie feigned offense as she withdrew her hand, turning her head away to drain the drink. Then she got up with me, and I paid the tab with a generous tip. Pushing back through the front doors, I stood in the sticky Florida darkness and inhaled a breath of salty air. The flush of heat in my chest had subsided a little since Sophie touched my arm, but it left a cloud of confusion in my mind.

Confusion, and discomfort. Only one other woman had touched me since I lost Mia, and that was of my own origination. It had been years since a drunk girl at a bar had come on to me, and I didn't enjoy it like I used to.

It wasn't Sophie's fault. I just wasn't looking for that kind of attention.

The door groaned open behind me, and Sophie appeared. She wobbled a little on her feet, fiddling with her car keys. Across the street headlights flashed from a parking garage as she signaled her Volkswagen. Sophie tossed her hair with a sloppy flick of her hand and shot me a dismissive glance.

"Well. Thanks for the drinks."

She started toward the street and I sighed. I wanted to let her go. I wanted to be back on the bike, roaring to the campsite by myself. But the burden of responsibility wouldn't release me. Sophie was hardly fit to drive.

"Hey," I said. "You need a ride?"

Sophie stopped. She glanced back, fiddling with the keys. Her teeth flashed over her bottom lip, biting just a little. She cocked her head.

"I think I'm good," she said coyly.

I laughed. "Sure you are. Come on...I'm parked in the garage. I'll take you home."

30

Sophie accepted my offer without further protest, trotting along the sidewalk and doing her best not to appear sloshed. It was a noble attempt, but unconvincing. She staggered a little. She suppressed a burp.

She looked like a drunk college kid stumbling home after a ballgame. It made me feel vaguely sad, and I couldn't put my finger on why.

We reached the garage where I left the Yamaha and I slung a leg over the seat. Sophie stopped, wrinkling her nose.

"Are you kidding me?" she slurred.

"It's got two seats," I said.

"And a *helmet?*"

"No helmet law in Florida."

I hit the starter, and the big engine grumbled to life with a throaty cough. It sounded good, cold. It sounded even better inside the confines of a concrete garage. Sophie hesitated a moment longer, uncertainty mixed with adventure dancing across her face. I disengaged the sidestand.

"Well? You coming or not?"

That was enough. She grinned and slung her leg over the pillion seat. The phone/wallet combo disappeared into a saddle bag, and her arms closed around my waist.

The rush of heat returned as I smelled vodka wafting over my shoulder. She pulled in close.

"Where to?" I asked.

"Pebble Creek. It's northeast of town—I'll tell you."

I mashed the shifter into first gear and rumbled out of the parking garage, accepting Sophie's slurred directions out of downtown and onto the highway. I wound the bike out the moment we hit the freeway, and the overbuilt motor didn't struggle in the least with the added weight. Sophie squealed with excitement as the speedometer raced to seventy, each consecutive gear unleashing new spectrums of power amid a roar of exhaust. There was no fear in her voice. No uncertainty. She clung to me and kept her face pressed close to my shoulder, hot wind sending strands of strawberry blonde whipping into my face.

The girlishness in her voice made me uneasy, at first. It made me feel old. But by the time we wound off the highway and into a dense suburb, I'd come to accept it.

She didn't just look like a kid. She *was* a kid—a college student out of college. A single young woman with a head full of confusions about life and a basket of growing disappointments. I still couldn't sort out what about her disposition made me sad, but I could feel the storm beneath her skin as surely as I'd detected the desperation in Ralph's eyes.

It takes one to know one.

Sophie directed me to a parking spot in front of a three-story apartment building sided with vinyl. I cut the bike off and she gave my waist another squeeze.

"That was *amazing*. How have I never done that before?"

The tenor of her voice had changed completely since the bar. Gone was the carefully crafted austerity of a big-city woman pretending not to be drunk. Sophie was all girl, now. All happy kid, bouncing off the bike and kissing me on the cheek before I could stop her.

I flushed, balancing the Yamaha between my knees.

"Come on up," Sophie said. "I'll fix you a drink."

She tugged on my arm and shot me a wink. The discomfort returned to my gut.

"No, thanks," I said. "I just wanted to make sure you got home safe."

She did the thing with her finger again, twirling her hair. Pouting just a little.

"Oh, come on...just one drink."

I clamped the clutch and flicked the starter. The bike roared back to life.

"Thanks, really. Have a great night."

I kicked off the asphalt to roll the bike backward, my face flushing hot. Sophie remained on the sidewalk, still smirking. She didn't look disappointed. She looked calculative.

"See you soon," she said with a little wave. Then she skipped up the sidewalk to a door on the first floor. I gunned the throttle, finding the highway, my tired thoughts again returning to my campsite. My hammock. Another quiet night.

And to Camilla. The inner circle. Every careless, drunken word Sophie had let slip. It was a lot to work with, but I still felt mired in mud, like every step was a fight.

I would return to the campsite. Rest. And then in the morning, I would call Sophie. Resume our conversation and dig a little deeper. Press a little harder.

Call Sophie.

My thoughts skipped away from our conversation in the bar, and into the saddlebag riding behind my thigh. I thought of the wallet/phone combo Sophie had deposited there, and pulled the bike into the highway's emergency lane. I didn't recall her removing the phone when I reached her apartment.

Twisting around, I dipped a hand into the bag. Sure enough, the phone was there. But not just the phone—Sophie's driver's license, credit cards, health insurance ID... everything a woman might keep in a wallet was found inside the phone's multi-purpose case. I snapped it shut with an irritated clench of my teeth, recalling the calculative look on her face as she watched me ride away.

She was *playing* me. Like a violin. She intended to leave the phone. She wanted me to return.

I sat astride the bike for a full minute, measuring my thoughts and half tempted to toss the phone into the emergency lane before roaring on back to the campsite. Leave Sophie to solve her own problems.

But no. I didn't like being toyed with, and besides, I still had questions. I'd backed off Sophie due to her inebriation, but if she wanted to play games, I would drive for checkmate. I'd demand real answers.

Pocketing the phone, I took the next exit and wound the Yamaha out on my way back to the apartment. I found the parking spot just down the hill from Sophie's apartment and cut the engine. I took the phone and jogged up the sidewalk, locating the first door on the right.

I made a fist and cocked it back to rap on the door.

Then I heard the scream.

31

The sound was muted and gurgling, followed by a crash of braking glass. Something hit the floor inside Sophie's apartment with a meaty thud. The scream repeated for a split second, then was cut short.

My heart rate spiked, and I reached for the doorknob. It was locked. I dropped back instead and launched myself off the concrete, driving with my right boot. Rubber met metal, and the doorframe exploded in a shower of cheap pine splinters. The door crashed open, revealing a dim living room paved in faux hardwood, illuminated by a single lamp. Dirty clothes and shards of glass littered the floor, and splatters of blood ran down the short hallway toward the bedroom.

Another thump resounded through the closed bedroom door. I sped down the hall, dropping the phone/wallet, and bracing my shoulder for the impact. Not even bothering with the knob. I lunged right and threw my entire body mass into the door, shattering the jamb and sending it rocketing open.

I saw Sophie first. She lay on her back over the bed, not dressed as I'd left her in a tank top and jean shorts, but instead wearing inky black lingerie that tangled over her stomach. Her head was laid back over the mattress, both hands clutched around her throat...

Where a leather belt sank deep into the skin.

I saw the second person in the room as a flash, diving through the open bedroom window just as I exploded through the door. They were dressed in all black, disappearing into the bushes outside long before I could make out a face or even a body type. Sophie thrashed on the bed and I rushed for her throat first, finding the buckle of the belt tangled up behind her neck and fighting to loosen it. It was tangled into some kind of slip knot, designed to tighten like a noose and remain that way. I wrestled it free and pulled it over her head just as an engine roared to life from the parking lot—fast and raspy, like a sports car.

Sophie gasped and shook, tears dripping down her face. She clawed at the bedclothes, then wrapped her hands around my arm and continued to shake as she fought to recover her wind. Her cheeks were pale, her lips as blue as the midday sky.

She'd been only seconds from strangling to death.

"Are you okay?" I asked, squeezing her shoulder. The car engine wound louder outside.

"I...I can't...I couldn't breathe..."

"Help is coming," I said. "Lie still!"

Then I raced for the window. I managed to poke my head out over the bushes just in time to catch the profile of a small black coupe jetting across the parking lot, crashing over a speed bump and headed for the exit. I only saw it for a split second, but the silhouette was impossible to misidentify for anyone even remotely familiar with cars.

It was a Porsche 911. Late model, rag top. Headed for the highway.

I burst out of the bedroom, leaving Sophie still sobbing as I returned to the breezeway. A couple of neighbors had detected the noise and now stood with their heads poking from doorways.

"Call an ambulance!" I shouted. "She needs help!"

Then I was back to the bike, firing up the big engine. Kicking away from the curb and burning rubber with a scream of amplified horsepower. I smelled asphalt and gasoline as the Yamaha slung me like a missile away from the apartments and toward the same exit. From two hundred yards back I spotted the coupe as it reached the intersection of the apartments' service road and the four-lane it connected to. The Porsche turned right, tires screaming and engine racing as it slid in front of a pickup truck. The pickup laid on its horn, and I laid on the accelerator. I leaned hard right coming out of the parking lot, and my right knee dipped toward the asphalt. Brand new Walmart jeans scraped pavement, and I ratcheted my left foot upward to reach third gear.

I could barely see the Porsche. It was now three hundred yards ahead, weaving through traffic with its lights off, little more than an inky black shadow. The modified four-cylinder growling between my legs was enough to match the speed of the turbocharged sports car, but the traffic gathered between us provided a steady stream of obstacles. I leaned left and right, gunning the motor at every opening and splitting lanes to close the gap. A four-by-four intersection blocked the path ahead, a line of traffic lights flicking from yellow to red as the Porsche neared the white line. Brake lights flashed, followed by a right-hand turn signal.

I didn't buy it. The strangler had yet to signal or to stop. I swung into a narrow gap between the left-hand lane and an adjacent turn lane and rode the dashed line, spiking the bike up to sixty miles per hour. The Porsche reached the white line and swerved right.

Then it yanked left, tires screaming as it launched straight into the intersection. Horns blared and brakes squealed. The Porsche slid, gliding through the turn and momentarily flashing its driver's side window across my field of view. I caught the profile of a shadowy figure pressed against the seat, both hands on the wheel, face turned away. Then the Porsche accelerated onto the intersecting four-lane, and I had a choice to make.

I pushed my chips in and twisted the throttle. The beastly Yamaha thundered, and I hurtled across the white line. More horns blared. An SUV squealed and rotated mid-intersection, spinning toward me. I leaned left and ignored it all, making for a gap in the traffic like Emmitt Smith racing for a hole in the defensive line.

The Yamaha passed the SUV with inches to spare, leaving me just enough time to relax my counter-steer and avoid the curb. Then I was through, and I gunned the motor. The speedometer spiked. I split lanes again and blazed past a semi-truck. The Porsche raced along barely eighty yards ahead. I wasn't sure exactly what I would do if and when I caught it.

But I wasn't letting it slip away.

Another intersection loomed ahead, a two-lane crossing our four-lane with a gas station on the left and some manner of large retention pond on the right, illuminated by a glowing fountain. This time the light was green, and the Porsche accelerated, its rear end squatting toward the pavement as the German motor dumped power to the wheels. I matched that power, the front suspension of the Yamaha lifting away from the street as weight transferred to the rear wheel. Hot Florida wind tore at my face. The air flooded with the thunder of exhaust, and cars on either side blurred out of existence. In a split second, I wasn't in Florida anymore. I was outside of Phoenix again. I was a kid.

And the bike was stolen.

The Porsche neared the intersection. The light turned yellow. I twisted harder on the throttle. The speedometer passed eighty. The gap between my front wheel and the Porsche's illuminated Florida license plate narrowed to thirty yards. The Porsche reached the white line.

And then I saw the van. It was one of those flat utility panel vans, printed with the name and logo of some local electrician or plumber. It was rolling up to the intersection along the two-lane to my right, preparing to make a right turn directly into my path of travel. The driver should have stopped and looked both ways.

But he didn't. He barely even slowed, and he most definitely didn't see me. The Porsche glided left into the fast lane, and the van turned right into my lane, the broad rear doors looming ahead like a block wall.

In an instant, I had another choice to make. It was too late to bleed off my speed. I had to swerve left behind the Porsche, or else swerve right into the road's shoulder. I chose left, but in the split second it took to make that decision, the driver of the Porsche detected my movement and made a decision of their own.

They laid on the brakes, squealing to a near stop and

matching the pace of the van. It was checkmate, in less time than it takes to blink. I was still hurtling along at over sixty miles an hour, with barely twenty yards to play with. Both cars blocked the lanes ahead, the Porsche swerving right toward the van to prevent me from riding the dashed line.

There was no time to stop. No time to think. I had to swerve, or else I was going to smack that van hard enough to turn bones into dust.

I chose to swerve, leaning right and rushing toward the edge of the road. I don't think the van driver ever saw me. The front tire of the Yamaha hit the road's shoulder at fifty miles per hour, heavy rubber tearing into grass and sand as I smashed down on the rear brake and clung on for dear life.

Once more my mind was snatched away from Florida. I remembered Arizona as the Yamaha teetered between my legs and started to crash right. Then I simply let go, lifting my leg off the bike a moment before it slammed sideways into the dirt. I hurled onward, flying over the handlebars like a cartoon character launched from a cannon. I cleared the ditch, cleared a low retention wall with barely an inch to spare...

And hurtled straight into the retention pond.

32

Black water closed over my head in a rush, a bone-jarring decrease in velocity driving a shockwave through my skeleton only a little softer than raw concrete would have. The air left my lungs and I went down, not even fighting until my boots sank into the gunky pond bottom ten or twelve feet beneath the surface.

I kicked off and blasted upward with a raw heave, a black sky polluted by city lights opening over my face as I gasped for breath. The dirty pond water lapped into my mouth and I kicked both legs, still gasping. Still not entirely sure what had happened. I saw the fountain thirty yards away, blasting a twenty-foot illuminated shower, with another multi-level apartment complex built behind it.

I wiped my face with one sodden blue sleeve, then rotated to find the shore. I'd flown well beyond the retention wall, but there was a sodden bank a few dozen yards to my left, overhung by the trailing limbs of a willow tree. I kept my face above the surface as I kicked for shore, dragging my brand-new Walmart clothes across the muck when I finally reached solid ground.

I took a moment just to breathe and flex each limb individually, inspecting for broken bones or shattered joints. I'd struck the water like a rocket, but miraculously, everything seemed to be intact. Some bruises and strained muscles, no doubt. Penalties I would suffer for the next few weeks. But the worst of it was losing the Porsche. The little black German coupe was long gone, racing away from the intersection even as a trio of cars stopped to check on the wreck.

A rustling caught my attention from a bush near the base of the willow. I rotated my head in that direction and caught a pair of bright orange eyes gleaming at me from the darkness. A three-foot alligator lay there, not blinking, its ugly mouth parted an inch or two as it stared at me like I had lost my mind.

"What?" I snapped. The gator closed its mouth, and I hauled myself to my feet. My clothes were ruined, and my head swam. But I could walk.

Returning to the ditch, I was greeted by a small crowd of frat guys with slicked-back hair and open-collared shirts. They all smelled like beer.

"Bro! You okay, man? You flew like a cannon ball!"

I waved them off, finding the Yamaha dug into the ditch not far from the retention wall. The right-side grip had sunk into the soil, and mud covered the wheels and the seat. The engine had cut off, and one mirror was knocked out of position.

Otherwise, the bike looked relatively unharmed. A near miracle.

"Give me a hand?" I asked.

The frat guys helped me to right the bike while they

continued to pontificate about my trip into the retention pond with increasingly hyperbolic similes. Somebody offered to call an ambulance, but I dismissed the idea and got the bike started again. The motor ran with as much aggression as before, a little mud exploding from the tail pipe. No worse for the wear.

I left the frat guys on the shoulder and returned to the road, working slowly up to highway speed. There was no sign of the panel van, and still no sign of the Porsche. I couldn't help but admire the swift thinking of my quarry. If I'd had just another ten yards of space, I might have been able to brake, or swerve left instead of right. Avoid the pond.

But the Porsche driver hadn't given me the chance. They had timed the application of brakes perfectly. It was brilliant.

I took my time returning to Sophie's apartment, partly because I couldn't quite remember the way. I had to resort to my phone and scan around on the map application before I eventually located the apartment complex. An ambulance and a trio of Tampa police cars sat outside, lights flashing. I parked the bike next to the curb and grunted a little as I swung off.

Already my limbs were stiffening. A lot had changed since my glory days in Arizona.

At Sophie's front door a smattering of neighbors stood at a distance while cops and paramedics walked in and out. I let myself in, accosted almost immediately by a skinny female cop wearing plastic glasses.

"Hold up there! Back outside—"

"Wait! He's with me."

Sophie sat on the couch, wrapped in a blanket, mascara-laced tear trails drying on her cheeks. Her hair was a disheveled mess, and one of the paramedics inspected her neck with a gloved hand. Two of the cops were busy in the back room, probably searching for fingerprints.

They wouldn't find any. I'd only gained a momentary glimpse of the strangler, but I'd noted gloves. That made sense, anyway. This wasn't a random, impulsive attack.

It was clearly premeditated.

"You were here?" the skinny cop asked.

I grunted an affirmation and shoved past her to squat next to Sophie. Her eyes still looked a little hazy, but she'd sobered up considerably since I dropped her off. She still wore the black lingerie, one shoulder strap visible beneath the edge of the blanket.

She stared at me with raw terror in her gaze.

"Are you okay?" I said softly.

Sophie's lip quivered. The skinny cop folded her arms and waited.

"He was going to kill me," Sophie rasped.

I nodded, but I didn't comment. I just retraced the sequence of events in my mind, from the moment I kicked the door open to the moment I flew over that retention wall. It felt like a blur, but there was an order to the chaos. A method to the madness.

"Did you see anything?" I asked. "Did you get a look at him?"

She shook her head. "I...I was just coming out of the bathroom. He attacked from behind. I never saw a thing."

The tears returned. I placed a gentle hand on her arm and gave it a squeeze. I smiled. "You're all right. Just let them check you out, okay? They'll take care of you."

"You're leaving?" Her voice was edged with panic.

"I'm just stepping outside. They'll want a statement."

Sophie didn't seem happy with that, but she let me go.

The skinny cop recorded my side of the story, from the moment I kicked the door down to the moment I returned covered in mud. She made a lot of notes and took down my name and phone number.

"You didn't get a good look at the suspect's face?" she asked.

"No."

"And the license plate?"

"Didn't have time. But I can guess."

The skinny cop squinted. "What does that mean?"

"Look up vehicle registrations for Camilla Cruz, local resident. She owned a late model Porsche 911."

"And what makes you think this is the same car?"

"Because Camilla worked with Sophie—and she was recently murdered."

33

The Tampa PD completed my witness interview, and I left Sophie's apartment after checking in on her. She was still strung out but appeared to have been medically sedated by the paramedics. She threw her arms around my neck and I awkwardly returned the hug. Then I was back astride the Yamaha and headed for the highway.

After consideration I modified my earlier plans to return to the campsite, finding a chain hotel instead and booking a room with a jacuzzi tub. The aches and pains of my flight into the retention pond were already setting in, and I knew I couldn't afford to be taken out of action by muscle cramps.

There was a killer on the loose. If I had been ten seconds later arriving to Sophie's front door, she would be as dead as Camilla. And I still didn't know why.

I filled the tub with cold water, then carted ice from the machine down the hall until the bath was frigid. I gritted my teeth as I settled into it, resisting the urge to gasp or spring back out. The cold quickly numbed my body from

the shoulders down, fighting against developing inflamma-
tion. By the time I toweled off, I felt a lot better. I cut the
lights, turned the AC down as low as it would go, and
stretched out over the king-sized bed. It was more
supportive than my leaky air mattress, and didn't groan
when I turned. I faced the ceiling and let sleep come slowly,
not focusing on any one thought. Not thinking too hard
about the truth.

Because I knew the answer would come. One way or the
other.

I AWOKE to the chime of my cell phone, which was strange,
because almost nobody ever calls me. The area code was 813,
the number unfamiliar. I set my feet on the floor and took a
moment to scrub the sleepiness out of my eyes. The bedside
clock read 8:14, but the blackout curtains held back the sun. I
could have slept another four hours.

"Hello?" I answered the call because I had no reason not
to. I figured it was a wrong number. Maybe a sales call. I
never expected the voice on the other end.

"Mr. Sharpe?"

I squinted. "Ava Sullivan?"

The voice was easily recognizable, but I didn't expect her
to call me by my real name. I'd only ever used the pseudonym Emmitt Smith with Ava. Then again, she had business with De Luca, and De Luca knew who I was. It actually
didn't really matter how she'd learned my name. I knew how
she got my number—I'd left her with it.

"Can you talk?" Ava asked.

I stood, biting back a groan as racing soreness ran down

my back and through my hips. Despite my preparation with the ice bath, I felt like I'd been hit by a truck.

"I can talk," I said, keeping my tone free of the pain. Ava took her time responding. I detected a hitch in her breathing. A raw tension.

"I'd rather talk in person," she said. "Are you still in Tampa?"

I squinted. "That depends. Are you gonna deploy more Italian gangsters to beat me over the head with a baseball bat?"

"I'm sorry about that," Ava said, making no effort to deny it. "It was a misunderstanding. I'm happy to compensate you for your pain and suffering. I just want to talk."

I considered, stepping to the window and peeling back the curtain. The sky was perfectly clear, bright with a blazing sun. The warmth on my face felt good.

"I'm not in the mood for any more games," I said. "I won't respond well if you yank my chain."

It was a promise, not a threat. Ava accepted it as such.

"That won't happen, Mr. Sharpe. I'll text you an address. Get here as soon as you can."

She hung up, and I looked for the address. It popped through as promised—some residential neighborhood on Pelican Island, a gated, waterfront community northwest of downtown Tampa. It wasn't far.

I showered before redressing in the same mucky clothes I'd worn into the retention pond. Then I raided the breakfast bar downstairs before finding the Yamaha waiting for me in the parking lot.

It was going to be a scorcher—I could feel that the moment I stepped through the automatic sliding glass doors and into the Florida morning. I guessed it to already be north of ninety degrees, without a breath of wind in the air. Not bad motorcycling weather.

I used my phone to navigate to Pelican Island, not bothering to hit Walmart along the way. I looked rough, but maybe that was a good thing. My appearance might serve to remind Ava who she was dealing with, and discourage any further games. The gate guard was expecting me, and directed me to Ava's house with a wave of one hand. I puttered along with sweat running down my face, admiring a long stream of million-dollar homes, many with Spanish tile roofs and white adobe siding. The pavement was blacktop, the grass vibrant green. Plenty of palm trees and shrubbery gathered around driveways populated by Land Rovers, Escalades, and Porsche SUVs. The neighborhood gave me the vibe of an upper middle-class community, certainly on the wealthier side of the city, but a far cry from being elite.

A million dollars isn't what it used to be.

I found Ava's house near the back of the loop, a two-story residence topped with the same Spanish-style tile roof I'd seen before. A semi-circular driveway ran past a two-car garage, with a Mercedes S-class baking beneath the sun. Automatic sprinklers watered the grass. The hedges were all neatly trimmed, the flowerbeds perfectly cultivated.

It had the look of a place whose owner paid through the nose for immigrants to maintain her property while she was never around. I deployed the sidestand behind the Mercedes and hit the kill switch. The bike died with a chug, and I sat for a moment regarding the front door.

Ava's call wasn't a wrinkle I had expected. I knew she had lied to me before. I knew somebody was targeting her girls. I knew she had links to De Luca and was in some way under his protection.

What I didn't know was why on earth she'd want to talk to me.

I left the bike and hit the doorbell, hands free at my sides. Ready for almost anything. Ava herself answered a moment later, dressed down from the last time I saw her, in jeans and a simple baby-blue blouse, hair pulled back into a pony tail. She was still a very gorgeous woman, but showed her age more than she had at the modeling agency.

She looked very tired, with black shadows beneath her eyes and lines in her forehead. Her eyes spoke to deep stress.

"Mr. Sharpe...thank you for coming."

She cast a glance across my disheveled appearance. I made no apologies, stepping right inside. The air conditioning was strong. The house smelled of lemon water, or maybe it was cleaner. Certainly, everything was spotless. The foyer was paved in tile, decorative furniture lining the walls alongside art housed in wood frames. I'm sure it was all very nice, but it wasn't my style.

"Please join me on the veranda. I have a little snack prepared."

I followed Ava through a sprawling open living room stocked with more expensive art and furniture, onto a screened-in porch that overlooked Old Tampa Bay. More fancy furniture, this time made of wicker, and a wet bar. A fan spun slowly overhead, not making a sound, and a doorway led to a wooden walkway which in turn led to a dock.

A yacht was parked alongside that dock—not a big yacht by Tampa standards, but there's no such thing as a cheap boat. I guessed it to be forty or forty-five feet in length, fully equipped with a swim platform and a covered cockpit. Not new, but not very old, either. The name *Snapshot* was printed across the stern in elegant gold script.

How cute.

I raised an eyebrow, and Ava fidgeted with her hands.

"Business has been good to me, Mr. Sharpe."

"Congratulations." I didn't mean it, not because I had any derogatory opinions about the nature of her business so much as the goose egg on my skull still hurt. Ava motioned for me to have a seat in one of the wicker lounge chairs. There was a coffee table arranged with finger sandwiches and a selection of sparkling waters.

Girl food.

I sat down and Ava sat across from me. She smoothed her jeans, breathing deeply. Her eyes twitched. Her lips looked tight.

I relaxed, fully prepared for any number of De Luca's inflatable thugs to pop out of the woodwork.

"I appreciate you coming," Ava said again.

I didn't speak. She sighed.

"I'll get right to the point. I'm in trouble, and I need your help. I want you to work for me."

34

It wasn't the statement I expected, but then again I hadn't made any assumptions about her request for a conversation. So I stalled, simply lifting a ham and cheese finger sandwich from the table and eating quietly.

It was bland. The mayonnaise tasted light, the ham lean. I revised my prior assessment of girl food to *skinny girl food*.

I finished the sandwich, and Ava still hadn't spoken. I cracked a sparkling water open. It was also bland.

"Before you ask any favors, you might start by explaining the thing with the baseball bat."

I jabbed a thumb at the top of my head. Ava dropped her gaze.

"I'm sorry about that. Like I said, it was a misunderstanding."

"So help me understand."

She picked at her jeans. Sighed. "We've had some... issues. Lately. With people stalking my girls."

"You mean your models."

"Right."

"And?"

"And when you turned up, I thought that's what you were."

"I made it clear that I wasn't."

"Well, I didn't believe you. I'm sorry."

"So you called your Mafia friends."

Ava locked eyes with me. She didn't blink.

"I met De Luca," I said. "Which you already know, because he gave you my name. It wasn't a friendly encounter. There was conversation of my being fed to alligators."

Ava flinched. "I'm sorry."

"I'm less interested in your apology and more interested in your explanation."

"About?"

"About why your modeling agency is under the protection of De Luca's crime ring."

Ava took her time responding. I sipped bland water.

"That's a complex situation."

"I've got time."

Her shoulders dropped. So did her gaze. "It sounds like you're familiar with a protection agreement."

"Yes."

"De Luca charges me a fee. It's a percentage of my profits. In exchange, his gangsters protect me."

"From themselves," I said.

Ava shrugged. "It's a complicated world we live in, Mr. Sharpe."

"No, it's not. Not that complicated. 911 is a simple number. It's not difficult to reach the FBI, either. Why haven't you?"

I already knew the answer, but I wanted her to say it. Ava squared her shoulders.

"For the same reason I called you this morning instead of the police."

"You don't want cops poking around your business," I said.

Ava shrugged.

"Why not?"

"I don't suppose there's a way we could leave it unsaid."

"Not a chance. Not if you want my help."

Ava settled into her chair, seeming to find her grit.

"When you came to me before, you made certain accusations against Camilla. That she had swindled Ralph Roberts."

"Right."

"Okay. So let's say that's true. Hypothetically."

I set the water down. "No hypotheticals. Give it to me straight, or I'm out of here. I owe you nothing."

Another momentary hesitation. A flex of the lips. Then, "Camilla swindled Mr. Roberts. Yes."

"And others?"

"Yes."

"And Camilla isn't the only one doing it, is she?"

Ava flinched. "What makes you say that?"

"Call it intuition. I'm guessing there's an organized system at play. You're the ringleader."

"Why do you think that?"

"Because I passed third grade math, and I have some idea what that boat cost." I jabbed a thumb toward the yacht. "Modeling work is lucrative, I have no doubt. But surely not *that* lucrative."

Ava turned a little cold. I didn't care.

"What are you suggesting, Mr. Sharpe?"

"I'm not suggesting anything. I'm simply observing.

You've got a rolodex full of beautiful young women at your beck and call who have already demonstrated their willingness to strip their clothes off for money."

Ava drew breath. I help up a hand. "I'm not judging anybody. Those girls only make money because sexy pictures make sales. That's the world we live in. I'm only recognizing the reality that your business extends beyond sexy pictures. Your girls also do a lot of live modeling work, like the work they're doing right now at the Tampa Auto Exchange. All skin-tight clothes and flirting. Snapping selfies with half-drunk old guys...very *rich* half-drunk old guys."

Ava didn't so much as blink, but the hint of a smirk tugged at her lips.

"I imagine Camilla was one of a few," I said. "One of an inner circle, let's say. A group of trusted girls who took their work to the next level. Make a friend. Get him drunk. See what happens. Maybe it spills into a hotel room. Maybe it spills into internet chats. But wherever it spills, there's a price. Most of that price your girls get to keep, but not all. You take a cut because you set the whole thing up. You led them to a barrel full of fish and handed them a shotgun."

I lifted the can of water. I sipped. Ava's smirk grew a little wider.

"You're very perceptive, Mr. Sharpe."

"I was a homicide detective," I said. "Apparently I have a knack for unraveling things."

Ava nodded slowly. Then she reached to the little shelf beneath the coffee table and produced a paper folder. She tossed it next to the bland sandwiches.

"I know you were," Ava said. "And that's why you're here."

I looked at the folder. Cocked an eyebrow.

"Go ahead," Ava said.

I set the water down and flipped the folder open. The first page was a black and white printout of a newspaper page. *The Arizona Republic*, dated for eighteen months prior. A single headline was highlighted in yellow.

HERO COP GUNS DOWN SCHOOL SHOOTERS, LOSES FIANCÉE.

I looked up, sudden heat rising through my face. I snapped the folder closed and pushed it back across the table. There were other printouts beneath the newspaper headline, but I didn't need to see them. I could already guess.

"After De Luca told me who you were I had a private investigator run your name," Ava said. "I'm very sorry for your loss."

My teeth clenched, and the heat intensified. I wasn't sure why. Maybe it was the intrusion into my privacy. Maybe it was the vague feeling that Ava was trying to manipulate me.

Whatever the case, I had better than half a mind to leave her to her skinny girl food.

"You believe Ralph Roberts didn't kill Camilla," Ava said. It wasn't a question, and I didn't answer it. Ava lifted her chin. "I think you're right."

I tensed. Ava plowed ahead.

"There is an inner circle. Camilla was the ringleader. Together with three others, she amplified my business profits. Significantly. Tampa is a target-rich environment for that kind of thing. Lots of loose businessmen from out of town who drop their pants at the first flash of a pretty girl's smile.

They're only too happy to pay a few grand in exchange for their wives not finding out."

"That's extortion," I said.

"That's *business*," Ava snapped, her lips quivering. "And it's no less than these pigs deserve. You cheat, you pay."

It was bent and twisted logic, but I didn't have the time to unravel Ava's worldview. I could already tell where this story was headed.

"The men don't usually come back, do they?" I asked. "Ralph is an exception."

The tension in Ava's face faded a little. She nodded. "Yes, he is. Usually, it's a few thousand dollars, and they're gone. They don't want contact. They want it all to go away."

"But Ralph was different."

"Camilla pushed too far with Ralph. My girls are trained to target married men. Single men are more difficult to manage. A guy like Ralph should have never been touched, but…"

"But he had money," I finished. "Camilla saw a lot of low-hanging fruit. She couldn't help herself."

"Yes."

I looked out over the water, arranging the facts in my mind. Racing toward an inevitable conclusion.

"Somebody else was pushed too far," I said. "One of the old targets. Somebody who snapped."

Ava didn't answer. I faced her again.

"That person is back," I said. "They're working down a checklist. They're targeting your girls."

Ava stood slowly. She walked to the veranda railing, arms folded. She watched the water. It shimmered beneath the summer sun. I could almost feel the heat wafting off it.

But Ava looked cold.

"You know about Sophie," Ava said. "About last night."

"I was there."

"So you know how close she came to...to..." Ava's voice quivered. She swallowed hard. Then she faced me.

"I can't go to the police, Mr. Sharpe. They'd pick my business apart... I'd lose everything. But if you don't help me, Camilla won't be the last, and neither will Sophie. Whoever this guy is, he won't stop until he's killed them all."

35

I spent another hour with Ava, asking my own questions about her business and her relationship with De Luca. The obvious solution to her present crisis seemed to be for her to call on her protection agreement with the Italians to prevent further murder attempts.

But according to Ava, she'd already made that call. De Luca had blown her off. He wasn't interested in running around-the-clock close personal protection for thirty-plus women, and he wasn't interested in hunting a killer. These were Ava's problems, which was why she'd thought of me. An ex-homicide detective with no place to be, and a vested interest in seeing Ralph liberated.

It was almost too logical.

"I kept files on all the targets," Ava said, handing me an accordion folder nearly an inch thick. "I really don't know where to start. I was hoping you would have an idea."

I took the folder and flipped quickly through it. The documentation appeared thorough, but something was still bothering me. "Sophie was never a part of this scheme, was she? The inner circle."

Ava shook her head. "No."

"And yet she was a target."

"I know. I can't explain that."

"Was she friends with Camilla?" I'd already asked Sophie about her relationship with Ralph's slain lover. I wanted Ava's perspective.

"Camilla wasn't really friends with anyone. She was reclusive. Mercurial. She didn't associate with the newer models."

I looked back at the folder. Sucked my teeth and evaluated. It was a bigger investigation than I had bet on when I agreed to help Ralph out of his mess, but nothing about my motivation had changed since then. He was still locked up. He still deserved justice.

"I'll pay you twenty grand if you can find this guy," Ava said. "Double if you get him to the cops without it leading back to me."

I snorted, flipping through the file again. Ava's notes were good—all kept on a computer, and now printed out. Tight recordings about the who, what, when, where, and how of the so-called "inner ring's" interactions with each of their targets. There were even snapshots of driver's licenses printed beneath the names. Those would have been taken with a cell phone camera while the guy was in the shower, I figured. They would be used to record legal names and addresses, which would be necessary during the next phase of the operation. The extortion phase.

What a clever little scheme.

"Is twenty not enough?" Ava asked.

I closed the folder and stood. I studied Ava for a moment,

measuring her features. The strain in her face and the way she picked at her fingernails.

She was afraid. Deeply so. And she had reason to be.

"Let me make this perfectly clear," I said. "I don't give a rat's ass about your modeling agency, or whatever little side scheme you're running. I know you've justified it in your mind, but it's petty theft and extortion nonetheless, which makes you a criminal."

Ava held her chin up. I kept going.

"I'm gonna take a look because there's an innocent man in jail, and because people like Sophie Wilson shouldn't live in fear. I'm not doing it for you. If and when I find Camilla's true killer, and Ralph is exonerated, you're going to make him whole. Every dime Camilla took. Every single red cent. He gets it back, without question. Otherwise, I go to the cops, and you can deal with them. Those are my terms. Take them or leave them."

Ava thought a moment. I wondered if she knew exactly how much Camilla had taken. Well north of a hundred grand, based on the Instagram messages alone. If there were any other avenues of communication Ralph shared with his pseudo girlfriend, there might be more money.

Ava was on the hook for all of it as far as I was concerned. She could sell her yacht if she had to. Ralph only wanted to find love. He never deserved any of this.

Slowly, Ava extended a hand. I shook it once, and then I turned for the door.

"You have my number," I said. "I'll keep you posted."

I TOOK the folder to a Waffle House and dug through it while consuming an All Star Special with bacon, hash browns covered and smothered, and chocolate chips on the waffle. Black coffee on the side. My go-to.

There were sixteen dossiers in total, and the notes about what had happened to each man were more detailed than I would have liked. In summary, they were exploited. Brutally. Sex wasn't always a factor in the equation, but it usually was. The general strategy was for one of Ava's "inner circle" to sit at the bar of a trade show and wait for somebody to flash an out-of-state ID. They looked for wedding bands and flirty eyes.

Then they conducted a little flirting of their own. They let the guy buy them drinks...just an innocent thing. Just friends talking.

One thing led to another, and eventually a compromising situation was arranged. Sometimes it took days. The girls obtained photographs of driver's licenses and sometimes photographs of other things. Things that wives back home would be devastated to see.

Farewells were exchanged—thank you and goodnight. The adulterer flew home, and then the message was sent, usually by text or by email. Pictures were attached. Demands were made. Five, ten, even twelve thousand dollars in one case. The girls kept seventy percent. Ava took the remaining thirty. All cash, of course, usually transmitted by mail. No paper trail, and no taxes.

If I weren't so disgusted by everything Ava and her secret ring of temptresses represented, I might have admired the genius of it all. It was a nearly perfect scheme...and maybe it would have remained such, but somebody had been pushed too far.

And presumably, that somebody had turned violent.

I took my time examining the files while the waitress kept black coffee coming. None of the driver's licenses were Florida-issued, which I expected. Ava deliberately instructed her girls to target people from out of state. There were plenty of IDs from New York, Illinois, and California.

But it was the lone ID from Louisiana that caught my eye. James Rossi, of New Orleans. His driver's license stood out to me for two reasons. First, there was the bold red label printed beneath his picture in all caps. It read: "SEX OFFENDER", and I'd seen such labels before. Several states require convicted sex offenders to be identified as such on their state-issued IDs. Apparently, Louisiana was one of them.

But the red label by itself wasn't enough to prove guilt of murder. "Sex offender" is a pretty broad term that covers everything from drunken lewd behavior to serial rape. It didn't prove that Rossi was a violent man.

It was the second thing which caught my eye that had me taking a closer look. I squinted at Rossi's picture, looking south of rich black hair and tanned skin to the breast of his polo shirt. It was barely visible, cut off by the edge of the image, but there was a logo embroidered there, and I recognized the silhouette of racing flags. Beneath them were stitched several gold letters.

N, O, C, T, A. With periods between each.

I retrieved my phone and ran a web search, typing "New Orleans" before adding the letters. The result was instant. One page appeared at the top of the stack, matching the letters perfectly. When I opened the website, I saw the same logo that Rossi had printed on his shirt.

New Orleans Chapter Track Association. It was a local

racing club, dedicated to drifting and stunt-driving in small sports cars. Specifically, small and *agile* sports cars. Not muscled beasts like the GSX Sophie had posed alongside.

No, these cars were more in the category of light and torquey European racers. Like Porches.

My mind flicked back to the night prior. The way the driver of the 911 had drifted through intersections and effortlessly timed his braking to force me into a corner. Quick, decisive driving.

It wasn't a smoking gun, but it was a solid lead. I chewed my lip and studied his picture a moment longer, still pondering. My gaze flicked back across the sex offender label, and then I had an idea.

The driver's license was old—already expired, in fact. Rossi may no longer reside in New Orleans, but if he had moved he would have been required to update his address on the sex offender registry. Just maybe...

I called up Florida's registry website. I typed in Rossi's full name. I waited.

And then a chill ran up my spine. There was a listing, all right. And a photo. It was the same man depicted on the driver's license, and a quick application of my phone's GPS called up his new address. It was a little property out in the sticks, in a county I was recently familiarized with.

Only a short drive outside of Tampa.

36

The address lay near Zolfo Springs, which in turn lay inside Hardee County. The ride was both bright and hot. I kept the Yamaha purring along just under the speed limit, weaving through Tampa traffic before I turned south. I stopped at a Walmart just outside the city for a change of clothes, opting for more fresh jeans and a dark T-shirt, then I took the same bridge across the bayou where I had ditched the Mercury.

There was no sign of cops—no sign of cranes or investigative teams. The car was invisible beneath the surface and would likely remain such for years to come.

Recalling my last encounter with De Luca's inflatable thugs also brought to mind Ava's explained relation to the Italians. It made sense, on face value. Somehow De Luca had discovered her little side business and had leveraged it against her. That hadn't made them partners, and he wasn't willing to run down a murderer on her behalf.

But he *was* willing to deploy his inflatables to run off a washed-up homicide detective living out of a pickup truck, and something about that bothered me. It would bear further thought once I checked out Rossi.

Zolfo Springs was even smaller in person than it looked on a map, little more than a wide spot in the road equipped with a post office, a couple of service stations, and a trio of churches. It was quaint, Old South America, as baking hot as the rest of the state. I cruised through a pair of traffic lights before I turned east, deeper into the county.

Then civilization faded almost completely, replaced as if by magic with sprawling fields and pastures surrounded by dense thickets of trees. Everything was a vibrant shade of green, the roads busted and faded by years of sunshine. Signs leaned on metal posts, some shot through by handgun rounds, others decorated by "missing dog" and "hay for sale" posters.

It was difficult for me to wrap my mind around how close the metropolis of Tampa lay, just over my shoulder. I could have been convinced I was in rural South Georgia or the middle of nowhere East Texas, save for the occasional palm tree joining the mix of hardwoods and pines.

The navigation on my phone led me down a deserted county road speckled with potholes and asphalt cracks that I was forced to wrestle the Yamaha around. The last home I passed was a trailer, propped up on blocks, with no skirt around the bottom, a pit bull chained to the hitch. That was a mile back, and now everything was sticky and still.

The driveway to Rossi's address was paved in dirt, mating with the asphalt next to a rusted mailbox that leaned atop a fence post. The mailbox's door hung open, and a wad of mail poked out. The numbers on the side were faded but matched the numbers on Rossi's sex offender registry.

I rolled to a stop and planted my boots on the asphalt,

inspecting the entrance to the driveway. It was dusty, a mix of red clay and gravel. There were fresh tire tracks running in and out. Wide and spaced evenly apart, like the back tires of a fast car.

I looked up the driveway, beyond a chained cattle gate to a narrow alleyway that ran between tangled hardwoods. It was dark, and I couldn't see a house. The road bent a hundred yards away, disappearing from my line of sight.

I wiped sweat from my forehead, thinking. Picturing Rossi at the bar of the convention center, talking up Camilla. Ava's documentation recorded Camilla as the model who targeted him, which could explain why he had killed her. Maybe she hadn't seen the red sex offender label when he flashed his Louisiana ID to the bartender. Maybe instead she had seen a sports car keychain or another embroidered shirt. Camilla liked fast cars. She owned one herself. It could be an easy opening line. A first step in a seduction that led to her hotel room...or his.

And then what? According to the dossier, the interaction occurred nearly three months prior. Camilla tapped Rossi for five grand. Had he developed a grudge? Or maybe an obsession. Would he have moved to Florida just to stalk her, murder her, and then steal her car?

Possibly. People are crazy. But how had Sophie become his next target?

I was missing something. Something big, and the only way to find it would be to dig a little deeper. But I wasn't about to simply rumble down Rossi's driveway, potentially throwing myself into the arms of a psychopath. This situation called for a little more strategy.

So I kicked off again, driving a mile and a half down the road before I found an abandoned lapboard church with a slouching steeple and a historic landmark sign posted to the door. The yard was overgrown, as was the accompanying graveyard. I parked the bike behind the church and took the keys before I set off into the forest, using my phone's GPS for guidance.

Rossi's property sat sandwiched between the county road and the Peace River, a muddy little tributary that ran south out of central Florida, through Hardee County, and eventually into Charlotte Harbor. I estimated there to be fifteen or twenty acres of dense forest in the block surrounding Rossi's place, with the driveway feeding directly into the middle of it. That meant I was in for a hike, but I'd rather hike than risk being shot in the head.

I made it a hundred yards into the trees before I reached a rusted barbed wire fence, running chest high. I climbed it with ease and slowed my pace between the trees, keeping an eye out for cameras or signs of humanity. My boots fell into a natural rhythm, ingrained in me by the Army's famed Ranger School, that kept me away from muddy holes and loud, snapping sticks. It wasn't difficult to glide amid the trees, working from one patch of shadow to the next, and using my phone to keep a bearing on where I thought the house should be.

I heard the noises before I saw any signs of life. Not one voice, but multiple. Growling and low, accompanied by irregular sounds of shifting items and slamming doors. The faint odor of gasoline engine fumes wafted through the trees, and I slowed my progress to nearly a crawl, crouching down low and choosing each step with care.

I still couldn't see anything amid the dense foliage. I descended all the way onto my stomach and crawled another thirty yards, just edging along amid the undergrowth, moving branches and bushes and making friends with the damp loam covering the forest floor. Sweat glued my fresh Walmart T-shirt to my back, and my brand-new jeans quickly soiled.

I was going to have to find a way to wash them. I was tired of trashing perfectly good Walmart clothes.

The voices and noises of movement grew louder, but my view was still obscured by a line of saw palmettos rising in a cluster out of the mud. I cut my pace in half and inched along, my head low, my heartbeat not rising above a resting drumroll. Despite my focus, a grin crept across my face.

Because I don't miss the army, but sometimes I miss being a soldier.

I reached the palmettos and stopped. I edged my fingers between a cluster of spiny leaves and pressed them apart, exposing a view of a clearing beyond. Dim sunlight cut through tall oak trees, spilling over the spot and the structure it contained.

It was a house. But it wasn't a residence.

37

The structure sitting amid the swampy Florida clearing may have been a hundred years old. It could accurately be described as both a farmhouse and a shack, and while the decades had failed to bring the building to the ground, time had not been kind to the squat little building resting atop a moldy brick base. Its lapboard siding hung clustered with mildew and moss, many of its windows fogged or boarded over. The front porch slouched on one side, half rotten away. The shingles were thick with more gunky green Florida residue, semi-illuminated by the sun but not threatened by it.

In the front yard a rotting rope that might once have suspended a tire swing hung from the limb of a giant oak tree. Fifty yards behind the house I caught a glimpse of the muddy Peace River, a floating dock jutting out over the water with a flat-bottomed airboat tied off to it. There were rusted clothesline posts and a rotting picnic table.

All the hallmarks of a once-happy family home, but it wasn't difficult to see that no family had occupied this property for years. The cluster of vehicles gathered around the side of the house were a mottled mix of pickup trucks and SUVs, all a little dusty from the long driveway, all wearing Florida license plates. I counted four in total, and none of them were a ragtop Porsche 911.

I couldn't see the people, but I still heard the voices. They came from the busted window panes, the barking of orders and grunting of acquiescence from whatever invisible occupants lay inside. I settled onto my elbows and watched the house for ten full minutes, not so much as budging. I didn't recognize any particular voice, but when the front door swung open and a bulky guy dressed in a skin-tight black T-shirt appeared, I did a double-take, my blood pressure spiking under sudden and unexpected recognition.

The guy was beefy. Almost inflated looking. He had bruises all over his face, particularly around his right eye. The injuries were familiar, because I had originated them. It was one of De Luca's thugs from Club Bolita. The guy I had pounded for information.

What?

I lowered my body another inch as the inflatable lit up a cigarette and blew smoke through his teeth. The sounds from inside the house were louder now that the front door stood open. More voices, just as gruff and abrupt as before, and this time further recognition dawned in my brain.

They were *more* of De Luca's thugs. I had somehow stumbled right into a hive of them, and the surprise of it all temporarily drove my mind off track. I forgot about Ava and her dossiers, mentally tripping instead over Rossi and the impossible coincidence of tracing his address to a house full of Italian mobsters.

Was Rossi himself associated with De Luca's gang? I

thought Rossi was an Italian name. Even if it wasn't, what
did it matter? De Luca had to hire outside his native lineage
sometimes. But what did that mean?

My mind buzzed as I sorted the pieces back and forth,
struggling to formulate a picture. I had built a case against
Rossi—at least a hypothetical one—but now that was out
the window. Now I had to factor in a potential association
with De Luca and ask deeper questions. Questions like: Was
De Luca involved in Camilla's murder? Was he involved in
Sophie's attempted murder? Was I still missing the forest for
the trees?

I blinked the thoughts away, focusing again on the house.
I could solve the riddle later. At present, I needed to focus on
the task at hand, which was gathering intel. New sounds had
reached my ears from behind the property, causing me to
look in that direction. A loud, grinding engine was churning
its way up the Peace River, approaching the house. The
inflatable thug on the porch stamped out his cigarette and
went back inside. Other inflatables appeared in the back
yard, all headed for the river.

I remained behind the palmettos, watching as a center-
console fishing skiff appeared beyond the trees, churning
through murky water and turning for the dock. It was about
twenty-five feet long, a heavy motor planted in the water, yet
another inflatable guy standing behind the controls. He
rotated the boat with ease, cutting the motor just in time to
allow the bow to drift against the dock without slamming
into it.

The party from the house greeted him. Among them I
recognized yet another face—a bandaged individual who
moved stiffly, his chest puffy beneath his shirt, his neck
mottled red and white.

It was Mr. Brutally Simple, my flare gun victim from two nights before. I couldn't resist indulging in a humored snort. He was not only still alive, but he was right back to work as though nothing had happened. I wondered if he told De Luca I was rotting in a swamp, my body torn by the long fangs of hungry alligators. Maybe he'd explained the burns as a horrible accident.

I couldn't imagine how he explained the missing Mercury.

The boat engine died and the crowd of thugs tied the vessel off to the dock. Then a line was formed, and big ice chests were heaved out of the boat and onto shore. Some were so large they required two men at a time to carry them back into the house. The procedure consumed nearly ten minutes, and at no point did I see inside any of the chests. When at last the boat was emptied, everybody went inside, and the work resumed. Heavy items slammed against tables, and orders were snapped. Somebody turned on a radio, and country music played.

But nobody came back outside. Nobody returned to the cars or the dock. I couldn't see through any windows.

Lying behind the palmettos, I gave momentary thought to my situation. It occurred to me that any one of the men now inside could be James Rossi. I had his picture, and I had yet to see his face, but it wasn't like I had personally met every one of De Luca's associates. Maybe he was inside, even now, and could be easily targeted for a mandatory interview.

The only thing I knew for sure was that I needed a closer look. Ralph's predicament was rapidly becoming a tangled web, and I was ready and willing to rip it apart.

38

I left the palmettos in a crouch and swung right along the tree line to gain a better view of the far side of the house before I entered the clearing. I didn't want to be surprised by any occupant of the parked vehicles, or anybody who might be lounging in an invisible camp chair.

Nobody fitting that description met my gaze. The vehicles were empty, as was the yard. My path to the house would weave between the tire-swing oak tree and the makeshift parking lot, landing me at the right-hand side of the front porch, which was the side not yet collapsed into the mud. I could shelter there, and if necessary, I could hide beneath it.

Beyond the porch, around the corner of the house, the grass was tall. There was an old brick chimney and several windows. They were all gunky or boarded over, but I figured at least one of them would provide a view of the home's interior. That should be good enough to reveal the goings-on inside and give me an idea of next steps.

I measured the tempo of voices inside the house,

checking for any break in rhythm which might signal a departing thug. Then I left the trees and moved like a ghost to the tire-swing tree, my feet barely making a sound as they found quiet patches of soft grass amid dry sticks and crunchy leaves. From the tree I waited only a moment before sprinting for the porch. The spot at the corner of the house was damp and clogged by weeds, but it wasn't difficult for me to fade against the slimy lapboard siding, crouching with my back to the exterior wall before easing my way toward the nearest window. It stood five feet off the ground, the bottom-most window pane about the size of a paperback novel, and completely covered in swamp grime. I couldn't see a thing through it, so I leaned in close to listen instead.

The voices were dim, little better than muted grunts, and in no way helpful. Words consisted of little more than "Hand me that," or "Where did you put the marker?"

I pressed my face nearer to the window and scrubbed with my thumb. The window pane shifted, and a dry piece of caulking fell onto my arm.

I still couldn't see anything. I'd need a pressure washer to remove enough grime to restore visibility to the glass, but a quick inspection of its perimeter confirmed that the caulking was all dry and ready to fail.

I dipped a hand into my pocket and retrieved my Victorinox. The Locksmith was warm from riding so near to the Yamaha's engine all day. I slipped my thumbnail into the slot of the little pointed tool built next to the screwdriver and flipped it out. It was what Victorinox called a *reamer*—a sharp, pointed little piece of metal a little like an awl.

It made short work of the dry caulk, scraping it away with barely a sound while the voices and blare of country music continued from inside the house. When the last of the caulk was gone, I switched the reamer for the Locksmith's bottle opener, which featured a flat-tipped screwdriver built into the end. The screwdriver slid beneath the glass pane, and I lifted and jiggled softly until the pane slipped free of the window frame and fell into my fingers.

I lifted the glass away with as slow a movement as I could manage. The resulting hole stood a few inches below eye level for me, requiring me to bend before I could peer through. Part of my view was blocked by the backside of a piece of furniture—a dresser, or a desk. But there was a one-inch gap, and that gap was enough.

The room spread out in front of me might once have been a living room, with the fireplace to my right and hard-wood flooring stretching out to dirty plaster walls. It was about fifteen feet square and was occupied by half a dozen beefy men all working around a series of tables laden with a dozen different types of electronic devices. Laptops, cameras, cell phones, flatscreen TVs, and video gaming consoles. Through a doorway into the next room I saw one of the large ice chests De Luca's crew had removed from the boat. It stood open, and one of the inflatable thugs was busy lifting more electronics out of it.

Across the room from the tables one of the guys I had brutalized at Club Bolita stood with a clipboard, making notes as he surveyed an organized string of electronics, sorted by type. Somebody else was busy scraping personalized stickers from the back of a MacBook. A pile of purses, backpacks, and wallets were heaped against one wall, and an office shredder ground like an airplane engine while another thug fed credit cards and driver's licenses into it, one at a time.

I watched for thirty seconds and wanted to laugh. I

wasn't sure what I expected when I approached the house—maybe a drug operation, or tables stacked with cash ready to be laundered. Whatever the case, I had seriously overestimated De Luca's criminal genius.

This wasn't a drug ring, this was a fencing operation—petty street crime rudimentarily escalated into a slightly more advanced scheme. The bags piled into the corner had been snatched from cars, unlocked houses, and park benches, probably all across Tampa. The captured electronics were then gathered at this house and sorted for resale, all indicators of previous ownership removed and shredded. Pawn shops and buyers from the classifieds would purchase the items. A small but tidy profit would be generated, like sifting gold out of river sand.

I'd seen it before as a beat cop in Phoenix, and it was such a far cry from the criminal empire that came to mind when I pictured the Italian Mafia that I was almost disappointed. This was bush league. Amateur hour.

And yet I was still hung up on the impossible coincidence of tracing James Rossi here. I had double- and even triple-checked the address listed on the Florida sex offender registry. This was the correct house. The picture on the registry matched that on the Louisiana driver's license. I had yet to actually *see* James Rossi.

But there had to be a connection. It was too many links in too tight a web. I needed to find Rossi, or at the very least, find Camilla's Porsche. That by itself might lead to tangible evidence sufficient to exonerate Ralph.

But where to look?

I never got the chance to develop the thought. Mr. Brutally Simple was dumping out a backpack full of stolen personal items when a cell phone skittered across the table and struck the floor. He grunted and stooped to retrieve it, his face pivoting naturally downward. I realized his line of sight was headed straight for the window only a moment before his eyes locked onto mine.

I froze, hoping against hope that he wouldn't register what he was looking at. That preoccupied thoughts—and perhaps, the pain of being roasted with a flare gun—would mute his mental faculties, and he would see me without actually seeing me. A phenomenon that happens all the time.

No such luck. Brutally Simple's brow furrowed in an instinctual moment of recognition blanketed by confusion, then his eyes went wide.

I snatched back from the window just as the house boomed with a panicked shout. "He's *here!*"

Adrenaline rushed my bloodstream. I moved quickly down the wall, abandoning any thought of concealing myself beneath the porch and planning instead to simply flee the way I'd come. The palmettos still offered a maze of potential concealment, and with strong legs and a relentless desire to survive, I was confident I could lose myself in the forest before Brutally Simple or any of his minions could find their way out of the house.

But again, my luck was cut short. Another vehicle was headed down the driveway just as I reached the front corner of the house. A truck, loaded down with two more inflatable guys, cigarette smoke rolling from the open windows. I saw them. They saw me. The front door of the house blew open and I slid to a stop, forced to recalculate.

Go the back way.

I turned and sprinted amid a chorus of shouts, running along the side of the house with my head ducked low to avoid any gunshots. It was a smart move—the window exploded with the thunderous boom of a shotgun just as I passed. I winced as shards of brittle glass rained over my back. I reached the chimney and swung right, glancing back to ensure I wasn't stepping into a field of fire. Brutally Simple and his chums had just found their way off the porch. They hadn't made the corner yet. I turned around, launching myself toward the back yard.

And ran headlong into the inflated chest of an Italian gangster.

39

I may have surprised my enemy as much as he surprised me. My right shoulder collided with his chest and he stumbled backward, thrown off balance. The momentum was on my side, but it took me a split second to break my charge and zero in on my target. He began to topple, arms windmilling in a desperate attempt to regain his balance, and I pounced. My elbow crashed into his jaw as he fell, striking fast and hard enough to ensure his collapse. The big guy struck the mud with a muted grunt, and I was on the run again, still headed for the back of the house.

But now it was too late. The storm of reinforcements breaking out through the front door had reached the corner of the house, and the gunfire began. A bullet zipped over my shoulder, and two more ripped into the home's lapboard siding. Just as I reached the house's rear corner I was immediately confronted by the bruised face of the guy whose eye I had gouged at Club Bolita. He exploded from the back door and skipped a trio of concrete steps, leaping toward me instead like a pouncing jungle cat, arms and legs splayed.

I ratcheted back against the wall, cocking a fist and catching him halfway between the door and the ground. Knuckles met nose, and blood exploded over my closed hand. Pain shot up my arm and his falling body slammed me against the wall. I shoved as his feet struck the ground, and he stumbled.

I grabbed him by the shirt and slung him right, straight into the faces of the three guys rushing around from the front of the house. They collided in a flailing mess of swinging arms and stumbling legs, a pistol shot cracking at random and spitting a slug into the concrete steps.

I left them to it and broke into a maddened sprint— across the mucky yard, beneath the trees, and straight for the only route of escape left to me. Not the forest. Hiding amid the trees was no longer a viable option.

I made for the boats instead.

The gunshots resumed as I reached the dock. A bullet zipped past my ear, and another cut my pants leg. Sodden wood exploded around my feet, and water shot skyward in muddy geysers. The two boats floated on either side of the dock—the center console on the right, and the airboat on the left. I made a split-second decision and chose the boat I knew would run. Jumping from the dock, I hurtled face-first into the center console as further gunfire cut the air in a crazed, unaimed storm. Shouts and confused commands rang from the hillside. I thrashed in the bottom of the boat to find my footing, then reached the console. The keys hung from the ignition. The engine fired up on the first twist. I clawed my way onto my knees and grabbed the throttle, yanking it into reverse.

It was only then that I remembered the rope tying the boat off to the dock. My gaze snapped to the bow, where the line ran around a cleat anchored to the boat's fiberglass hull before tangling around a matching cleat screwed into the dock. The line went tight, and the boat jolted, slamming me into the driver's seat. Pain radiated up my ribcage, and I thought about the razor-sharp blade of the Victorinox riding in my pocket.

There was no time. Half a dozen of De Luca's inflatables were thundering toward me, handguns brandished, still firing with maddened disregard for accuracy or ammunition conservation. A bullet shattered the boat's windshield while half a dozen more blasted through fiberglass and ventilated the seat cushion only inches from my face. I yanked the throttle backward, all the way to max reverse power. The outboard engine howled, and water sloshed. The line tensed like a guitar string, and the cleats strained.

I cut the wheel, driving the back end of the boat against the dock and leveraging the front end against the line.

That did it. The cleat anchored to the rotting deck planks exploded free, and the boat surged backward into the river. Mucky water exploded over the stern and washed against my legs. I remained in a semi-sheltered crouch, fumbling with the controls from the floor of the boat as the vessel spun into the middle of the river and continued to hurtle backward. I found the throttle again and rammed it to all-ahead full. The boat chugged and the bow snapped upward. The next hail of careless shots rained over the console, shattering gauges and blasting the top of the throttle away.

It didn't matter. The boat rocketed ahead, quickly rising to plane as I steered it up-river. The steroid-muscled men gathered on the dock rapidly shrank to dots as their errant bullets flew wider and wider. I pulled myself to my knees and grasped the bottom of the steering wheel, damp wind blasting my face and blurring my vision. The river turned just ahead, and I pulled the wheel to match it. The dock and the gangsters vanished behind, and I looked over my shoulder with a triumphant "*Ha!*".

Then the motor choked. My gaze snapped to the outboard as a cloud of dark black smoke rose from a shattered plastic housing. Oil streamed from a series of bullet holes and coated the transom, and the once-perfect purr faded into an inconsistent cough. Power bled away, and the nose of the boat dropped toward the water.

I scrambled onto the bench seat and fought with the broken throttle, backing it down in an effort to calm the engine. The RPMs dropped, and the coughing continued. Speed plummeted, and the boat lost plane. All around the bow mucky water sloshed against bullet-ridden fiberglass, and when I looked down I noted half an inch of water now sloshing across the floor.

Then I heard another sound—a howl of mechanical fury mixed with the snarl of a giant blade tearing through the air. I looked over one shoulder, heart rate spiking. Then the airboat roared around the bend, loaded with De Luca's thugs.

There wasn't time to think of a clever escape plan. With my own vessel gathering water and losing power, I couldn't match half the speed of the approaching airboat. The gangsters were four hundred yards back, but according to quick mental math, that gap would evaporate inside of twenty seconds.

I rammed the throttle back to max, no longer caring about an oil-drained engine overheating or locking up. The bow rose a little, and I tore the wheel to the left. The next bend in the river was followed by a reverse turn, back the other way. The rear end of the boat tore through the water, swinging wide as a gathering lake of murk sloshed around my feet. It was up to my ankles now, and I could feel the extra weight in the boat's lethargic steering.

Think.

I kept my breathing calm and pulled through the next bend, pumping the throttle to overcome a choking sound behind me. The air clouded with black smoke. I could barely see.

But I saw the bridge. It was a county road bridge, with simple steel guard rails running along its outside edges and giant metal I-beams supporting it from beneath. It stood maybe ten feet off the river's surface, no vehicles in sight.

I looked over my shoulder and couldn't see the airboat. It must have slowed to negotiate the double-hairpin turns, but that wouldn't last long. The moment that giant fan motor opened up again, I was toast. They'd run it down my throat.

But maybe that was a good thing.

I focused my attention on the bridge again. It was fifty yards away and drawing nearer. The motor behind me clacked and banged, turning at barely ten percent speed. I swept my gaze down the gunwales of the boat until my gaze landed on the fuel inlet, planted near the bow of the craft. A four-inch, stainless steel cap.

Bingo.

I dropped to my knees in the gathering flood of river water and ripped through the glovebox built beneath the console. There were maps, markers, a flashlight...and a half-empty box of cigarettes, with a lighter tucked inside. I jammed both into my pocket, then ripped my brand-new Walmart T-shirt off and hurried to the front of the boat.

The bridge was nearly overhead. The motor behind me was dying. I held the T-shirt by either end and spun it into a tight roll, then popped the fuel cap off and pushed that roll through, immersing half of it into a sloshing tank of gasoline before removing it, rotating the roll, and dropping in the dry end. I left half of the shirt draped over the bow, then rotated quickly to look for the bridge.

It was just passing overhead, a foot out of reach as I stretched from the bottom of the boat. I stepped quickly onto the bow and waited until I had passed to nearly the far side of the bridge. The motor on my boat died, and downriver at the second hairpin turn the rush of the airboat thundered like a helicopter.

I lunged upward and caught the final I-beam of the bridge with both hands. My bodyweight descended on my shoulders, and I gritted my teeth. Then I wrenched upward, pulling my chin level with the beam and kicking out with both legs. I caught the underside of the next I-beam with my feet as the boat spun in the current beneath me, then started to drift back under the bridge.

Now hanging by one hand and two feet, I used my other hand to reach around the outside edge of the bridge and grab the base of the steel guard rail. Muscles tensed until my arms quivered, and I moved my second arm into place, also latching onto the rail. Then I kicked off from the I-beam and jerked upward.

I almost fell. My hands wrenched against galvanized steel, and I bit back a scream. I clung on by sheer willpower, muscling my way up and over the low guard rail before landing on the concrete bridge with a thud.

There was no time to celebrate my aerobatics. The airboat's engine was roaring in, winding down a little as it approached the bridge. I scrambled to my hands and knees and kept my head beneath the guard rail. I made it to the far side of the two-lane bridge just as the stern of the center console passed back into view. There was a solid foot of water flooding the cockpit, now. The current was pushing the boat back the way it had come, but not quickly.

The bow was coming—bringing a gasoline-soaked T-shirt with it.

I retrieved the cigarettes and lit one up, puffing until tobacco turned bright orange. The airboat reached the bridge with a lot of production. Half a dozen gangsters were gathered at the bow, all brandishing guns and shouting variations of "Where is he?".

They still hadn't seen me lying on my stomach behind the guard rail. They wouldn't see me until it was too late.

I took another puff, grimacing a little. I enjoy the occasional cigar, but cigarettes have never been my thing. The airboat stopped ten yards downriver. The center console drifted out from under the bridge, the bow passing only eight feet beneath me.

I blew smoke between my teeth, extended the cigarette beneath the guard rail, and dropped it.

The reaction from the airboat was instantaneous. Maybe they saw my arm, maybe they saw the rush of flames as the cigarette ignited the gasoline-soaked T-shirt. Desperate cries and demands to "*Go back! Go back!*" rang across the river, joined by a couple pot shots at the bridge.

I didn't wait for them to figure out how to reverse an airboat. I returned to my feet and ran—as hard as I could, straight off the bridge. I made it barely a yard onto the blacktop before the center console detonated with a thunderous *boom* ripping through the forest, accompanied by a rush of flames and a shockwave strong enough to send me hurtling to my hands and knees. I rolled onto my back in time to see parts and pieces of the boat exploding into the sky, escorted by flames and smoke.

And no shortage of screams.

My grin returned as I slowly picked myself up off the blacktop. By the time I stepped back onto the bridge, the center console was gone. Flames burned on the water's surface. The airboat was overturned and rapidly sinking.

And De Luca's gangsters were swimming for their lives.

40

I hitchhiked shirtless back to the Yamaha, riding the majority of the trip on the running board of a beefy John Deere tractor with a sweat-smeared kid driving it, listening to country music blared from a boombox. He didn't ask about my partial clothing or muddy face, but he did ask if I'd heard an explosion a few minutes back.

I suggested there could be a storm rolling in, and he rocked his head beneath the tractor's awning to peer up at a cloudless sky.

"Rainless thunderstorm," I said with a shrug.

He nodded knowingly, and we didn't speak again before he dropped me at the abandoned church with a two-finger salute.

The Yamaha fired right up. I enjoyed the hot summer sun on my bare chest as I rumbled through Zolfo Springs and took the same route to Tampa that I had run in the captured Mercury. I thought about the inflatable guys bobbing in the river, burning water on every side, their floundered airboat quickly vanishing from view. Maybe they thought about alligators and being eaten alive.

I would have grinned again, but I didn't want to catch a bug in my teeth.

By the time I stopped at a gas station south of Tampa my temperament had sobered considerably. The sun I had initially enjoyed on my bare back was starting to burn, and thoughts of De Luca's floundering idiots were replaced by the deeper questions that had driven me to the house by the river in the first place.

Questions about James Rossi, and how De Luca's army connected to Camilla's murder. Even in the harrowing moments of dodging bullets and makeshift bombmaking, I'd gotten a pretty good look at each of the men following me. Mr. Brutally Simple was there. So was the guy I had eye-gouged, and a few other faces I recognized from my visit to Club Bolita.

But James Rossi wasn't one of them. I never saw him.

I stuck a fuel nozzle into the Yamaha's tank and enjoyed the shade, taking my phone out for the first time since leaving Ava's place earlier that day. The folder full of evidence she'd given me still rode in one of the Yamaha's saddle bags. I thought about retrieving it, but when I opened my phone I noted a missed call from Ava. I went ahead and hit redial, figuring there had been enough developments to justify a report. Maybe Ava could be helpful.

"Mason?"

"Yep."

"I was just checking in. I did some digging through those files I gave you, and a name caught my eye. He's a sex offender—"

"James Rossi," I said. "I know."

"Did you run a search?"

"Yep."

"So you know he moved to Florida." Ava's tone strained with suppressed agitation. She sounded like she was fighting back a mental breakdown. I remained calm.

"Don't panic. I already checked it out."

"Did you find him?"

"No. He wasn't there. But your friends from downtown were—quite a few of them. Any reason you can think of why De Luca would be linked to Camilla's murder?"

A pause. Ava's voice faltered a little. "I...I can't think of anything. She never dealt with him. I'm the only one his people talk to."

I nodded slowly, still pondering. Now evaluating this problem in reverse, and wondering if I were still going about it from the wrong angle. There could be a link to De Luca, now, but without hard evidence such a link would be useless in exonerating Ralph. I was *still* missing the bigger picture.

"I'm gonna take another look at Camilla," I said. "Maybe speak with her brothers again. I'll keep you posted. Have you heard from Sophie?"

"She checked out of the hospital this morning. They kept her overnight. I can't get her on the phone."

"Let me know when you find her."

I hung up without further comment, rotating the phone in my hand. The pump clicked off over a full tank, but I ignored it.

I thought of the house by the river. The petty fencing operation—stolen laptops and cell phones. Small-time crime. Much less than I would assume from a man like De Luca. Maybe the Mafia had been suppressed by modern law enforcement more thoroughly than I imagined.

But that didn't answer my chief question—the question that nagged at me from the moment I recognized Mr. Brutally Simple on the front porch.

What am I missing?

I STOPPED by yet another Walmart for a fresh shirt—because why take apart a clock that's ticking?—then I turned the bike for Tampa.

The nagging thoughts in the back of my mind about James Rossi and the house by the river wouldn't leave, but I was starting to think that I needed to take a step back. Reevaluate each of my leads and ensure that I wasn't missing the obvious. My routine run-ins with De Luca's people were starting to draw my attention away from the core problem. The problem that had started me down this path in the first place.

Who killed Camilla Cruz?

It may have been James Rossi. It may have been any one of the fifteen other men detailed in Ava's files. It could be somebody completely different. In theory, it could even be somebody other than Sophie's would-be strangler.

But all those questions rested on the micro level, and my gut told me I had raced right past something much more significant. Not the how. Not the when, the where, or even the what.

But the *why*.

Why would somebody kill Camilla Cruz? What had she tangled herself into? A conflict with De Luca? A blackmail victim she couldn't control?

What if Rossi *did* work for De Luca, or maybe alongside

De Luca? Rossi himself could be De Luca's equal, responsible for Mafia operations in New Orleans the way De Luca
was responsible for operations in Tampa. Maybe Rossi
switched his sex offender registration address to an obscure
property in Hardee County as a way of flying under the
radar with Louisiana police. Maybe De Luca owed him a
favor, and Rossi was embarrassed by his dealings with
Camilla, so he cashed in that favor.

De Luca axed Camilla.

It was plausible, but it still didn't feel right. Aside from
the fact that nothing about Camilla's death felt like a professional Mob hit, there was still the question of Sophie. Who
had come after her? And why?

That was the problem that bothered me most, but
without understanding a motive for Camilla's killer, I
couldn't expect to find one for Sophie's failed killer. It was
too many layers. I needed to step back and recover my bases.

I needed to know more about Ralph's slain girlfriend.

41

There was a stray contradiction in what I knew about Camilla that had bothered me from the start. It had to do with the fact that Camilla hadn't driven her Porsche to Ralph's motel. She had taken a cab. That by itself wasn't the peculiar part. She probably didn't want to park a nice car in front of a ratty motel. Whoever killed her could have stolen the car at another time.

The bigger question had to do with where she had taken the cab *from*. That was where the contradiction came in. Sophie had mentioned that Camilla lived in downtown Tampa, but Emilio Cruz said that his sister had just purchased a condo in Clearwater, on the coast. In a brand-new condominium.

Both could be true, of course. Maybe the condo was a recent purchase, and Camilla was in the process of moving out to Clearwater. If so, the cops may not have searched her Clearwater address yet. There could still be evidence.

It was worth a look.

I turned the Yamaha back toward Harper Springs. Traffic

was heavy, and it was late afternoon before I made it into town, at which point the traffic worsened. Backed up through the heart of the city, stretching past the barbershop alley where I'd made my second encounter with the Cruz brothers, brake lights blocked my path. There was some kind of jam up ahead, and as I slowed to a stop behind a minivan, I smelled woodsmoke on the air.

The cloud of black drifting aimlessly above the buildings only reinforced what my nostrils had already informed me. I shifted down a gear and hopped the bike up onto the sidewalk, bypassing the clog of cars and weaving down alleyways. The smokey smell grew stronger, and now I heard a commotion of voices. Red lights blinked against the side of a building. I wound around the corner and slid to a stop, planting both boots onto the pavement and killing the engine.

Havana Seafood Restaurant lay in an ashen heap, bright red trucks gathered around it while firefighters dumped jet streams of water across the rubble. It could barely be recognized as a restaurant anymore, save for the charred sign standing next to the curb.

Fresh Seafood Caught and Cooked Daily.

The entire structure was gone. The outdoor dining. The shed out back. Only smoldering timbers and the hulks of stainless-steel ovens remained. Even with the deluge of water drowning out the last of the flames, I could feel the additional heat on my face from the mountain of embers remaining.

It had been a hot fire. A fast fire.

I deployed the sidestand and swung off the bike. Amid

the swarm of firefighters and paramedics were a crowd of kitchen workers and onlookers. I recognized Rosa among them, but I didn't see the Cruz brothers.

Stepping around a bright orange traffic cone, I approached an ambulance just as a familiar face appeared from the back. It was the bodybuilder paramedic who had given me the painkillers. The one who wanted me to visit a hospital.

"What happened?" I asked.

The paramedic shot me a look, clearly recognizing me and not remembering me fondly.

"Stand back, sir," she barked, extending a hand.

I obliged, taking a step back as she opened the second rear door of the ambulance and turned her face toward the crowd. I followed her line of sight.

And then I saw Jorge. The bigger of the two Cruz brothers lay on a gurney, writhing in pain as additional paramedics worked to hold him down. He was badly burned, with a melted synthetic shirt sticking to a scalded chest, and cherry-red marks running down his arms and up his neck. Emilio jogged behind, talking earnestly to his brother in Spanish while Jorge continued to resist the paramedics.

My stomach tightened as I watched the group approach. The stretcher reached the ambulance as Jorge howled in pain, then the paramedics worked to load him into the vehicle. Emilio tried to climb in, but the bodybuilder pushed him back.

"There's no room, sir. We'll meet you at the hospital."

Ambulance doors slammed. Emilio stumbled back, his caramel-colored skin smeared dark with soot and dust. He looked like something out of a movie about settlers battling prairie fires.

Vacant brown eyes watched as the ambulance pulled away, red lights flashing.

I remained on the curb as the cops appeared, clustering around Emilio and cutting him off on his way to the Dodge Ramcharger parked down the street. I recognized Mack, the local police lieutenant. I saw the anger in Emilio's face. The confusion. The disbelief.

The heartbreak.

I let the cops finish their interview before I approached. The air was still rank with smoke. Everyone was sweaty. Emilio shook Mack's hand, his eyes red rimmed, his face smeared with dirt. Mack saw me and held my gaze but said nothing. He retreated with his partner to the waiting police cruiser, and I turned to Emilio.

"What happened?" I said, softly.

Emilio stared into the ashen mess of his restaurant, mouth hanging half open. His shoulders slumped. I couldn't be sure if he were thinking of his brother, or his lost business, or of nothing at all.

"Gas leak," he said, simply.

"Jorge?" I asked.

Emilio gritted his teeth. Shook his head. "Stupid fool. Ran back in there to get a photo off the wall...our parents."

A tear slipped down his face. I felt his pain. I'd done a little mad dash of my own to save a photo recently. It rekindled my own indignation, but didn't leave me with a lot to say. I put a hand on Emilio's shoulder instead and squeezed. Then Emilio turned away, swinging aboard the Ramcharger and firing up the big engine. I watched him go, retracing my thoughts back to Camilla...then Sophie.

And now Jorge.

James Rossi—whoever he was—might well be at the

middle of this mess, as could any of the other names in Ava's accordion file. But whatever was happening here, it was bigger than them. Somebody, or several somebodies, had declared all-out war on a seemingly random list of targets.

Seemingly random—except there was one common denominator. Camilla Cruz.

42

I wound the Yamaha out on the way back to the campsite. The thunder of the big motor pounded in my ears, but it couldn't overcome the storm of thoughts surging around inside my skull.

I had to end this. Whatever it took, and as quickly as possible. I'd danced around the problem long enough. It was time to get violent. Time to choke this thing to death before death visited another victim.

The campsite was abuzz with all the usual activity of late afternoon as I roared up to the shed where Hank kept his motorcycles and parked the bike in the back. I replaced the cover with care, then routed directly for my campsite. My GMC sat unmolested, still grimy with lagoon gunk, and missing a window. The hood was propped up, just the way I'd left it. Hank's tools lay littered around the front bumper.

And Sophie Wilson's red Volkswagen Beetle was parked alongside it.

She sat curled up in the driver's seat, hugging herself, when I approached. She didn't see me, and I tapped gently on the glass. Sophie jumped, wide and panicked eyes snapping toward me. Then she exploded out of the car and threw her arms around my neck. I stood a little awkwardly, patting her on the back, while Sophie buried her face in my chest and sobbed. And shook. And didn't let go.

At last, I pried her arms free and pushed her back far enough to see her face. Tangled strawberry blonde hair surrounded cheeks smeared with old makeup and tear trails. There were black bags beneath her eyes—those pools of green looking a little vacant, despite the fear.

"Are you okay?" I asked.

She swallowed. Nodded slowly.

"I...I didn't know where to go."

"You should have stayed at the hospital."

"I was afraid..." Her lip trembled. She fell into my chest again, and this time I simply held her. It was still awkward, at least for me, but maybe it was what she needed.

When Sophie finally released me I led her to the picnic table and offered her a bottle of water. Then I returned to my truck and reassembled the carburetor. I climbed beneath the bed and found the fuel line running out of the tank. I filled five-gallon buckets from Hank's shed with polluted gasoline. I inspected brake lines for damage, and cleaned debris away from the wheel wells.

Two hours of steady work restored the truck to operational order. Hank brought me a two-gallon can of gasoline, and I worked the choke and pumped the accelerator a few times before the rough grumbles built into something more sustained. It took me nearly ten minutes to get it started, but once it finally ran, the black smoke pouring from the tailpipe thinned out, and a cheer rang from around the campsite. I cut the motor off, and handed Hank his gas can back.

"What's my balance?" I asked.

Hank wrinkled his brow. "Huh?"

"On the lot." I jabbed a thumb at the gravel the truck was parked on. Hank shook his head and waved a hand.

"Don't worry 'bout it. We're square."

I peeled three hundred-dollar bills from my pocket and poked them into Hank's shirt pocket before he could stop me.

"Thank you," I said. "For everything."

Hank nodded dumbly, then extended a greasy hand.

"I don't suppose you'll be back?"

"Maybe. I don't know. Right now I just need to be someplace else. I've pissed off some violent people. I don't want them coming here."

Hank stepped back, and I slammed the hood of the pickup. It closed with a metallic *thunk*, like a watertight door on a battleship.

They don't make them like that anymore.

At last, I circled to the back of the GMC, where Sophie stood playing with her keys. Her fingers shook. Her face was a little pale. She looked exhausted.

"Have you got someplace to go?" I asked quietly. "Family?"

Sophie shook her head.

"Then you should get a hotel," I said.

Another shake of her head. "Please don't make me go. I'm... If they come again..."

A heavy tear splashed on the gravel. She scrubbed her face and dropped her chin. I looked to the Beetle, then to Hank. Something gnawed in my gut—unanswered questions, mostly. Things I still wanted to ask Sophie.

But more than that, I couldn't leave her to fend for

herself any more than she wanted to fend for herself. It wasn't in me.

"Hank, you got a place to stick that Beetle?"

The grizzled old Marine nodded. "Sure. I'll put it in the shed."

"If anybody comes looking for it—" I began.

"They're gonna meet my shotgun," Hank said bluntly.

I patted him on the shoulder. Sophie passed him the keys with a whispered "thank you". Then I loaded the rest of my camping gear into the back of the GMC. I took down my hammock and wadded it up on top of the air mattress before I lowered the glass on the rear of the camper shell.

Sophie piled onto the passenger's side of the bench seat. It was still wet, but she didn't seem to mind. I slid in behind the wheel. The GMC fired right up like it hadn't recently doubled as a submarine. I shot a two-finger salute to Hank and beeped the horn for the campground.

Then we were off. I didn't know where we were headed.

I only knew it was time to force a showdown.

43

I selected another campground twenty miles inland of the coast. It was a branded, chain place, with a steep nightly fee and a lot of "amenities". I asked for a camping spot near the back and was offered a smooth concrete pad surrounded by towering oak trees, within earshot of children laughing on a playground.

I could have picked a hotel, but the GMC is a conspicuous vehicle, and I thought De Luca would check hotels first. I didn't like the idea of having to drive all the way to Orlando just to get a good night's sleep. At least this way, I could hang my hammock in the forest fifty yards from the truck and keep a weathered eye on it. If the Italians did somehow find us, it would be easier to lead them away from innocent civilians in the midst of a forest than it would be in the middle of a city.

In such an event, all bets would be off. I was done playing nice, not only because they would have killed me if they'd ever caught me up on the river, but because I had to assume they had burned Havana Seafood Restaurant to the ground...and nearly killed Jorge Cruz.

Sophie said nothing as we drove, riding with her wide eyes fixated on every passing car. She looked somehow even younger in a state of fear than she had trouncing around in mermaid makeup. Twenty-one, she said, but age isn't measured in months or years lived. Sophie's soul felt locked in artificial youth, perhaps by hardship.

But she was growing up fast.

I strung up the hammock away from the pickup while Sophie unloaded the cookware and spread it across a picnic table. An application of my hand pump added pressure to the air mattress. It still had a slow leak, but under Sophie's slender frame it should be okay.

"If you put your pillow on the tailgate, you can see the stars," I said.

Sophie rubbed her elbows and looked at the ground. She seemed to have leveled off a little since leaving Hank's place, and I detected a hint of embarrassment in her posture. Shame, perhaps, for having to ask a relative stranger for help.

But maybe still enough fear to keep that shame silenced.

"Why don't we talk?" I motioned to the picnic table. Sophie sat without objection, and I fished a pair of water bottles out of my ice chest. They were almost gone, and the remainder of my food had been lost in the submersible pickup incident, but the campsite featured a little grocery store. They should have something for dinner.

I guzzled half the bottle while Sophie sipped hers. She wouldn't meet my gaze. Her eyes darted to every noise in the woods, every laugh of a child or shout of a parent at the playground.

It was traumatized paranoia, and even though her near-death experience was ample justification for such behavior, I couldn't help thinking that Sophie's level of emotional breakdown surpassed what I would have expected from such a recent event. I've seen a lot of trauma in my day—a lot of really horrific situations. Soldiers got blown apart in Afghanistan, and cops stumbled on the decomposing bodies of children in sprawling state parks outside of Phoenix.

It gets to you, all of it. It sinks into your soul and leaves a mark...but generally that takes time. Usually, there's a period of dull shock at first. Disbelief. The mind shuts down. The heart won't acknowledge. The brain blankets itself in denial in the interest of self-preservation. You go numb.

Sophie had skipped all that. She had jumped straight to the emotional phase, when all those images and paranoias come surging back in waves, and you don't know how to cope. Self-preservation breaks down. Reality hits hard.

Maybe she simply processed faster than the average Ranger or cop. But I didn't think so. If I had to bet, I would say there was something else. Something deeper, something before.

Something ugly that the would-be strangler had simply triggered.

"Are you okay?" I said.

Sophie turned vacant eyes on me, looking a little zoned out, as though she were inebriated. I remembered the previous night at the bar. How quickly she'd become drunk off just a few drinks.

Some medications have that effect. The mental kind of medications.

"What are you taking?" I kept my voice just strong enough for her to hear.

She swallowed. Her eyes watered.

"Prozac," she said.

"Antidepressant?"

She nodded.

"I'm so sorry."

Sophie looked down. The tears kept bubbling. She opened her mouth and closed it a few times without a sound.

"You don't have to talk about it," I said.

Sophie didn't answer. She picked at her nails. Then she looked up, and the fog in her eyes parted a little.

"I...want to."

I offered a reassuring smile—because I wasn't sure what to say. I wasn't sure what I was walking into. I simply waited.

Sophie laid her hands on the rough wood of the picnic table. She took her time. I didn't rush her.

"I never went to Atlanta," she said. "My mother died when I was young. Drug overdose. My father...he...was not a good man. He abused me."

She looked up. Her gaze was lifeless. "In every way."

I winced. I couldn't help it. The mental image made me want to clench a fist. It made me want to wrap my hands around some psycho's throat and squeeze.

But I remained relaxed because none of that would help her. Sophie just needed to talk.

"I went to college," Sophie said. "It was good, at first. You know. Being away from home. A nice big school. I liked art and theater. Music. I liked to study."

She blinked hard. Her hands trembled.

"There was a frat party one night. All the girls were invited. I went... I didn't plan to drink. I only had a couple, but it was like they all hit me at once. I blacked out. And when I woke up..."

She pressed her hands into the table to stop the shaking. She clamped her eyes closed. Her voice was barely a whisper.

"He was on top of me. One of the frat boys. Two of his friends were watching, laughing. They had me tied down. And when I tried to scream...he choked me. And kept choking me."

She faced me again. "I thought I was going to die."

The picture was clear in my mind. Again, I remained calm. I didn't nod or speak. I didn't reach for her hand, because she probably didn't want to be touched.

I just waited, giving her that calm space to talk. Sophie sniffed and wiped her nose. She looked down again.

"I told everybody I got a job offer in Atlanta. An acting job." She snorted a laugh. "I had to leave. I mean...I had to get out of there. Away from school, away from home. I needed money, and I didn't have a lot of skills. I found an ad for a modeling job in Tampa. The ad said experience wasn't necessary. I've always been told I was photogenic. So, I applied. I drove down. Ava hired me. And...here I am."

Sophie smiled sadly, and the pit in my stomach deepened. I felt every note of the heartbreak melody playing in her soul. I felt it in my very bones. Not because it was anything like my own, but because a wrecked world is a wrecked world. It hurts us all in different ways, but hurt is hurt.

"I'm sorry," I said simply. It was the only thing I knew to say. Sophie's jaw trembled. She swallowed again. Her eyes bubbled.

"Please don't let them hurt me."

"Nobody's going to hurt you," I said. "You have my word on that."

44

W e made a campfire and I cooked dinner on my camp stove. Hamburger helper with breakfast sausage and sliced apples. Not a gourmet meal, by any stretch, but a solid one. A marching meal, the army might have called it.

Sophie ate about half of hers and finished the water bottle. She'd stopped crying and seemed to feel better after getting the pain off her chest. I wondered if she'd ever told anyone that story before, or if the antidepressants had been administered by a therapist who was also providing counseling. Certainly, Sophie needed counseling, but I was in no position to judge anybody for muscling their way through recovery.

As the sun set and the campground descended into that hum of slowly dying social activity unique to all campgrounds, I turned my mind back to the problem at hand. To the issue of who the enemy was—who had killed Camilla. Who had tried to kill Sophie. Who had burned the Cruz restaurant down.

The three items could still be unrelated, but I didn't think so. It didn't sit right with my gut. It was too many coincidences, too closely packed together.

"You play cards?" I asked Sophie.

She set her bottle down and wiped her lips with the back of one hand. It was a casual sort of gesture. Her entire body language had transformed since dinner. She seemed like a different person. Less of the big city, fancy model girl. More of the backwoods southern country girl I always detected in her accent.

It was a good look on her.

"Not really," Sophie said. "I mean...I play Go Fish."

She blushed.

I dug into my camping bin. There was a deck of worn playing cards in the bottom. I'd lost a lot of money to Hank and the sunburnt bartenders playing Texas hold 'em over the last few months. They'd lost a lot of money to me, also.

I shuffled the cards and dealt seven to each of us. Then I placed the deck on the table.

"What's this?" Sophie asked.

"Go fish."

She laughed. "It's a child's game."

"So? It's a great game." I tipped my head. "Ladies first."

Sophie rolled her eyes, but she sifted through her cards, arranging by suit or face value. Then she shot me a smirk.

"Do you have any two's?" Her voice carried sarcasm.

"Go fish," I said. My voice carried no sarcasm. Sophie reached for the deck.

"I want to talk to you about the agency," I said.

"Okay." Sophie's voice dropped a notch. I kept my posture loose—casual. Just playing a game.

"The first night we met, at the bar, Ralph came there looking for you. Because he was looking for Camilla."

Sophie said nothing.

"Any fives?" I asked.

"Go fish."

I dipped into the deck. A seven—no use.

"What are you asking me?" Sophie said.

I thought she knew what I was asking her. Just the way she knew this question would come up, eventually, because it was too great a coincidence for Ralph, Sophie, and the Cruz brothers to all turn up at the same bar in the middle of nowhere at the same time, all ready to fight each other.

I'd played that bar for months, and I'd never seen any of them. There had to be a common denominator.

"When did Camilla ask you to lead Ralph there?"

Sophie's gaze dropped. She bit her lip.

"Any kings?"

"Shoot." I passed her two kings. Sophie laid all four on the table with a triumphant flash of her eyes. I waited expectantly, and the triumph faded.

"That day," she said.

"What was the ask?"

Sophie shifted uncomfortably. I flexed the cards in my hand.

"I'm not judging, Sophie. I'm just trying to figure out what's happening."

"Camilla and I..." Sophie hesitated. "We weren't really friends. I mean, we were friendly. But Camilla was always... well. I don't want to speak ill of the dead."

"Just say what you know."

"Camilla was always superior. She was top girl. Ava's favorite. She only worked when she wanted to, and she still somehow made a ton of money. She drove the nicest car. She was *it*. Obviously, I wanted to be her friend. I wanted help. Camilla would be nice, sometimes."

"She strung you along," I said.

Sophie shrugged.

"What did she want that day?" I asked.

"She called and said she wanted to go to dinner. Give me some tips on my stance and smile. Modeling stuff. And then she asked for a favor—a one-girl-to-another kind of thing. Something she couldn't trust anybody with."

Blatant manipulation.

I thought it. I didn't say it.

"She said there was a creep she couldn't shake," Sophie continued. "Some old guy. He wasn't dangerous, just annoying. She said her brothers were going to take care of it, but it had to be outside the city. Someplace quiet."

"You arranged the meeting?"

Sophie nodded. "She gave me a number to text. I told the old guy I could help him find his girlfriend, and that we should meet. That's what Camilla told me to say. I got to the bar... He got to the bar. Camilla said he might get handsy but I shouldn't worry. Her brothers would be there. But he never made a move. He just wanted to know where Camilla was. He kept pushing. He was so..."

"Desperate," I finished.

Sophie nodded.

I tapped the cards on the table and pondered. Sophie's story was pretty much what I expected—she was the only person at the bar who wasn't directly linked to Camilla outside of work. It stood to reason that she had been somehow thrust into the mix. Her loneliness and desperation for belonging were vulnerabilities Camilla could easily target to make use out of her.

But none of that told me anything beyond what I already knew—that Camilla was a bad egg, dishonest and manipulative, and clearly up to her neck in some kind of trouble. Obviously, she'd bitten off more than she could chew with Ralph. He wouldn't leave her alone. She needed him gone.

But how had that led to her murder? And why did Camilla's killer also need Sophie dead, or the Cruz brothers' restaurant destroyed?

It was staring me right in the face. I knew it. But I couldn't put my finger on it, no matter how hard I tried.

"Your play," Sophie said.

I looked quickly to my cards. "Any nines?"

Sophie passed me a nine. I only had two. She asked for sixes and I told her to go fish.

And then I squinted, because another thought had occurred to me. A brief memory. Something not very important at the time, but now it rose to the surface.

"You don't have a boyfriend," I said.

Sophie looked up. She flushed a little. The hint of a bashful smile played at her lips.

"No..."

I flushed also. "That's...not what I meant. I just mean, the second night you came to the bar, when I was playing, a guy came in. He sat with you. You seemed to argue, then he left. I thought he might be a boyfriend, but..."

Sophie grew very still. I waited.

"I'm not supposed to talk about that," she whispered.

I set the cards down. "Who is he?"

She shifted. Looked across the darkened campsite, then back to me.

"It's not related."

"It might be."

"It can't be. He's a good guy."

"What kind of good guy?"

She hesitated. "He's FBI."

I cocked an eyebrow, replaying the image in my mind. The burly guy talking to Sophie. The tension in their conversation. His body language.

Because lips can lie, but the body never does. I've interacted with plenty of FBI agents, and this guy acted like none of them. His demeanor felt more akin to De Luca's inflatable thugs.

"What's he want?" I asked.

Sophie sighed. She put her cards down and ran both hands through her hair. She looked exhausted.

"It's something about Ava. About the modeling agency. He's investigating money laundering, he said. A routine search, just making sure everything is above board. He just wanted to ask me some questions."

"About?"

"About her practices, I guess. About whether she kept cash around. About whether she'd made any big purchases recently, or if any money was made off the books."

I squinted. "What did you tell him?"

Sophie shrugged. "Nothing. There was nothing to tell. But...he stuck around. Kept wanting to talk. Kept pushing on me to poke around the office."

"And you've not seen him around here before?"

"No. He's definitely not from Florida. He's got a pretty heavy accent...like in the movies. Like he's from New York or Boston or something."

"When did you first meet him?"

"I don't know. Couple of weeks ago, maybe. It was right after the big jewelry expo at the convention center. It was a lot like the car thing...standing around indulging creepy old guys. Except I got to wear a nice dress and model fancy jewelry."

Sophie smiled. It was a girlish smile. Very innocent, but still a little tarnished by the abuse she'd been afflicted with. It made me sad.

It made me want to throttle somebody.

Sophie caught me staring at her, and she shifted uncomfortably. She flashed a smile. "Your play."

SOPHIE KICKED my ass at Go Fish, and then we cleaned up. I made up the air mattress for her and explained how the tailgate and camper shell latched, in case she wanted to close them. It was boiling hot, even after dark, but I thought she might want some privacy. She simply nodded as I retreated to my hammock and swung inside. It sagged against its straps, and I stared up at an inky black sky lit by a million pinholes of light.

An owl hooted softly from someplace amid the forest. A bullfrog croaked a sad blues song from a drainage ditch. A hundred yards away, somebody played a guitar gently, barely loud enough to hear. I closed my eyes and tried to relax. Tried not to think about all the messy problems lying in my lap, and to simply let them rest.

I would unravel them in the morning, one piece at a time. I would pull at each individual thread until something broke loose...as long as it took.

I was almost asleep when a gentle hand touched my arm.

My eyes snapped open and my body stiffened instinctively, my left fist closing and ready for a lightning hook. I was already twisting for the ground.

And then I stopped. Sophie stood next to me, strawberry hair falling over pale shoulders. The T-shirt she'd worn before was gone, replaced now by a simple tank top. Goosebumps rose on her skin, but she didn't look cold. She didn't shiver.

Her green eyes watered, and her lip trembled. She removed her hand and stood awkwardly next to the hammock, avoiding my gaze.

"I..." she started. Then stopped.

I didn't make her explain. I took her hand and helped her into the hammock. The straps groaned under the additional weight, but her slender body fit easily next to mine. I let her rest her cheek against my shoulder, and I wrapped an arm around her back. I gave her a little squeeze.

Then we both drifted slowly to sleep. Two lost souls, keeping each other close for the night.

45

I didn't have to break any bones that night. If De Luca's thugs or Sophie's would-be strangler were searching for us, they didn't find us. I slept like a baby in the hammock with Sophie pressed up next to me, and when the sun finally broke through the trees we both woke up at once.

We didn't talk. We just lay there and let our bodies come to life slowly, not in a hurry to move. When we finally tumbled out and shuffled to the campsite, I went to work on a breakfast of eggs and more sliced apples while Sophie visited the bathhouse. I thought I could use a shower myself, but maybe that could wait until I'd resolved my other priorities.

Priorities that were likely to leave me much dirtier.

Sophie returned and we ate quietly, clearing our plates and washing up. She looked better than she had the night before, with a freshly washed face and a relaxation to her body that defied the mental turmoil she must be facing. I kept quiet as she subtly slipped a pill from her purse and finished her water.

Then she faced me. "What now?"

I'd been contemplating that question all morning, but the answer was a simple one. I had to dig into Camilla, deeper than I had before. I had to know why somebody would want her dead.

"I'm going to Camilla's place. I want to have a look."

"In Tampa?"

"No. In Clearwater."

Sophie frowned, lips puckered. Then a strange light illuminated behind her bright green eyes.

"She had a place in Clearwater?"

"Her brother said so. Do you know the address?"

Another pause. Then Sophie nodded.

"I think I might. Camilla said she lived downtown, but one time she asked me to bring her something from work, and she gave me a Clearwater address. It was one of those occasions when she was being nice to me, like she wanted to be friends." Sophie shrugged.

"Where did you go?"

"Someplace on the beach. A condo. There were lots of girls there...I mean, the elite girls. That's where I first got the idea that there was an inner circle. I stayed a while, but then it got weird...like they didn't want me around. It was a nice place. I assumed it was a rental."

Nice place, I thought. *Nice like stolen money nice?*

"Can you recall where it was?"

Sophie shrugged. "The address should still be in my text messages."

She went to work on her phone, and I waited. It didn't take long. I recorded the address in my own GPS application and mapped out a route. It would take nearly an hour to drive there.

"What are you going to do?" Sophie asked.

"I'm going to have a look. See what I can find."

"You have a theory?"

I had been waiting for that question. Sophie was smart—smart enough to work problems in reverse, like any good investigator. She had to be asking herself by now, if Ralph hadn't killed Camilla, who had? And *why?*

"I have a theory," I said. "I think Camilla was mixed up in a scam ring. All the inner circle was. Ava pretty much confirmed it."

"You spoke to Ava?"

"I did. She wanted to hire me. She thinks Camilla exploited the wrong target and he came back to bite her."

Sophie squinted. "But...why would he want to kill me?"

"That's my question. Can you think of a reason?"

Sophie pondered. Her top teeth worked her bottom lip in a little pucker. It was cute.

"I've never done anything," she said at last. "I just model."

"But you and Camilla were friends."

"I thought so, but...I think she just used me."

"I think she used a lot of people, and I think she made money doing it. That's the kind of thing that could put anybody on a kill list."

"And me?" A hint of fear edged into Sophie's voice.

"I don't know," I said. "Let's cross one bridge at a time. Are you willing to help me investigate?"

"Of course. Anything."

"Great. I need you to go back to Tampa. Return to the tower and tell Ava you need to dig through the company's client logs. I need details on every client Camilla worked with over the past year, no matter how small. The devil is always in the details."

"We've got the auto expo today. I'm supposed to be there...everybody is. Ava won't even be in the office."

"So call in sick. Do you have a key to the office?"

"There's a door code."

"Use it. Help yourself to the files. Call me when you have a list of every client Camilla has worked with in the past twelve months."

Sophie nodded slowly. Her fingers worked the edge of the picnic table, and I noted that suppressed nervousness returning to her body. A sort of raw tension. I thought I knew why.

"You're going to be okay," I said. "You can trust me. I've done this before."

"You've hunted killers?" Sophie asked. Her voice was barely above a whisper.

"More than I'd like to admit," I said. "And they all have one thing in common—they all make mistakes, eventually. I'm the guy waiting with a noose when they do."

That seemed to hearten Sophie a little. I shot her a smile I didn't quite feel.

"Come on. It's gonna be a beautiful day—you can roll the windows down on that Beetle."

46

I knew I was right about the killer screwing up, but I was dead wrong about the weather. By the time we returned to Hank's campsite the bright morning sun had vanished behind a bank of storm clouds rolling in from the coast. They were ink black, and sort of boiled together as though a heavenly giant were blowing the storm from the tip of an immense cigar.

Sophie kept the windows up on the Beetle as she departed for Tampa, promising to keep me updated. I ignored the blown-out window of my GMC as I set the phone on my lap and navigated for Clearwater—into the storm.

The address Sophie gave me was for a second-floor condominium in the midst of a stretch of identical condos, all directly facing the gulf. The lineup of expensive cars parked on the leeward side of the complex told me everything I needed to know about the cost of such a residence. Jaguars, BMWs, Escalades, and Mercedes SUVs. I didn't see a hatchback or a Japanese import anywhere. It was like a luxury car lot, and it was protected by a gate. I drove the GMC three blocks away before I found a convenience store with ample enough parking to leave my truck. I took a pair of mechanic's gloves and a lockpicking kit from the GMC's glovebox before stowing my backpack in the bed and padlocking the camper shell gate to the tailgate.

Then I returned to the condos, jogging as darkening clouds rumbled overhead and a steady breeze poured in from the ocean. It was salty, and hot. An American flag standing outside the gate of the complex blew steadily inland, fabric snapping with every gust.

I sidestepped the gate and circled the parking lot. Much of the perimeter was protected by tall shrubs, not a fence. It took a little work to find a place where I could squeeze between them, but I didn't have to sneak. Nobody was around—the windows facing the parking lot were all covered by shades, the sidewalks empty of vacationers and tourists.

Maybe the storm was a good thing.

I took the stairs to the second floor of the complex, moving along an exterior walkway to the door marked by the address Sophie gave me—number 206, a faded beige in color with a video doorbell unit affixed next to it. The swollen doorframe and visible layers of paint told a story of an old building, frequently remodeled and refreshed to serve demanding new generations of wealthy expats from the northeast. Only a "nice place" because of the location.

The door was dead-bolted, with a knob locked by thumb latch. I glanced over my shoulder, then tugged on my gloves before slipping the lockpick kit out of my jeans pocket. The tools slipped with ease into the deadbolt, but it took time to feel out the tumblers and manipulate the keyhole. It was a new bolt, and more complex than the simple bolts I had learned on a decade prior.

The thumb latch was easier, and two minutes later I slipped inside a darkened foyer paved in tile. The condo was perfectly still, an assortment of women's shoes standing in a neat row along one wall. The gloves ensured I left no prints as I flipped a wall switch. Bright light flooded the hallway, illuminating a kitchen and a bar to my right, a living room straight ahead, and a doorway leading to what I assumed to be a bedroom standing just to one side of a sixty-inch flatscreen TV.

The condo was immaculate—not just clean, but well updated. Granite counter tops, all stainless-steel appliances, and pseudo-hardwood flooring stretching to double glass doors covered in vertical blinds. Every piece of furniture was posh and stylish, like the demo room at an exclusive furniture store. A shelf held an assortment of books altogether too clean and color-matched to be anything more than decoration, and a wine rack contained half a dozen expensive-looking bottles just inside the kitchen.

It was a city-woman's paradise. Feminine in its touches, but not overly personal. The theme was more *elite* than customized, almost as though this unit itself were a demo.

But it wasn't. I knew that by the lone photograph held by magnet to the refrigerator. It was faded, depicting a landscape any Arizona native would be well familiar with—the Grand Canyon, spilling out to the horizon with the brilliant southwestern sun blazing down.

A family stood next to it. I recognized Emilio as a youthful teenager. Jorge a couple years younger, but already two inches taller than his brother. Camilla only four or five, dressed in a bright sundress and a brighter smile.

And parents—two of them. Grinning and holding their children. Posing for the camera.

My stomach twisted, and I scanned the remainder of the kitchen. There were empty glasses in the sink, stained by red wine residue. A cereal box left on the counter. When I opened the fridge, I found produce and fresh groceries. A package of deli meat dated for the day before Camilla died. A utility bill with Camilla's name on it lying next to a cup of pens and a checkbook.

She hadn't known her life was in danger when she left the condo. I could feel the average oozing out of every care-less detail. This had been a normal day...but something had to be different. Dramatically so.

My phone buzzed and I checked the messages. Sophie had reached the modeling agency and said that Ava wasn't there, but she had found the client files in a shared computer cloud folder. She would update me shortly.

I pocketed the phone and pushed through a short hallway into the bathroom. The counter was much less clean than the living room had been, strewn with all the usual female products. Hair sprays, a curling iron, a lot of makeup. Nothing to see.

Next I checked the bedroom. My heart rate spiked when I twisted the knob and it wouldn't budge. It was locked by key, and the doorknob didn't match the fixtures of the rest of the apartment.

Who locks their bedroom?

My lockpick set made short work of the thumb latch. The room on the other side was dark, and I flipped the wall switch. Bright yellow light spilled from a ceiling fan, cascading over an unmade queen-size bed. A dresser strewn with more feminine hair items, drawers half open and drip-

ping with ladies' undergarments. A TV with a dusty black
screen mounted to the wall. An open door with a walk-in
closet crowded by colorful clothes and rack upon rack of
shoes.

Nothing unexpected, and yet the door had been locked. I
moved carefully through the room, searching the drawers
and closet space. I found abandoned hair bands, creased
gossip magazines, and a box loaded with lotions and skin
products. There was another empty wine glass on the nightstand next to a tablet computer. An empty wine bottle rested
on the floor. The window overlooked the beach—but a
curtain covered it.

It wasn't until I opened the nightstand drawer that I found
my first clue of why the door may have been locked. Beneath
an assortment of well-worn smut novels lay a Smith and
Wesson J-frame revolver—nickel-plated, with an exposed
hammer, I immediately recognized it as Smith's 637 model. A
new gun, loaded with five rounds of .38 Special hollow points.
The box the hollow points had been taken from lay next to it,
along with a half-empty box of target loads.

I left the gun in the drawer and chewed my cheek,
thinking slowly. There was nothing particularly unusual
about finding a handgun in a bedside table. It didn't neces-
sarily *mean* that Camilla feared for her life. She might have
proactively purchased the gun just like millions of other
security-conscious Americans.

But something didn't sit well with me. It was the locked
door. Camilla lived alone, and there was no reason to think
the gun would fall into the wrong hands with the main
entrance already locked. So...

I swept the room again, inspecting the dresser drawers

and the closet. Tapping my foot over worn sections of faux hardwood, searching for a hollow sound that might conceal a compartment. Rapping on the wall with my knuckles, looking for the same.

I found only dirty clothes and more smut novels stacked in the closet, so I returned to the bedroom and fished my Streamlight out of my pocket to inspect beneath the bed. It was dusty down there, a pair of additional empty wine bottles rolled out of sight beneath the bedframe. Stray threads hung from the bottom edge of the box spring, and clusters of dust shifted under my breath.

But it was the bulge that caught my eye. Barely detectable but by the blast of my Streamlight. The fabric stapled to the underside of the box spring sagged a little...as though something hefty were weighing it down.

I returned quickly to my feet and placed my gloved hands on the mattress, heaving to shift it away from the box spring. It slid with effort, pivoting off the bed and swinging into the far wall.

The box spring was revealed beneath, looking perfectly normal at first. Undamaged. But as I heaved to push the mattress another six inches, I saw the tear ripping through the box spring's cloth-covered top, a cavity opening beneath. I pushed the mattress until it bent and spilled off the side of the bed, and then I saw the duffel bag.

My heart jumped. I looked impulsively over my shoulder. The hallway and the kitchen beyond were both empty. I used the duffel bag's nylon straps to lift it out. It was heavy, and even before I pulled it free of the box spring cavity, I knew what it contained. The weight, mass, and shifting profile of the contents were all unmistakable.

I unzipped it anyway, because I had to know for sure. I flashed the Streamlight over the open top.

It was cash. American one-hundred-dollar bills, wrapped in ten-thousand-dollar bands.

Dozens of them.

47

I sifted through the bag with a gloved hand, but even near the bottom I only uncovered more of the same. Not tens, not twenties, not fifties. Only hundreds, and only ten-thousand-dollar bands. I stopped counting when I hit five hundred grand and I wasn't more than halfway through the bag.

It was a million plus, easy. Maybe one point five. All cash.

I settled onto my knees and just stared for a moment. It wasn't the first time I'd seen a large quantity of cash hidden beneath a mattress—I'd actually seen this a number of times, both in Afghanistan and Phoenix.

The troubling thing was, I'd never seen such circumstances apart from criminal behavior. As a rule of thumb, the larger the pile of cash, the larger the corresponding illegality of whatever had put it there.

And I'd never seen north of a million.

What did you do, Camilla?

My gaze drifted back to the revolver and paused. Then I again noticed the tablet computer, blank screened. Turned off, but a quick tap of the power button produced a lock screen depicting a beach scene, with a request for fingerprint ID.

I stopped. I thought of the things that tablet might contain. Messages, or emails. Photographs. Web searches.

And then I thought of the refrigerator.

Returning quickly to the kitchen, I used the Streamlight to pour bright light over the face of the stainless-steel appliance at an angle, focusing on the handles. The flashlight highlighted dust collected over the surface of the brushed silver, gathered around scuffs and smears and sticking over fingerprints. A lot of them.

I leaned in close and searched through the mess for a clear print. I thought about the tablet and the position of the power switch where the finger print reader lay. It was on the top, on the right-hand side, just above the camera. I pictured myself holding the device, and instinctively moved my right index finger into a curling motion, as if I were pressing it.

The index finger.

I returned to the prints. I craned my neck around the back side of the refrigerator handle and shone the light, imagining a woman of average height curling her hands around the handle to open the door.

And then I found it. Perfectly clean and unmarred, sticking to the stainless steel a few inches above the bulk of smudged prints that gathered near the bottom. A random high-grab, outside the median point used to open the door.

A sudden blast of thunder shook the windows from the direction of the coast, but I barely noticed. I moved to the kitchen drawers, searching instinctively for that one drawer every kitchen has—the junk drawer. The drawer with all the screwdrivers, matches, picture frame nails.

And tape.

I found a roll of misted Scotch tape beneath a flashlight and tore off a two-inch length. I returned to the refrigerator, moving slowly now. Focusing. Stretching the tape across the dusty fingerprint, I pressed it uniformly against the steel. The tape peeled away with a stretching, popping sound. It brought a lot of dust with it—and one very clear fingerprint.

I sat on the edge of the box spring and peeled my gloves off. I needed bare skin to operate the tablet's touch screen, and I figured I could scrub my prints away later. I pressed the back of the tape across my own finger, then mashed the sticky side against the unlock button.

The tablet's display shuddered, denying entry. I adjusted my press, rolling my finger. It shuddered again. I placed my T-shirt between the tape and my finger.

The tablet unlocked, displaying the same beach scene as before, this time dotted by application icons. Photos, emails, and a web browser full of search history. I tabbed quickly through it all, wading amongst the usual slew of junk emails and random pictures. Selfies at the beach, artistic photos of Camilla's nails and shoes. A search history full of makeup tutorials and mortgage advice.

And investing questions. *Lots* of investing questions.

How to invest a million dollars.

What to do with a large quantity of cash.

Does the government track large cash deposits?

It was so blatant I couldn't resist a derisive shake of my head, not because the questions were so basic, but because

Camilla didn't know better than to search these things on a device registered in her name.

Because, yes. The government can track large cash deposits, just like they can track web searches. It was a moronic oversight on her part, but it told me very little about where the cash originated, or how it led to her death.

I transitioned to her messages, and then the dam finally broke. The message pane was surprisingly simple, with only half a dozen contacts exchanging texts with Camilla over the past ten days. Emilio was there, as was Sophie. Brief and curt conversations of a mostly utilitarian nature. There were a trio of contacts labeled as "guy from bar" or "Tinder date". Those messages were overtly and almost exclusively sexual in nature. Pictures and innuendos that I moved quickly beyond.

And then there was the top contact. A single name, followed by an emoticon of a witch riding a broom.

Ava.

I tabbed into the contact, and my heart rate spiked. There weren't dozens of messages. There were *hundreds*. Ranging back to months prior, generally populated by clipped questions and even more clipped responses. But it was the most recent message that caught my eye. It was dated for the morning Camilla died. It was sent by Ava—five simple words loaded with the sinister undertone of distant thunder.

You better bring the money.

My gaze snapped across the room again, checking instinctively for intruders. There was nobody. I used my finger to fast-scroll up the column of messages, scraping to a stop a week prior when I recognized a name.

Ralph.

Ava wrote:

I told you this would happen. When you suck too hard, you draw blood.

Camilla: I'm not here to scrape together pennies on your crummy photo shoots. I'm here for the real money. Don't fault me for having the gumption to go get it.

Ava: I can fault you when you're stupid. You got greedy. Now the old man is a problem, but he's not my problem. Deal with it.

The messages were exchanged a week before I met Ralph. I thought back to his Instagram conversations with Camilla. All the talk about her being in Cuba and trying to get family out. How she went silent. How Ralph panicked.

It only served to reinforce what I already knew. She'd been drilling him from the start. He'd pushed too hard. She needed to get away. So why in the world would she meet him at his own grungy motel room?

I scanned onward. The next collection of messages concerned scheduling for the upcoming auto expo. Ava wanted Camilla present, complaining that she hadn't appeared in the office in two weeks. Camilla was obstinate, refusing to "fool with that crap" any longer. She told Ava she wanted more—a bigger cut of the "bigger fish".

And then the threats started.

Camilla: I know about the Italians. I know about their percentage, and I know you've been shorting them. They're getting a fraction of what you owe. Imagine what would happen if I paid them a visit...

Ava: You arrogant little wench. You think I'm cowed by you? I built this business without you, and I don't need you now. You better get back to the office and help with the expo, or you're finished.

Camilla: You think you can threaten me? I know things, remember? And I'm the one doing the dirty work. You're nothing more than a glorified scheduler. You don't deserve fifty percent. I'll give you twenty.

The messaging quickly broke down into a long stream of vulgarities, pitched back and forth like a tennis ball over a net, and leading to an eventual termination in contact for a period of two days.

The next message came from Ava—the night before Camilla died.

Ava: You ignorant whore! What did you do?

Apparently Camilla didn't respond, because Ava kept texting.

Ava: You better answer my calls. This is important.

Ava: Pick up the phone!! You have no idea what hornet's nest you kicked.

Ava: Camilla, I'm not screwing around. ANSWER THE PHONE.

At last Camilla messaged back.

Sorry, been asleep. Not talking on the phone right now. What do you want?

Ava: You know exactly what I want. I just got off the phone with our client from Boston. The jewelry expo two weeks ago. WHAT DID YOU TAKE?

A five-minute gap passed. Ava sent additional demands for a response. Finally, Camilla said:

I don't know what you're talking about.

Ava: Stop lying to me! The client has already pulled security footage from the hotel. He says he's got proof that you left the bar with one of his guys...and that guy misplaced a bag later that night. What did you take?

A cold tingle ran up my spine. My gaze snapped to the duffel bag resting next to me. I immediately thought of Sophie. The "FBI agent" who'd been interviewing her. His Boston accent. A million-five in hundred-dollar bills. A jewelry expo.

It was a mess of facts I couldn't immediately unravel, but it didn't take a genius to make a guess. Camilla's response was obstinate and forceful.

Camilla: You know what? It doesn't matter what I took.

*What I earn on my own time is my business. Pound
sand!*

*Ava: You stupid slut. You think this is about percentages?
You don't realize who you're messing with. These guys
aren't business people. They'll freaking kill you.*

Camilla: What are you talking about?

*Ava: You need to give it back. Whatever you took. Every
dime. I'm not messing around.*

*Camilla: Ha! You think I was born yesterday? You've
underestimated me, you old hag. And you know what? I
don't need you anymore. I'm striking out on my own. You
can keep your stupid expos and trashy models. I've got
my own thing going.*

*Ava: Camilla, you better listen to me. They will KILL
YOU, and they will KILL ME. I don't want a cut. I don't
want a dime. We can renegotiate your contract. You
HAVE TO GIVE IT BACK.*

*Camilla: This coming from the skank who's ripping off
the Italians.*

*Ava: You're right. We'll sort that out. I just need you to
come in. Work with me. This is life and death, Camilla.*

The message thread descended into a five-minute gap.
Ava kept messaging increasingly desperate demands.
Camilla ignored them.

Finally, Camilla said:

I tell you what. If you want my help, you've got to do something for me.

Ava: You've got to be kidding. I'm trying to save your neck!

Camilla: Sure you are. But it's like you always say, business is business, right? One hand washes the other. So meet me halfway or I'm out of here.

Ava: What do you want?

Camilla: This idiot from New Jersey flew down to Tampa. I can't ditch him. I need him gone.

Ava: Are you seriously asking me to…?

Camilla: No. Maybe. I don't know. I just need him gone.

Another pause. Ava returned after five minutes.

Ava: I've got an idea, but you're doing the dirty work.

Camilla: What else is new?

Ava: He's in Tampa now?

Camilla: Yes. I tried to have my brothers run him off. No dice.

Ava: He's staying in a hotel?

Camilla: I don't know. I guess.

Ava: Okay. Here's what you do. Message him and arrange a meeting wherever he's staying. You're going to drop your pants.

Camilla: Excuse me?

Ava: He's going to rape you out of his obsession.

Another pause in the messages. My stomach tightened.

Camilla: And then?

Ava: And then you're going to call the police, and he's going to go away. I'll be ready to meet you immediately afterward. Bring what you took—every last dime. I'll get you out of this. Then we'll talk about everything else.

Three minutes. Then Camilla said:

Okay. Help me with the old guy. Then we'll talk.

Ava: You better bring the money.

48

I t was the last message Camilla received before she died. I sat with the tablet in my lap, staring blankly at the screen. Mind moving slowly through the pieces.

Camilla. Her brothers. De Luca and his fencing thugs. James Rossi. The unidentified man from Boston. The pile of cash resting on the bed next to me. One murder followed by an attempted murder.

Sophie. My mind ground to a stop, slamming headfirst into the block wall of the strawberry blonde from South Carolina. And suddenly, it all made sense.

There were a lot of players, but only one person connected with everybody. I had sent Sophie straight into the lion's mouth.

I yanked my phone out and dialed. I hadn't received any message from Sophie since she texted to say she had arrived at the modeling agency. Now her phone rang and rang before sliding to voicemail. I called again. A third time.

At last the line picked up, and Sophie's Carolina drawl answered. "Mason?"

"Sophie, thank God. Where are you?"

"At the agency..."

"Did Ava show up?"

"No. She must be at the auto expo. I'm working through files. Mason, there's something going on with Camilla. I found bank records. They don't make sense. Camilla was paying *Ava*."

"I know. It's because she was ripping people off and cutting Ava a percentage. I don't have time to explain. You need to get out of there, *right now*."

The phone clattered against Sophie's ear. A door shut. Leather squeaked and an office chair rolled along the floor as Sophie stood.

"Ava?"

My heart nearly stopped. "Sophie, don't!"

It was too late. The phone hit the floor. I heard it as a clap, followed by a scuffle. Sophie screamed. Glass broke. Then the phone clattered again.

"Ava?" I shouted.

Rough breathing filled the microphone. Nobody spoke. Sophie screamed again.

Then the call cut off.

I lunged to my feet, smashing redial. The phone rang only once this time before switching to voicemail. Somebody had shut it off.

The ice rushing through my blood all morning turned to hot fire. Outside the condo a flash of lightning blazed through the blinds, followed almost immediately by a blast of thunder. Rain pounded on the glass. My heart hammered.

And I saw Ava bent over Sophie, a gun to her head. A leather belt wrapped around her neck, ready to strangle her. I saw Ava as the black shadow vanishing through Sophie's window, rushing to the Porsche. Ava as the driver who slammed on her brakes and drove me into the retention pond. Ava as the murderer who turned up at Ralph's motel just as Camilla was prepping to call the police and report a rape.

Ava who demanded the bag of cash Camilla hadn't brought, triggering Camilla to become obstinate and confrontational. Ava who then turned desperate as that confrontation turned physical. Ava who snapped and grabbed a wine bottle. It broke over Camilla's face. The Cuban girl fell, maybe not yet dead. But Ava didn't stick around. She kept the bottle neck and she ran, maybe escaping just before Ralph returned.

She'd sent the Italians to mug me and shove my truck into the lagoon because I wouldn't stop proclaiming Ralph's innocence. She'd turned up to strangle Sophie because she probably assumed Sophie knew something and was helping me. After Sophie's murder failed, Ava hired me as a way of keeping tabs on me. Handed me the folders to keep me busy...

But no. It was deeper than that.

The sex offender registry.

I gritted my teeth and bit back a curse. Pivoting to the nightstand drawer, my gaze fell over the Smith 637. It glinted in another flash of lightning, fully loaded with five rounds of lethal hollow points. I snatched it out and rammed it into my waistband, and then I was gone. Back through the living room, abandoning the cash. Bursting through the door and out onto the landing.

The atmosphere outside the condo had transformed completely since I lock-picked my way inside. The sky was black, roiled with clouds. Rain beat down in torrents, pelting my back as I returned to the convenience store for the GMC. I hurled myself inside and landed on a sopping-wet seat. The broken driver's side window, compliments of Jorge Cruz, let in a deluge that filled the floorboards and streamed from the steering wheel. I ignored it and started the motor. My single working windshield wiper scraped across the glass, dumping water in sheets but unable to keep up with the rain.

I threw the truck into reverse and roared out anyway. The suspension bounced and camping gear slammed into the side of the bed as I turned instinctively east, away from the coast. Toward downtown Tampa.

Traffic lights swung in the wind as I navigated through town, pushing the aged inline-six to its limits at every acceleration, heedless of the low visibility or the fogging windows. My knuckles turned white around the wheel, and rain beat against my exposed shoulder. My spine tingled as though electricity were shooting up it.

I pictured the tenth floor of the high rise. The empty modeling agency, all of Ava's personnel dedicated to the ongoing auto expo. Sophie all alone, Ava getting the jump on her. Maybe pulling a gun or going straight for the throat.

If Ava still wanted to kill Sophie, then Sophie was likely already dead. But a lot had changed since the night of my rocket trip into the retention pond. I hadn't known things then—I knew them now. If Ava was smart, she would keep Sophie alive as a bargaining chip.

Maybe.

The light turned green and I mashed the accelerator. Water exploded under the crush of the front tire and washed over my chest. I could barely see through the windshield. Sparse traffic passing around me blew their horns and swerved to rush by. I remained fixated on the road, counting the passing seconds and estimating the distance to Tampa as Clearwater faded around me.

There was a bridge leading across the bay. I'd need my phone to locate the correct high rise—I still didn't know Tampa well enough to find it on my own.

A light ahead turned yellow. I mashed the gas. A panel van appeared in my rearview mirror, headlights running on high beams and blinding me. I shoved the mirror to one side as the van roared and rushed to my right. I slowed to let him pass, but the van slowed also. It paused next to me. I glanced right but couldn't see anything through the fogged passenger's window. We both glided through the intersection as the light turned red.

Ahead I saw the bridge, five hundred yards distant. The road lanes condensed, with the panel van's lane evaporating. The guy hit his blinker and surged ahead, cutting in front of me. A deluge of water erupted from his back tires and exploded over my hood, temporarily obscuring my windshield. I squinted into the mess, hands rigid around the wheel.

Then red brake lights flashed from ahead, only yards away. I released the accelerator and slammed on the clutch and the brake at the same time, even as the van came to a complete halt. The nose of the GMC dove toward the pavement and the wheels locked. Tires screamed. The back end slid sideways, and the truck kept going. It was too much mass moving at too great a speed. There was no chance to stop in time.

I hit the rear of the van with a bone-jarring thud, and my forehead slammed into the GMC's steering wheel. I saw stars, my head spinning. The windshield blurred and even the crash of thunder faded out of relevance. Momentary disorientation took over, and I couldn't move as the front doors of the van exploded open.

I saw the figures coming as blurs—giant, muscled, inflatable blurs. I reached instinctively for the revolver in my pants, but it was much too late. De Luca's first thug shoved a handgun through the open window gap. The weapon pressed under my chin and rammed my head back. Then the door was open, his hands closing around my arms. The revolver was wrenched away. The second guy belted me over the skull with the butt of another handgun, sending my mind cartwheeling into further darkness. I could barely see at all. The GMC faded from around me.

Then a rolling door rushed opened. I was thrown through the side of the van onto a cold metal floor. My wrists were pulled behind my back, and handcuffs cinched down.

The door closed. An engine surged. A boot collided with my ribcage, and I rolled over.

De Luca himself stood over me even as the van thundered forward, grinning down with that pearly white smile, not an ounce of mercy to be found in it.

"You're a hard man to find, *Mr. Sharpe.*"

49

D e Luca grabbed me by the shoulder and hauled my body up. Then he drove a fist straight into my jaw, hard enough to send my skull bouncing back against the steel door I had just entered through. Stars closed in again. My head swam, and I spat blood. De Luca followed his blow with a knee to my stomach, ramming so suddenly and so hard I thought he might blow my spine out. I doubled over, the wind driven right out of me, choking and gasping.

De Luca released my shoulder with a shove, and retreated to a bench seat that ran along the far side of the van. I leaned against the closed side door and continued to gasp, head still spinning. I saw De Luca as a body mass, not really a discernible figure. His son, Marco, sat next to him, fists closed over his knees. The two inflatables who had grabbed me now sat up front—a driver and a passenger. As my vision started to clear, I recognized the passenger.

It was Mr. Brutally Simple himself—because of course it

was. He glowered at me through bloodshot eyes, his chest padded thick with bandages.

"You know what burns me?" De Luca snarled. "My boys were gonna let you go the other night. The alligator talk was just me having fun. A few good bruises, a broken bone or two, and you would have been left in a ditch. But now—now I'm missing one car and two boats, with half a dozen of my men pounded and half-drowned. I'm done having fun!"

De Luca flicked a hand, and Marco rose off the bench, slick black hair plastered back like a helmet. His lips curled in an ugly snarl, and brass knuckles appeared from his pocket.

"Wait!" I choked.

Marco hit me anyway—right fist pivoting with the full force of a trained boxer.

Emilio Cruz may have only busted my nose, but Marco De Luca *shattered* it. My head slammed against the door with a thud, and this time the stars were blood red. The pain was both immediate and absolute—consuming. It flooded my head and crowded out any conscious thought. I couldn't see. I couldn't breathe. I choked on blood as tears streamed down my cheeks.

Marco leaned close, teeth bared as the van rumbled across the bridge. Hate consumed his eyes—hate, and violence.

"You're gonna wish you were never born," he snarled.

I spat blood and finally caught my breath. The agony in my skull was so absolute I couldn't really tell what was hurting. I decided to block it all away under sheer willpower. I played my ace.

"Ava's stealing from you!"

Marco cocked his arm back. De Luca caught him by the

elbow, an iron grip clamping down. I slouched against the door, still gasping for air. Even as the cataclysmic throbbing radiated from my shattered nose, my fingers moved slowly toward the invisible pocket in the back of my belt.

De Luca jerked his head, and Marco returned to his seat with a rebellious growl. The Mafia boss leaned forward, so close I could smell his breath.

"*What?*"

I ran my tongue over my upper lip, mopping blood away as it streamed from my nose like a river. My sinus cavity felt like it was on fire, but I continued to block it out. I focused instead on De Luca, and my belt. My fingers had already found the Velcro compartment, and I was busy slowly tearing the hooks and loops apart, methodically enough that the ripping sound couldn't be heard above the beat of the rain on the van's metal roof.

"*Speak,*" De Luca snapped.

I spat blood into my lap. "She's shorting you," I said, simply.

"Ava?"

"Yes. She owes you a percentage, right? Based on profits."

I kept my voice calm, none of the sarcasm or disgust I wanted to vent boiling into my tone. My right index finger touched the handcuff key, and I slowed my movements.

I would be a dead man if I failed now.

"How do you know?" De Luca demanded.

"I saw her records," I lied. "She's got separate books. Hundreds of thousands hidden in offshore accounts."

De Luca flinched, the tendons in his neck flexing. I twisted my right hand, and the handcuff key fell into my palm.

"You're bluffing," De Luca snarled.

"I can prove it," I said. "Take me to her office. I'll show you the records."

I pinned the handcuff key between my fingers and rotated one wrist, fishing for the keyhole. Taking my time.

"She's running, De Luca," I said. "She knows she's busted. Take me there now, and I'll show you."

De Luca squinted. I could see the gears turning behind his eyes. But then he laughed.

"You're a slick SOB, aren't you, Sharpe? An ex-soldier. An *ex-cop*. I read all about you, after our last little encounter. I'll bet you've never played checkers in your life, am I right? Only chess. Only three and four moves ahead."

The tip of the handcuff key scraped the keyhole just as the van hit a bump in the road. I winced, almost dropping it.

"I'm not playing games," I said. "She's stealing. Let me help you."

De Luca snorted. "I think you already have. And you know what else I think? There will be plenty of time to deal with Ava once I'm finished dealing with *you*."

De Luca tilted his head to Marco. The brass knuckles appeared again, shiny with my own blood. The mobster's son stepped across the van, steadying himself with his free hand. Cocking back the knuckles, face dripping with violent zeal.

I moved just a little quicker. The handcuff key twisted as he stepped. The left cuff ratcheted open and cleared my hand as he cocked a fist. My right hand caught the free cuff and I closed my fist around it, sharp stainless steel encircling my fingers.

A little like brass knuckles.

Marco swung, and I swung, leaning right and rocketing toward his face. Panic flashed across his eyes as brass knuckles raced over my shoulder and plowed into the metal door with a bang. The handcuff glimmering around my right fist shot out and up, right past his lowered left arm and straight into his face.

Blood sprayed. I lunged off the floor and struck again, like a machine gun, just pounding and tearing into his unprotected cheekbone. Marco screamed, stumbling back. My next blow caught him in the windpipe, crushing his trachea and compromising his airflow in an instant. He gargled and fell, and then I was on De Luca.

The Italian crime boss was flailing for a gun when my left hook caught him in the jaw, slamming his head against the wall. Mr. Brutally Simple ratcheted around from the front passenger seat, clawing for his own gun as I grabbed De Luca and manhandled him off the bench. I threw him forward, straight into the muzzle of Brutally Simple's handgun.

Just as he fired.

De Luca took the bullet in his back, and his eyes went wide. I dropped his limp body as blood surged across the floor. The van squealed and shrieked on the wet pavement as the driver laid on the brakes. Brutally Simple raised his pistol, and I struck him in the face with the handcuff. The steel broke his nose, and then my free hand was on top of his gun, pressing the slide back, driving the weapon out of battery. He clamped down on the trigger, but he was too late. The pistol wouldn't fire. I hit him again, and the then a third time. The nose was broken and skin hung in shreds. He didn't even fight as I jerked the pistol free and pivoted it left —toward the driver.

The van had just stopped when I pulled the trigger, spitting a 9mm slug straight into the guy's thigh. He screamed and wretched, and I shot him again in the other leg.

Then I was turning, wiping my soaked T-shirt across the grip of the pistol to scrub my fingerprints away before I hurled the weapon down.

De Luca was dead. Marco couldn't breathe. Brutally Simple choked on his own blood while the driver just screamed.

I found the handcuff key. I found Camilla's fallen revolver. I kicked the side door open, exploded from the van, and ran.

50

We were someplace in downtown Tampa. I didn't recognize the street, but it wouldn't have helped if I'd been born here. The rain beat down so hard it obscured the street signs, while low-hanging clouds gathered around the tops of skyscrapers. I sprinted down the sidewalk with the revolver jammed into my waistband, using the handcuff key to unlock the other half of the cuffs before I slung them down a rushing storm drain.

My head pounded. Waves of pain radiated from my sinus cavity. My crushed nose continued to gush blood, but none of it mattered. The only thing I could think about was Sophie—and getting there in time.

There weren't any cars, and there weren't any people in the business district. Tampa was a ghost town as lightning flashed overhead. I tore my phone out and navigated to the Queen City Modeling Agency high rise. It stood three blocks away, and I kept sprinting. By the time I reached the correct block I was winded and my legs burned. Blood still ran from my nose and splashed over my saturated T-shirt, but I barely noticed. Racing around the corner, I spotted Sophie's Volkswagen Beetle parked on the street near the building's front entrance. I tore past it and blew inside. The elevator was just closing as somebody exited. They shot me a crazed look as I stuck my arm through the door to stop it, then smacked the tenth-floor button.

The elevator rose. I breathed hard, muscles tensed. Not even thinking about De Luca and his thugs. The cops would find them. There would be an investigation. It would get ugly.

I didn't care about any of that.

The elevator dinged on the tenth floor, and I rushed out with one hand under my shirt, wrapped around the grip of the Smith. I routed toward the entrance of the modeling agency, remembering how Sophie had said she used a code to gain entry. I didn't have the code, but as it turned out, I didn't need it.

The glass door of the agency was completely shattered and stood open. I skidded to a stop as thousands of glass shards glistened up at me, the largest section held together by Ava's business logo—that suggestive female silhouette, orbited by the initials of Queen City Modeling Agency.

My hand dropped beneath my shirt and I drew the Smith, stepping quickly over the mess and pivoting into the reception area. The blonde with the neon blouses was gone from the receptionist's desk. The floor beyond was vacant of stylists, photographers, or models. Open windows looking' out over Tampa Bay ran with rain, the lights off, an eerie sort of stillness hanging over the room.

And *everything* was a wreck. Upturned desks and makeup stations, overturned tripods, and spilled file boxes. Portions of the walls were caved in, and ceiling panels were torn down. Ava's office looked like a tornado had ripped through it.

Somebody had sacked the entire floor, and it wasn't difficult to guess why. They were looking for something.

Or, more accurately—over a million somethings.

My gaze snapped to Ava's office, where further shattered glass lay on the floor amid scattered papers. The desk chair was overturned. One of Ava's glass plaques lay broken on the floor.

And then I saw blood—just a trace, staining the wall next to Sophie's abandoned car keys and cell phone. I recognized the phone in an instant by the case/wallet combo, but Sophie wasn't there, and neither was Ava.

I looked over my shoulder, surveying the chaos. There was no way to really know for sure when the place had been ransacked, but it couldn't have been long ago. Sophie had been here barely forty minutes prior, searching the computer system unmolested. Ava had arrived, but Ava wouldn't have wrecked her own office space, and this mess was far too extreme to be caused by a two-woman struggle.

No, the force of nature that unleased the carnage was bigger than Ava, bigger than Sophie, and maybe even bigger than De Luca and his thugs. It was the demon on the loose that Ava so desperately feared when she messaged pleas of reason to Camilla, which could only mean one thing.

Ava was now *running*.

As if on cue, my phone rang. I snatched it out of my pocket to see Ava's number lit up on the screen. I smashed answer without thinking.

"Don't you lay a finger on her!" I snapped.

"We're way past that, Mr. Sharpe." Ava's voice was distorted by the blast of heavy wind. I thought I heard a whimper or a cry someplace on the other side of the phone, but I couldn't be sure. It could have been my own desperate hope, working in overdrive.

"I know what you did," I said. "I know you killed Camilla, and I know why."

"You don't know anything!"

"So enlighten me," I spoke through gritted teeth.

Brief pause. Ava's breath ran ragged. She sounded like a cornered animal.

"They're coming for me," she rasped. "They're coming right now, and if you don't get them off my back, they'll kill us both!"

"Who's coming?"

I already had a pretty good idea. Maybe not of the specifics, but definitely of the general.

"The *Irish*," Ava snapped. "The Irish Mob! Camilla stole from them. They think I have the money—"

Her voice broke off in a storm of wind and another female scream. Now I was certain it was Sophie.

"Where are you, Ava?" I said. "Let me help you. We can figure this out—"

"No!" Ava screamed. "I'm done negotiating. Now you listen to me!"

There was something in her voice. An animalistic desperation. I'd never heard her talk this way, but the hallmarks of a mental breakdown were all there. I'd seen it before, as both a cop and a soldier. When people are suddenly and absolutely pushed into a corner, all sense of rationale goes out the window.

"I want you to kill them," Ava snapped. "You kill them all, and then you get the girl. That's the only deal!"

"I'm not killing anybody," I retorted. "But I can help you. I know what they want—"

"You were a soldier!" Ava roared. "You took care of De Luca's thugs down in Hardee County well enough."

Hardee County.

The comment didn't surprise me. It only served to confirm what I already suspected.

"*Where are you?*" I repeated.

"Someplace you'll never find me. Now get it done! You kill them all, or I swear I'll dump her so far out you'll *never* find her. Do you hear me?"

"I hear you." I kept my tone low. "Just stay calm. We can talk—"

"Text me when it's done," Ava snapped.

The phone cut off, and I coughed on blood running into my mouth. My head buzzed, my face on fire with pain. I hit redial. The call was bumped immediately to voicemail. I dialed again.

Nothing.

Gritting my teeth, I ran back to reception and dug through the desk, locating a box of tissues. I rammed multiple tissues up each of my nostrils to stem the blood flow while my mind spun.

Irish Mob. A stolen bag of cash. A jewelry expo.

Stupid. Ava, Camilla, and me. All of us, so *stupid.*

Spitting blood across the carpet, I looked back out the windows and thought quickly, racing ahead to the next step. The only step that mattered.

Save Sophie.

There was no doubt in my mind that Ava would kill her. No doubt in my mind that we had advanced far beyond reason. With a hostage situation and madmen on the loose, I couldn't afford to play checkers with anybody. I had to think three and four moves ahead, just like De Luca said. But not just my moves—Ava's moves. I had to think like a desperate woman on the run. I had to ask myself where she might flee.

The answer was obvious. Standing in reception, looking out through the rain-soaked windows, I was staring right at it.

51

I took Sophie's keys from the floor and returned to the street. The wind had picked up in the short time I was inside. It beat against the sides of the little Volkswagen, sounding like an earthquake as the turbocharged engine whined to life.

I didn't need to use my GPS to route my way out of the city and back to the burned-out hulk of Havana Seafood Restaurant. The path was committed to memory by now, and I found the ashen pit of the old building swimming with rainwater when I arrived.

Emilio was there, just as I knew he would be. The oldest Cruz brother worked frantically to cover the surviving stainless-steel ovens and friers with tarpaulins to block out the rain. It was a fruitless effort—the wind tore them out of his hands and buffeted against the strap. I ran from the Beetle and lent a hand to tie down one corner, but even with the tarp in place, it provided little protection.

"I need your boat!" I shouted.

Emilio scrubbed rainwater out of his eyes, squinting

against the gusts. He didn't seem surprised to see me. I wasn't sure if anything could surprise him at this point.

"What?"

"Your *boat*." I pointed to the still-standing Havana Seafood Restaurant sign planted in the sidewalk ten yards away. They letters were faded, and one end was smoke-blackened, but the little tagline at the bottom was still visible.

Fresh Seafood Caught Daily.

I remembered what Emilio had said the first time I ate at his restaurant. About how he had risen at four a.m. to catch the fish. He definitely had a boat, and I needed one.

"I know who killed your sister," I said.

That got Emilio's attention. He tensed, dropping the tarp line. Something crimson crossed his face, and I held up a hand to calm him.

"It was Ava Sullivan—Camilla's boss. Your sister stole some money from the wrong people. The Mob was coming after her, and Ava was caught in the middle."

"The *Mob?*" Emilio feigned confusion. I didn't buy it. Emilio was a smart man. He didn't actually believe his restaurant had succumbed to a gas leak...why would he? That would negate the point of the threat.

"I know somebody came to see you, Emilio. He wanted to know about your sister, just like I did. But you didn't talk, did you? And now this."

I tilted my head toward the restaurant's burned-out hulk. Emilio's jaw locked closed, and he didn't answer.

"There's all kinds of players mixed up in this thing," I continued. "But we can talk about that later. All that matters is catching Ava. She's kidnapped a girl and headed out to sea. I need your boat."

"In *this?*" Disbelief crept into Emilio's voice. I remembered again what Ava had said—that throwaway line about what she would do to Sophie if I didn't comply.

"I'll dump her so far out you'll never find her."

It wasn't difficult to put myself in Ava's shoes and know what she would do. With the Irish Mob ransacking her business and out for blood, Ava had descended into panic mode. Nothing about the storm bearing down on Tampa was scarier than the jaws of death snapping at her heels.

"Ava has a yacht," I said. "She ran out to sea to hide. If we don't catch her now, she's gonna kill again."

Emilio looked instinctively toward the coast, dark eyes flashing as his mind spun. I could see the mental math almost as though it were being written across a chalkboard. The uncertainty. The frustration. The anger.

Jorge wasn't here. I could only assume he was in the hospital. Camilla was someplace worse. The restaurant was gone. Emilio had a lot to be angry about.

The Cuban faced me again. "You're certain this woman killed Camilla?"

"Completely."

Emilio held my gaze. Lightning flashed, and he didn't so much as blink.

Then he nodded once. "Okay. Come with me."

I abandoned the Beetle as Emilio led the way to the dripping Dodge Ramcharger. The elevated beast sat in the parking lot, and Emilio hauled himself into the driver's seat while I took the passenger's side. The engine thundered to life, and Emilio drove like a madman, lunging on the gas and yanking the wheel while giant ice chests slid back and

forth across the steel cargo bed. Everything smelled like
fish.

The drive from the restaurant to the coast took less than
five minutes as Emilio blew through stop signs and red
lights. The marina he stopped at sat in a little cove right on
the gulf coast, north of Clearwater, sheltered a little by
Dutchman Key. I saw it all on my phone's map application
while I guessed the location of Ava's yacht.

Pelican Island sat inside Old Tampa Bay, nearly twenty
miles southeast of our position and sheltered by the Pinellas
Peninsula. It was nearly thirty nautical miles from Ava's
house, down the length of that peninsula, to the mouth of
Tampa Bay, and there was no real reason to assume she
would have put out into open waters, especially in this
storm.

Except—she was desperate. Maddened. Terrified. I
heard it in her voice. She was running now, not just from me,
but from the owner of that duffel bag full of cash Camilla
had stolen.

Ava had indeed put out to sea, risking dangerous open
waters in favor of risking the killers on shore. I guessed the
cruising speed of her yacht to be no more than twenty knots,
and checked the call log on my phone to estimate how long
she may have been at sea.

An hour and a half. Almost on the dot. Ava was just now
reaching the mouth of Tampa Bay.

"Over here," Emilio said, throwing his door open.

I dropped out of the Ramcharger and endured the rain
as Emilio led me down a rickety wooden walkway onto a
floating pier. The marina was relatively small, equipped with
two dozen slips, most of which contained medium-sized

charter fishing vessels tied off, with bumpers riding their gunwales.

Emilio turned left down the line of boats and didn't stop until he reached the end. When I saw the slip he was headed toward, I almost stopped. I almost turned back. I almost resorted to an act of piracy instead, stealing somebody else's boat.

The vessel was no more than thirty feet long, and completely open. A center console featured steerage and engine controls, and two Suzuki 150-horse engines hung off the back. There were fishing rod lockers and net apparatus spread across the rear deck behind the console. The floor was faded and stained and looked rotten. Three inches of water swam in the recess just forward of the twin Suzukis.

The boat looked forty years old. It looked one hurricane away from landing upside down in a grocery store parking lot.

It looked ready to sink.

Emilio leapt aboard without comment and went to work untying the bow and stern lines. There was a rage in his eyes that I'd only ever seen in one other place—the mirror.

I made a split-second decision and jumped in. Emilio put a key in the ignition and fired up the twin engines. Three hundred horsepower thundered to life with a throaty snarl, and he backed us out of the slip. We left the marina in a surge of black water, and I didn't look back.

Emilio and I only looked ahead—straight into the storm —as the bow of the fishing boat arced upward, and thunder rolled.

52

The moment we cleared the southern tip of Dutchman Key I knew we'd made a terrible mistake. The waves ran five and six feet high, crashing in from the gulf like the fists of underwater giants. Emilio followed my directions to navigate for the mouth of Tampa Bay, and he rammed the throttle all the way to the max. The Suzukis thundered above the wind, and I clung to the console next to him as one wave after another exploded over the bow, temporarily blinding us before we plummeted into the next trough.

There were no life jackets, and we lost the fishing nets barely ten minutes into the ride. Emilio clung to the wheel and piloted like a madman, his feet braced against the fish-gut-stained deck. He barely blinked with each flash of lightning, never taking his eyes off the course ahead.

There was something stone-cold in his gaze that chilled me to the core. I wondered if he was thinking about his dead parents. The family they had left him to protect.

And how he had failed them.

"She's running aboard a small yacht!" I screamed over the wind. "Forty, maybe forty-five feet. She'll be alone—just her and the girl. I'll deal with them. You get me close."

Emilio turned away from the bow for the first time, those hellfire eyes landing on me.

"You get the girl—the woman is *mine*."

Before I could argue, the next wave broke across the bow like a mini tsunami. Water ran between my legs and swept my feet out from under me. The old fishing boat groaned and turned at the top of the crest, both motors popping out of the water with a rushing surge of spinning propellers. I clung to the bottom of the console while Emilio stood unmoved behind the wheel, managing it with perfect calm.

"Another coming!" he called.

I braced myself for the blast. It was softer this time, but still left six inches of water swimming across the deck. Emilio flipped a switch and the bilge pumps clicked on, shooting jet streams of water back into the gulf. Lightning flashed and thunder rolled. I hauled myself upright again.

"How far?" Emilio asked.

I clawed my phone out and checked the screen. We had made it south of Dutchman Key. To my left, the Florida coastline was still visible. To my right, it was nothing but an empty wasteland of white tops.

"Fifteen miles!" I called.

The first hint of uncertainty crossed Emilio's face. He glanced over his shoulder at the straining Suzukis. I wondered about fuel, but I said nothing.

Fifteen miles...maybe twenty knots of speed. Forty-five more minutes.

"If she's far outside the bay I won't be able to overtake her!" Emilio said.

"She won't be—she'll want to be within cell signal. Just keep going."

Emilio gave the boat a little more throttle. I couldn't tell if it made a difference with the steady crash of waves rocking the boat. We could be sailing into the wind or with it—alongside the tide or against it. The ocean was so torn and the sky so dark, nothing made sense.

I elected not to worry about it, using my waterlogged phone to chart the course ahead. Checking the shoreline to my left for passing landmarks. Keeping one hand always on the console rail to brace myself against the next wave. The seas didn't calm—but they didn't worsen, either. A steady shower beat down from overhead and soaked my Walmart clothes.

I only thought of Sophie, tied up in the bottom of that yacht. Smashing her head against a wall every time Ava ran the craft into an oncoming wave. Alive with fear. Knowing she was about to die at the hands of a psychopath.

But not if I got there first.

"Two o'clock!" Emilio's voice cracked thirty-eight minutes later, and he pointed across the bow. The boat rocked violently beneath my feet as he adjusted heading, but even when I shielded my eyes I couldn't see the yacht.

"Where?"

"Just over the horizon. We lost her in a swell. Keep looking."

I squinted. Emilio wrestled the wheel.

And then I saw the yacht. Forty or forty-five feet long, wreathed in sea spray and diving into a trough, it was three or four miles away, bobbing like a cork in a creek. Ava had sailed through the mouth of Tampa Bay and much deeper into open water than I initially estimated she would. The waves out there were high—six, sometimes eight feet—and capped in white. When I glanced sideways I saw Emilio's hand riding the throttle, further uncertainty crossing his gaze as he backed the motors down.

I didn't say anything. The wind beat at my face, and rain flooded my eyes. I waited as Emilio judged distance, time, and weather.

"You're sure that's her?" he shouted.

I nodded once. "That's the boat."

He spat water from his lips and faced me. "And she killed my sister?"

"Without a doubt."

Emilio jammed the fishing boat to full throttle.

53

The last three miles almost broke us. Emilio had navigated most of the coastline between Dutchman Key and the mouth of Tampa Bay at an angle—sailing not quite perpendicular to the waves, but not quite parallel to them, either. The technique minimized the force of each wave while also preventing us from being swamped by them.

But now that the swells were rising to deadly heights, there was no other choice. Emilio was forced to swing the bow of the old boat perpendicular to each swell, pushing the engines to full power while we both clung to the console for dear life. With every wave the bow of the boat rose skyward, sometimes so high that I could no longer see the ocean. Then the wave passed beneath midship, and the boat balanced at the crest of the white top. The engines rocketed out of the water, and propellers whined. For a perfect moment, like a roller coaster at the top of its track, we hung motionless. The world stopped. I felt weightless.

Then the bow dropped, hard. We surged into the next

trough like that same roller coaster rocketing toward a tunnel. The motors caught. Water exploded over the bow. We hit the bottom so hard and so fast I *knew* we would dive straight down or explode on impact. Instantly be swamped.

But every time, the boat found a way. Buoyancy took over. Emilio held the wheel rock solid to keep us from turning at the bottom of the trough. The Suzukis strained.

And the cycle began again.

After twenty minutes I could make out the yacht clearly, noting details like the strapped sun chairs shaking just above the swim deck, and the Florida flag snapping at the top of a stern mast. Its windows were dark, and it managed the swells a lot more gracefully than the fishing boat did, rocking and bobbing but never diving. The engines were running—I could tell by the bubbly wake kicked up at the yacht's stern—but it wasn't making much headway. I wondered if Ava was at the wheel, or if some manner of autopilot had taken over. Either way, this desperate flight of hers couldn't last much longer. She would have to turn back to shore to avoid being swamped by increasingly severe waves.

I would catch her before then.

"Get us behind her!" I called.

Emilio measured the tempo of the incoming waves before tacking left. I checked Camilla's revolver in my waistband and found it streaming with water, but undamaged. The sealed defensive cartridges held in each of its five chambers would fire without a hitch.

I hoped I wouldn't need them.

"When we get close I'll go aboard. You hold off the stern and wait for me."

My next command wasn't as well received as my last.

Emilio turned his hellfire eyes on me. "You hold the boat—
I'm dealing with the woman."

A crash of thunder cut off my next line of argument. The
fishing boat rocked, and the yacht appeared atop the next
swell. Two hundred yards and closing. I put a hand on
Emilio's arm and leaned close.

"You'll *get* justice. Hold the boat. We need a way to run if
things turn south."

Emilio hesitated. Then he ground his teeth and yanked
the wheel. The bow swung westward, circling as the Suzukis
howled. Then we were riding in the yacht's wake, a hundred
yards back. I held the starboard gunwale as I inched my way
to the bow. Each heave of the fishing boat sent shockwaves
through my legs like an earthquake. Fiberglass groaned.
Soggy decking sagged beneath my feet. But the waves were a
little calmer, broken by the yacht. Looking ahead I could see
that Ava was still headed out to sea, her engines still turning.
Still running.

I waved once to Emilio, beckoning him ahead. He
touched the throttle, and we ground a little closer. Lightning
flashed, reflected across the yacht's name printed in that
fancy gold script. *Snapshot.* The fishing boat ducked just as
the yacht lifted atop another swell. I put one foot on the bow
and braced myself. Emilio cut the wheel, turning left as we
surged home. The bow slammed into the swim platform of
the yacht.

And I jumped.

I landed just beyond the deck chairs, catching myself on
the sundeck's railing as the yacht rocked violently to starboard. Then I was back on my feet, the revolver clearing my
waistband. I reached the open stern lounge, lined on all
sides by cushioned couches covered in vinyl streaming with

sea water. The cockpit lay directly ahead—covered, but open in the back. A low step followed by two chairs, with the controls on the right.

I could already see that nobody stood at the controls. The throttle levers were fixed at about three-quarter power, and the deck beneath my feet vibrated with the churn of heavy diesels while the wheel adjusted slowly left and right.

Autopilot was engaged. The big screen to the left of the wheel was illuminated with a charted course, leading straight out to sea.

But I wasn't looking at the cockpit, I was looking at the closed door that led down into the belly of the yacht. The cabin—dark and uncertain.

I inched my way forward and leaned close to the door, pressing one ear against it. Even as I struggled to shut out the pound of the wind and the chug of the diesels, I heard nothing from the other side. It was a completely blind leap —guaranteed death if a proven killer waited on the other side with a gun.

I lifted the latch anyway, standing to one side and throwing the door back. No shots cracked from below, but bright yellow light glimmered across the shellacked teakwood steps that led into the cabin. I risked a peek and saw a lounge dead ahead—a couch running along the left side wall, a counter on the right. There was a room directly beneath me, behind the stairs. I couldn't see that way, but the steps were completely open. If I walked downward, my legs and back would be fully exposed.

It was an ugly risk. I decided to shout instead.

"Ava!"

A crashing sound rang from beyond the door, joined by a muted scream. The noises came from the bow, not the stern.

I gritted my teeth and decided to roll the dice, rushing sideways down the steps with the revolver pointed backward. The rear of the cabin, beneath the cockpit above, consisted of another couch and a TV. The space was empty, but before I could rotate back toward the bow, the first gunshot cracked.

Hot lead zipped across the cabin as I threw myself sideways, toward the counter. I pivoted forward as a muzzle flash marked a handgun jutting through a gap in a half-open door. Raising the Smith, I yanked the trigger and spat a .38 caliber slug directly into the ceiling. I didn't even try to engage the shooter sheltered behind the door. There was too great a chance of hitting Sophie. My gunshot was only intended to announce my own firepower, and it worked. The gun poking through the door vanished, and the door slammed closed. I jumped on instinct, landing on the counter and pressing myself against the hull wall even as the pistol cracked again —once, twice, five times. Bullets zipped through the door, blasting veneer and particle board across the floor before burying themselves in the stern wall of the cabin. I leaned as close to the wall as I could, barely escaping the line of fire. I couldn't actually *see* the bullets blazing past, but I imagined I felt their shockwave. The cabin rang with the gunshots even as the yacht rocked hard, dropping into another swell.

I kept my hand wrapped around the underside of an overhead cabinet, suddenly feeling very under-gunned with only four rounds of .38 Special remaining. From beyond the bullet-ridden door a low cry reached my ears, followed by a thumping sound. Then another cry.

"Shut up!"

It was Ava's voice. Her footsteps crept across the floor. The yacht shuddered and rocked, but I remained on the counter.

She was going for the door again, maybe to check for a body. If I let her open it, she would see me immediately. She might start shooting before I could obtain a clear shot.

"Not another step!" I bellowed.

The footsteps stopped.

"I've got a shotgun," I called. "You open that door and I'll blow you in half."

It was a bluff, but a good one. I knew what it would make her do. Ava would retreat away from the door and think about her own competitive advantages.

"Is that you, Sharpe?" Her voice was hoarse and desperate, the same tone I'd detected over the phone.

"You better believe it," I barked, slowly lowering myself off the counter. Still leading with the revolver, and still thinking about Sophie.

I figured Ava was running through the usual string of panicked questions any person defaults to whenever they're hit with a sneak attack. Questions about how I found her, and how I reached the yacht. They were logical inquiries, but if Ava was smart, she would disregard them quickly, because they no longer mattered. This had now become a tactical engagement, and the only thing that matters in a tactical engagement is how a person can overpower their opponent before their opponent overpowers them.

My logic was confirmed by the next sound exploding from the cabin—a muffled shriek, young and female, without any identifying characteristics. But in my mind, I thought I detected a Carolina accent.

"You come through that door and I'll kill her!" Ava screamed.

I edged toward the door, keeping my back against the

counter, my body mass pressed as far as possible away from Ava's direct line of fire.

"You don't want to do that," I called back. "Sophie is innocent of this mess, and you know it."

"I don't care who's innocent, Sharpe. You come through that door and I'll blow her pretty little face off!"

I stopped. The Smith and Wesson rode near my face, still loaded with four rounds of a relatively underpowered cartridge. A quick inspection of the door told me two things —Ava had fired five times, and judging by the size of the bullet holes, she was shooting a handgun chambered in .40 Smith and Wesson. It's a midsized cartridge, a little bigger than 9mm, and a little smaller than .45 ACP. I knew that most full-sized service pistols chambered in .40 S&W hold fifteen rounds.

Which meant Ava still held a definite advantage in fire-power. More than two rounds for every one of mine, and they would do a lot more damage.

"I know you're not running from me, Ava." I kept my voice calm. "I visited your office—the place was ransacked. Those Irish mobsters are right on your heels, and they aren't messing around."

Ava didn't respond. I thought I heard desperate breathing beyond the door, but the groaning of the yacht was too loud to be sure.

"I found the cash Camilla took," I said. "Over a million dollars—but you already knew that. That's why they're coming after you. Let Sophie go and I'll help you. We'll get them the money and straighten this thing out."

"Straighten it out?" Ava choked on a crazed laugh. "We're way past that, Mason! You get off this boat and you finish them off, or we're *all* dead!"

Ava's voice exploded through the door. Sophie unleashed another muffled scream—she sounded like she might be gagged. I placed one hand on the wall to steady myself as rainwater rushing through the open door to the cockpit ran across the floor. The storm had calmed a little.

But only outside the yacht.

"I'm not an assassin, Ava. I'm just a guy. The only way out of this is for you to do the right thing. We'll take care of the Irish, then we'll take care of the thing with Camilla. I'll put in a good word for you. We can figure it out."

I kept my voice calm and reassuring, but there was no answer from beyond the door. I waited. I thought I heard Sophie sob.

"Ava?" I called. "Let me open the door. I just want to talk. You'll have your gun on me... There's no risk. Okay?"

Another muted sob from Sophie. Still no word from Ava.

She was keeping me in the dark. Forcing my hand. It could well be a trap...

Or it could mean that she had fallen into a mental deadlock. I'd seen it happen in hostage situations before. The kidnapper panics. They lose the ability to speak. They freeze up. It can be a useful thing, so long as it lasts. The bad part is, whenever the deadlock breaks, it almost always results in sudden and violent action.

I weighed my options. I thought about five more rounds of heavy .40 caliber ripping through my chest. Then I thought about Sophie. The girl from Carolina. The abused child, and the violated college kid. The lost young woman, now held with a gun to her head.

It was an easy choice to make. I held the revolver at my side and reached for the doorknob.

54

Thunder rolled just as I swung the door open. I didn't snatch it. I didn't rush. I just pulled smoothly, keeping the Smith next to my thigh, and stepping into Ava's line of fire.

Ava didn't shoot. I saw her the moment my line of sight opened into a narrow hallway—a shower stall to my left, a toilet to my right. A single cabin with a queen-sized bed directly ahead.

Both Sophie and Ava lay on the bed, a pile of pillows heaped up in front of them like a wall of sandbags—but not half as effective. Sophie was bound hand and foot with duct tape, her mouth covered with the same. Mascara ran from bloodshot eyes as Ava clutched Sophie's body in front of her own like a shield. A Smith and Wesson M&P handgun trembled in Ava's grasp, the muzzle jammed into Sophie's temple.

Ava's eyes were wide, her lips parted. She breathed like a sprinter straight off a one-hundred-meter dash, sweat running down her face despite the chug of an air conditioner. Waves beat against the side of the yacht and rain pounded against the bow deck.

I kept the revolver pointed down, finger on the trigger and thumb on the hammer. And I waited.

Ava's index finger rode the Smith's trigger, depressing the hinged mechanism to within a few pounds of firing. Her face was tensed, most of her body invisible behind Sophie and the pillows. Sophie moaned and squirmed. Ava held her close, a single hot tear sliding down her face.

I spoke softly. "Let her go, Ava. You don't want to do this."

"You have no *idea* what I want," Ava snarled. Her own makeup ran with sweat. She suddenly looked a lot older than she had previously. Older, and more savage. Like a dog backed into a corner. A mother bear ready to protect her cubs.

"You're a businesswoman, Ava. Not a killer. Camilla was a terrible mistake, but you don't have to make that mistake twice."

Sophie thrashed. Ava rammed the pistol into her temple. I lifted my free hand in a calming motion.

"Don't move, Sophie. Be calm... She doesn't want to hurt you."

Ava laughed. A dry, vicious sound, like a coyote coughing. "Is that what you think? Think again, *Sharpe*. I'd love nothing more than to carve her face off. Cute little lollypop-smacking girl next door. I've seen a thousand of them— they're all the same. No respect for what they have. No respect for what they *take*."

I kept my hand up. Sophie sobbed and quaked.

"Ava. Listen to me. Whatever your issue is with Sophie, or Camilla, or anyone—it doesn't matter. Not until we resolve this issue with the money. I know where it is. I'll give it to you, and you can give it to them. But first you have to let her go."

Ava breathed through her teeth, a stray trail of saliva sliding down her chin. Her eyes wide and darting. She shook her head.

"It's too late for that. They'll kill me anyway."

"You don't know that."

"And you don't know *them!*"

I didn't move, just watching. Ava continued to breathe like a winded bull and I thought about the man Sophie had described—the fake FBI agent with a Boston accent. Had it been ten grand or even fifty that Camilla stole, the Mob might have let it go. It might have been too difficult or too expensive to track down the thief.

But over a million? They had deployed considerable assets against this chase. They'd had to work for it. Ava was likely right—they wouldn't let her live, even if they got the money back. But that wasn't my problem. My only problem now was keeping Sophie alive.

Ava ran a dry tongue over her lips. She swallowed. Her next question took me off-guard.

"How much?"

"How much what?"

"How much *money?*"

"I didn't count it. A million five, maybe."

Ava's eyes widened, just a little. I saw something I hadn't before. A greedy flash, followed by a sudden tear. She shook her head in disbelief.

"There was a day when a million five wouldn't have fazed me. Like pocket money." She choked a laugh. "Back when I was a New York model—when I was a *real* model."

Sophie squirmed, and Ava turned hard. She rammed the gun into Sophie's face so hard the girl squealed.

"You know what happened, Sharpe?" Ava screamed. "You know how I lost *everything?*"

"No," I said. "How did you lose it?"

"A *man*. A drooling, dog-faced brute I should have never fallen for. He couldn't keep it in his pants—not even when he was dating a supermodel. He cheated on *me*, but when the divorce came, *I* was the one who lost it all. Every penny I ever worked for. The penthouse on the upper east side. The Maserati. The fame. The respect. I had to run all the way to *Florida* before he was finished!"

Ava was both screaming and sobbing now. Hot tears streamed down her face, but she never lifted her finger off the trigger. My heart rate spiked with each jerk of her shoulders, bracing myself for a thunderclap and an exposition of blood across the wall.

It didn't come. Sophie remained rigid. Ava just shook.

"I'll never bat an *eye* for ripping a man off. I'll take every dime I can get my hands on. I'll watch their marriages burn to the ground. I'll dance in the ashes, and I'll never apologize!"

The sobs worsened. I extended my calming hand. "Listen to me. The only way out of this is for you to work with me. I can help you."

"Help me?" Ava scoffed. "Here's how you help me, you meddling fool. You bring me that money! Every last dime. The girl stays with me until I have it, then I'm gone. I'm never coming back!"

More hot tears and enraged trembling. The ocean crashed against the yacht and the vessel rolled, forcing me to catch myself against a wall. Sudden rage boiled up in my chest. Frustration, long suppressed, but finally breaking free.

I'd danced at the ends of Ava's puppet strings long enough. She'd manipulated me, nearly had me killed, attempted to kill Sophie, and had successfully murdered Camilla. There wasn't the shadow of a chance that I would help her escape with stolen Irish Mob money. This was going to end—right here inside her own yacht.

"You knew about the Italians' fencing operation in Hardee County, didn't you?" I demanded.

Ava said nothing. Her jaw locked.

"That was a clever little stunt you pulled with James Rossi. What with the Italian surname and the sex offender registry. You knew I'd look him up to see if he'd ever lived in Florida. You said yourself that you had a private eye investigate me—I'll bet that same private eye faked a registry on the Florida sex offender website. Gave Rossi a new address, right at the heart of De Luca's operation. Rossi was never a part of that. He was just some fool businessman Camilla swindled five grand from."

Now Ava's eyes sparkled. Her lips spread into a tight smile, heavy with smugness.

"You *wanted* me at that house in the woods," I continued. "Not because you needed to find a killer. You needed help getting rid of *me*. That's why you called De Luca and tipped his thugs off. I didn't think of it at the time—I was too busy trying to stay alive—but when one of his guys saw me, he said 'he's here'. Not '*Sharpe* is here'. Just *he*, because they were already on the lookout for me. You made sure of that."

"You were a thorn in my side from day one, you washed-up grunt," Ava snarled. "Now I'm done playing games. Put your gun down, or Sophie gets it. This is the end of your line!"

My knuckles tightened around the grip of the revolver. I shook my head.

"No."

"*Do it!*" Ava screamed. "I'll kill her!"

"And then I'll kill you. Or maybe I won't—maybe I'll look up the Irish Mob and tell them where to find you. Let them drag you into a basement and tie you to a chair. See what creative ways they can imagine to get their money back. Except you don't know where the money is. Only I do. And you *need* that money."

Ava's teeth ground. Her vision darted. She licked her lips.

"Tell me," she snapped.

"No. Not until you release Sophie. Once she's off the boat, then I'll tell you."

"You'll tell me *now*," Ava snapped. "Or I'll blow her knee off."

The M&P shifted abruptly, the muzzle pointed down across Sophie's body. Sophie screamed behind the tape and jerked her legs. Ava shouted.

"Tell me, Sharpe! Tell me now!"

Her voice was overpowered by a crash of thunder. Lightning blazed from outside, illuminating every window on each side of the cabin. Then the thunder faded...but the growling roar remained. The sound originated from our port side, rushing in like a tornado. The lightning flashed again, and my gaze snapped left.

I saw the power boat streaking toward us, half a mile away. Fighting the waves. Rising and falling over each crest, jet black with a white phone number printed across the hull. A rental company's number. The cockpit was open, and behind the glass four figures stood in the rain, fixated on our position.

And one of them wielded a rifle.

I turned back to Ava, speaking through my teeth. "Looks like you're out of time."

Ava's body quaked. The lightning flashed again. Panic flooded her eyes.

Then the M&P moved. It rose across Sophie's body, arcing toward her head. Sophie's panicked green eyes locked onto it, terror flooding her face. Ava's jaw clenched. Her cheeks flushed scarlet. Her finger curled around the trigger, again engaging the hinged mechanism. The muzzle pivoted toward Sophie's face.

But I was quicker. I cocked the hammer on the little revolver and raised my arm all in one fluid motion. The sights aligned, my arm stopped, and my finger twitched. It happened in the blink of an eye, but the shot was perfect. The little .38 spat a hollow point at nearly a thousand feet per second, fire and the flavor of gun smoke erupting inside the cramped cabin like a belching volcano. The gun kicked back in my hand, sending a shockwave up my arm and through my shoulder.

And then the round struck, blowing through Ava's elbow and shattering bone in an instant. She screamed and dropped the M&P, falling back against the mattress. Blood sprayed across the sheets, and I rushed forward. The revolver found my waistband. The Victorinox appeared from my pocket, three inches of stainless-steel blade snapping out. I reached Sophie and cut her legs free first, then her hands. Outside the roar of the power boat neared. I closed the knife and helped Sophie up.

"Hurry!" I shouted. "We gotta go."

Sophie tore the tape from her lips but didn't speak. She shook like a leaf as I helped her toward the door.

From the bloody sheets behind me, Ava called after us in an agonized wail.

"Don't leave. They'll kill me!"

I paused, my gaze sliding across the gun on the floor. I thought of Camilla, bludgeoned to death in the motel room. Ralph left to rot for the murder. Sophie choking on the floor, panicked and desperate.

All that pain. All that hurt. All so that Ava could remain atop her castle of glass.

"That's between you and them," I said flatly.

Then I shoved through the door, pushing Sophie ahead. She reached the ladder and ran up it. From the swim deck outside the thunder of the power boat was louder than ever, but it circled in from the bow.

Emilio stood on the deck of the fishing boat, riding the swells with a line connecting his vessel to the rear of the yacht. Panic flooded his eyes. He pointed toward the power boat.

I pushed Sophie ahead, and she leapt from the swim deck of the yacht. Emilio caught her just as I landed in the fishing boat's bow. My Victorinox snapped open again, and the razor-sharp blade tore through Emilio's line.

"*Go!*" I screamed.

Emilio hesitated next to the console. He looked back to the boat.

"The woman?" he called.

I closed the knife and shook my head.

Emilio's lips tightened into a hard line, and he jammed the throttle open. The twin Suzukis howled, and the fishing boat rose out of the water. A wave crashed over the starboard side, and Sophie ran into my arms. She clung to me while I clung to the console and Emilio drove.

I looked back as we turned for the mouth of Tampa Bay. The black power boat ran alongside the yacht, and three men jumped out. Two carried shortened AR-15s. All three made directly for the cabin.

We were three hundred yards away before the gunshots cracked across the open water. A series of desperate pistol shots, returned by a barrage of rifle fire.

And then nothing.

55

The next day dawned bright, beautiful, and extremely hot. Whatever the nature of the sudden storm from the day prior, it hadn't seemed to leave much of a mark on coastal Florida. I began my day by borrowing Sophie's Beetle for a trip to a local urgent care facility, where I paid cash to have my nose reset. The doctor recommended surgery, stating that multiple fractures had occurred, but surgery sounded expensive. I talked him into putting everything in order the best he could, a process so painful that by the end of it I was pretty sure I was the one who should be compensated. He gave me a funny little mask-like nose brace and an over-the-counter painkiller, then stated that I should be all healed up in six to eight weeks.

Back in the Beetle I discarded the nose brace onto the floorboard, swallowed the painkillers dry, and drove to the heart of downtown Tampa where I found a riverwalk and a cluster of recreational rental companies. There were all kinds of vessels available for hire. Pontoon boats, and jet skis. Fishing charters, and little sailboats.

And power boats. Some of them long and black, with multiple engines and white numbers printed across their hulls. I made an inquiry with the rental manager. He was reluctant to talk, but I wormed the truth out of him eventually.

Then I drove back to Clearwater, passing along the same bridge where De Luca's life had reached a sudden and absolute end the previous afternoon. I passed the spot where I left my truck, also, but it wasn't there. I figured it was probably in an impound lot. I'd have to pay to get it back.

Problems for later.

At Camilla's apartment I picked the lock again. I took care to leave no prints as I replaced the Smith and Wesson 637 in her bedside drawer, freshly cleaned and scrubbed of any finger oil. Then I took the bag packed with one point five million dollars in hard cash and loaded it into the trunk of Sophie's Beetle. After the smoke of the last few days had cleared, I planned to notify Emilio of the apartment's existence. He could claim the contents as Camilla's next of kin—he and Jorge would want the family photograph pinned to the refrigerator. Maybe it would bring them a little closure.

Departing Clearwater, I navigated for the Emerald Bay Hotel, a twenty-story high rise sitting amid downtown Tampa. I handed off Sophie's keys to the valet and took the duffel bag with me to the front desk. I made another inquiry. The manager made a call.

The call didn't last long. I was given a room number. I took the elevator, my shoulders loose, the bag as unimportant to me as though it contained phone books.

At the fifteenth floor I got out. I found the door for room 1543—a suite, no less. I knocked, then stepped back so that the peep hole could catch a full view of my body. I kept my hands out of my pockets.

The door opened, revealing a tall guy with an iron face. Close-cropped red hair. Piercing blue eyes and muscled arms.

I'd seen him before, and he wasn't an FBI agent.

He regarded me without comment, then his gaze dropped to the bag. His lips puckered, and he tilted his head. I walked in and dropped the bag. Two other guys in jeans and black T-shirts appeared out of nowhere and rammed me face-first against the wall. They patted me down, but found nothing other than my wallet, my Streamlight, and the Victorinox. They took everything and propelled me at gunpoint into the sitting room of the suite. There was a minibar, and a picture window providing a sweeping view of Tampa Bay.

The water sparkled, the sun blazing down from a cloudless sky. It was perfect.

I relaxed in my seat, hands on my knees as the gangster behind me kept a gun pointed at my skull. From the far side of the room, a door opened. A man in his mid-fifties appeared, black hair turning rapidly gray, shoulders muscled but not bulky. He wore slacks and a button-down shirt, open at the collar. He regarded me without comment for a moment before stepping to the minibar. He poured two glasses of Jameson, then took the seat opposite me. One glass rested on his knee, the other landed with a click on the table between us. He nodded once. I bent to accept the glass and took a long pull.

The whiskey was good. It was Irish.

To my left the guy I'd seen before appeared with the duffel bag in one hand. He dropped it next to the older man. The older man gave it a cursory glance, swishing his whiskey in his glass. He slurped a drink, then turned back to me.

"Who are you?" His voice was calm. A hint of a Boston accent, but nothing overpowering.

"Nobody," I said evenly.

"Nobody," he snorted. "A nobody with a million five of my money."

"I didn't steal it," I said.

"Who stole it, then?"

"Camilla Cruz. She found it in a hotel, I imagine. In the custody of one of your men."

The man sitting across from me cocked an eyebrow. "Do you know why?"

I did know why—or I could guess, anyway. I remembered what Sophie had said about a jewelry expo at the Tampa convention center, similar to the antique auto expo I had witnessed. Millions of dollars' worth of rare and exquisite pieces up for auction. Some of those pieces might be stolen. They might have been acquired from all around the world at the hands of one crime group or another, before eventually being funneled to the Mob. It was a fencing operation, just like the Italians' little scheme at the house in the woods.

Except, jewelry turned a bigger profit than laptops and gaming consoles. Sometimes that profit might be collected in cash. Maybe in a duffel bag, kept by a "businessman" on site to manage things. A businessman who had found an attractive Cuban-American to share his bed for the night.

I suspected it, but there was no need to say it. So instead, I said, "I came to return your money."

"Evidently. But what I do not know is *why*."

"Because it's not mine."

The man grunted softly. He leaned back in his chair. "An honest man returning a bag full of cash to a room full of gangsters... Some would say that's a strange thing."

"Some would say," I replied.

He tapped one finger slowly against the side of his whiskey glass. He seemed to be considering. Then he sucked his teeth.

"It never pleases me when things get ugly. It's always unfortunate when...third parties are involved."

"Like Havana Seafood Restaurant?" I asked.

He shrugged.

"Your business with the Cruz brothers is your business," I said. "They never knew about your missing money, or what their sister was up to. The loss of their restaurant was unnecessary. A smart businessman might consider making a contribution toward their pain and suffering. Maybe a little bonus to go with the insurance money."

His eyes narrowed, but a smile played at the corners of his mouth. He grunted.

"And you? What do *you* want?"

"I want to be left alone," I said. "I want my peace and quiet back, and I want to not have to watch my back. I had a little brush-up with your Italian friends down here. Their boss was killed—not by me, but I was there. I'd like to know that they won't be coming after me. I'd like to know that *nobody* is coming after me." I said the last part slowly, not blinking. Holding his gaze. "Or Sophie Wilson."

A long pause. I gave him time.

At last, he lifted his chin. "You're leaving Tampa?"

"As soon as I pack my bags."

A slow nod. Then the man leaned down, lifting a band of ten thousand dollars from the bag. He tossed it into my lap.

"Gas money," he said. "Don't come back."

56

L iberating Ralph turned out to be a lot easier than it might have been. In the end, it all circled back to Camilla's missing Porsche. After confirming Ava as the killer, I had to admit to being impressed with her driving skills the night of my cannonball trip into the retention pond. I wouldn't have guessed her to be the sport driving type, but guessing why she would have taken the car in the first place was easy enough. She hated Camilla, after all. This was personal. Maybe Ava was trying to feel young again, or was satisfying her frustration by seizing one of Camilla's prized possessions.

Whatever the case, it was no great riddle as to where Ava would have stashed the stolen sports car. How many places could there really be?

I called a tip into Mack, the Harper Springs police lieutenant, while I was picking up my GMC from the impound lot. A shattered window and a saturated seat, plus a one-hundred-fifty-dollar bill for the towing. The guy at the counter didn't ask questions, and Mack and his crew didn't either. They investigated Ava's place on Pelican Island and found the jet-black Porsche 911 parked in the garage.

The tires were roasted from a late-night car chase. Ava's prints were everywhere. And wrapped in a branded motel towel inside the car's narrow trunk, smeared with dry blood and more of Ava's fingerprints, was the broken neck of a wine bottle.

Not *technically* a smoking gun. But I would take it.

Mack finally released Ralph four days later, just after the guys at the glass shop finished repairing my busted driver's side window. I drove to the police station to pick him up, and he gave me a big hug at the door.

His eyes were bloodshot. He'd lost significant weight. He was free...but he didn't look happy.

I drove him to the bus station on his request and sat with him on a bench while we waited for the number 115 bus to arrive—Tampa to Newark. The breeze was hot. The city humming with distant traffic and subdued voices. Ralph didn't talk while he sat with his hands in his lap, what meager belongings Camilla had left him with tucked into a worn backpack. Haunted eyes looked across the parking lot toward the afternoon sky, and the hurt in that gaze cut me with the same needle of pain that had started this entire mess.

I breathed deeply and wondered what to say. Wondered what essence of all the hard lessons I had learned over the last eighteen months could be distilled into advice or kindness strong enough to lift him out of the pit he cowered in. What could give him enough hope, or enough strength, just to go on another day.

But I knew hope didn't work that way. It's not something you find in other people, or in their words of kindness, no matter how sincere they may be. Hope is something you find inside yourself. It's a belief. A conviction. It's validated sometimes by the behavior of others, and we credit them for that.

But if it's not strong enough to handle the storm, it's not real. Only Ralph himself could decide if the hope would be real in the end.

"I have something for you," I said.

Ralph faced me blankly. I dug into my cargo pocket and liberated a roll of cash. Five thousand dollars in Irish Mob banknotes. I tucked them into his pocket without comment.

"It's not much," I said. "But it'll get you back on your feet."

Ralph's eyes watered. He smiled a weak thanks, then we both looked back to the sky. After a while the bus came, but neither of us stood. Passengers offloaded. The driver stretched his legs.

Ralph just stared into the sun.

"You think...you think there's a heaven, Mason?" he said, at last.

I cocked my head, surprised by the question. It brought to mind Mia's water-damaged Bible, the pages still sticking together. The words of the Psalms, praising a Creator bigger than it all.

A world beyond the clouds. A hope more eternal.

"I do," I said. "I really do."

Ralph smiled a little broader than before. I offered my hand. He pulled me into another hug instead, and I didn't resist.

Then the paint salesman from Jersey started for the bus.

"Hey, Ralph," I called out.

He looked over one shoulder.

"Go, Giants," I said. "Pick a better password."

Ralph grinned.

57

My old GMC ran well on the road back to Harper Springs, where I had reestablished temporary residency at Hank's little corner of paradise. Sophie was already there, the bright red Beetle parked near my lot. The story of her kidnapping and subsequent rescue had circulated quickly amid the beat-up Winnebagos and refurbished Airstreams, gaining embellishment and hyperbole with each wagging tongue that told it.

Nobody really knew, exactly, *why* Sophie had been kidnapped. Nobody cared. Hank had declared me a campsite hero and nailed a picture of my pickup truck to the bar wall alongside photos of Willie Nelson and Jimmy Buffet. He called for a campsite barbecue in my honor. Everybody brought meat and beer. The grills circled the picnic area. By the time I arrived, the sun was setting over the lagoon but the party was just getting started.

They greeted me like the hometown quarterback, with cheers and good-natured "were you outa your minds?" alike.

I accepted it all a little bashfully, eager for everyone to get drunk enough to start telling their own tall tales again. It didn't take long.

By midnight the party had finally wound down to the stubbornest old-timers who drank whiskey straight from the bottle while they competed for the wildest war story. Hank sat right in the middle of them, three sheets to the wind, droning on about good times in the Marine Corps.

I took Sophie's hand and led her to the tailgate of my truck. It faced the same gently sloping hill and open lagoon where my pickup had taken a bath the previous week. Again I thought of Mia's Bible, now fully dry but crinkly from water damage. I thought about finding an expert in a big city who might be able to restore it.

It seemed like a reasonable next step.

"It's so peaceful here," Sophie said. Her voice was calm, that Carolina drawl unhampered by stress or fear. I imagined she'd popped a few anti-depressants since returning to shore, and the alcohol certainly helped. But there was a strength and stability in her eyes that rose above all the supplements. A natural courage, stronger than I'd seen in many soldiers.

It looked great on her.

"There's places like this all over the country," I said. "Forgotten little spots the world just rushes past. I've found a lot of healing in them."

Sophie squeezed my hand. "Have you needed a lot of healing?"

It was a bit of a loaded question. I knew what she was really asking, and a part of me wanted to be honest. Wanted to tell her the truth, just like she'd told me, all about the love lost and the future ripped away. The angel in my arms, evaporating like morning mist under a Florida sun.

A part of me wanted to recount the pain, and the recovery. To tell myself that I could help Sophie on her own path to healing.

But another part of me said no. Not because I minded talking about it, or because Sophie couldn't handle it. I said no because some things don't need to be said. Because, if my travels since leaving Arizona had taught me anything, they had taught me that pain isn't exclusive. It isn't unique. Heartbreak is something everyone experiences—some just a little, and others a lot. And it all matters.

But you don't always have to say it out loud to share the burden. Sometimes silence is the greater medication.

I squeezed Sophie's hand in return, and I smiled gently. The application of facial muscles ignited burning pain in my brutalized nose, but it was worth it. She laid her head on my shoulder, and we just listened to the frogs for a while, watching as the water rippled with every flipping fish.

And then Sophie said, "I think I'm going to Atlanta."

I looked down. A smile broke across my face before I could stop it. "Yeah?"

She nodded. "Yeah. I think...I'm ready to take a risk."

The smile remained on my face, and a warmth rose in my chest. Not the awkward, unwelcome warmth I'd felt in many of my encounters with beautiful females since losing Mia.

This felt more like a brotherly warmth. A protective, proud warmth.

I dug into my pants pocket and liberated another roll of five thousand Irish Mob dollars. I laid them in Sophie's lap with a gentle pat.

"What's this?" She sat up with a little surprise.

"A vote of confidence," I said. "Go chase your dreams, Sophie Wilson. It's a beautiful life."

ABOUT THE AUTHOR

Logan Ryles was born in small town USA and knew from an early age he wanted to be a writer. After working as a pizza delivery driver, sawmill operator, and banker, he finally embraced the dream and has been writing ever since. With a passion for action-packed and mystery-laced stories, Logan's work has ranged from global-scale political thrillers to small town vigilante hero fiction.

Beyond writing, Logan enjoys saltwater fishing, road trips, sports, and fast cars. He lives with his wife and three fun-loving dogs in Alabama.

Did you enjoy *Flash Point*? Please consider leaving a review on Amazon to help other readers discover the book.

www.loganryles.com

ALSO BY LOGAN RYLES

Made in the USA
Middletown, DE
29 January 2024

48747050R00217